'The new political satire-cum-thri[ller]
by senior National Press Gallery jo[urnalists ... and Chris]
Uhlmann, should be required rea[ding for anyone in]
media or politics, or contemplating [...]'
Verona Burgess, *Australian Financial Review*

'Seasoned political journalists Steve Lewis and Chris Uhlmann have come up with a satirical political thriller designed to tell a ripping yarn at the same time as it confronts issues to do with power and leadership, our relations with China and the United States, and the changing face of the media and political reporting.'
Gia Metherell, *Canberra Times*

'The novel is regularly hilarious, inserting much fiction into a perfectly factual Canberra setting ... and teases unmercifully the readers' perceptions of Australian politics and the secret world.'
Tony Wright, *National Times*

'The book's blurb says it's a romp through the "dark underbelly of politics" and for once the blurb doesn't lie ... The result is *The Marmalade Files*, a banquet of bastardry.'
Don Woolford, *Daily Telegraph*

'It is indeed a romp – often hilarious and always great fun ...'
John Affleck, *Weekend Gold Coast Bulletin*

'Part thriller but mostly satire, *The Marmalade Files* is a deliciously fun look at Australian politics and the characters of Canberra ... If you're not a political junkie *Marmalade*'s wickedly mischievous take on Capital Hill's antics is for you. If you are a political junkie I hope you're not in it!'
Latika Bourke

'The new political satire-cum-thriller, *The Marmalade Files*, written by senior Canberra Gallery journalists Steve Lewis and Chris Uhlmann, should be required reading for anybody studying the media or politics, or contemplating a career in Canberra.'
— Verona Burgess, *Australian Financial Review*

THE MARMALADE FILES

STEVE LEWIS & CHRIS UHLMANN

FOURTH ESTATE

Like all works of fiction, this story was inspired by events in the real world, but it is a work of fiction and none of the main characters in this book really exists and, more importantly, none of the acts attributed to these fictional characters ever took place. So please do not interpret anything that happens in this book as a real event that actually happened or involved any person in the real world (whether living or now deceased).

Fourth Estate
An imprint of HarperCollins*Publishers*

First published in Australia in 2012
by HarperCollins*Publishers* Australia Pty Limited
ABN 36 009 913 517
harpercollins.com.au

Copyright © Steve Lewis and Chris Uhlmann 2012

The right of Steve Lewis and Chris Uhlmann to be identified as the authors of this work has been asserted by them in accordance with the *Copyright Amendment (Moral Rights) Act 2000.*

This work is copyright. Apart from any use as permitted under the *Copyright Act 1968*, no part may be reproduced, copied, scanned, stored in a retrieval system, recorded, or transmitted, in any form or by any means, without the prior written permission of the publisher.

HarperCollins*Publishers*
Level 13, 201 Elizabeth Street, Sydney NSW 2000, Australia
Unit D, 63 Apollo Drive, Rosedale, Auckland 0632, New Zealand
A 53, Sector 57, Noida, UP, India
1 London Bridge Street, London SE1 9GF United Kingdom
2 Bloor Street East, 20th floor, Toronto, Ontario M4W 1A8, Canada
195 Broadway, New York, NY 10007, USA

Lewis, Steve.
The marmalade files / Steve Lewis and Chris Uhlmann.
978 0 7322 9474 8 (pbk.)
978 0 7304 9965 7 (ebook)
Satire, Australian – 21st century.
Australia – Politics and government – Fiction.
Uhlmann, Chris.
A823.4

Cover design by Natalie Winter
Cover image by Bob Stefko/ Getty Images (200428221-001)
Author photograph by Gary Ramage, News Ltd
Typeset in Baskerville Regular by Kirby Jones
Printed and bound in Australia by Griffin Press
The papers used by HarperCollins in the manufacture of this book are a natural, recyclable product made from wood grown in sustainable plantation forests. The fibre source and manufacturing processes meet recognised international environmental standards, and carry certification.

*For Flint, Charlie, Rosie
and Harry – my love for all time*

For Gai Marie, sursum corda

O, what a tangled web we weave,
When first we practise to deceive!

Sir Walter Scott

June 16, 2011

It was a brutal morning, the mercury close to zero, the sun still in a foetal position. Canberra was snap-frozen in a harsh winter embrace, cold enough to tease an ache from your throat every time you drew breath. The freeze lay like frosted glass across the national capital, yet to wake from its public service slumber.

The time was nudging 6.30 a.m. this June 16, a Thursday if you really want to know.

Harry Dunkley, a press gallery veteran with an instinct for trouble, nursed a thermos of coffee and a grade-three hangover as he coaxed his '97 LandCruiser along the sweeping lake road. He chased the volume from the news and drove in silence, save for the steady beat of his pulse hammering inside his head.

Despite a layer of thermal clothing and a heater cranked to high, the cold bit hard as he turned right towards the muddy waters of Lake Burley Griffin.

'Fuck global warming,' he muttered, with the soft croak of the ill.

Harry's face, still handsome despite an encroaching fifty-third birthday, wore the signs of a morning-after-the-night-before. And some night it had been. The Press Gallery Midwinter Ball, the one night of the year when politicians and journalists could enjoy that rarest of commodities in the capital – camaraderie.

Dunkley had unquestionably enjoyed himself, drinking too much of a good red – a 2006 Barossa shiraz, from memory. He'd chatted up the odd MP – one Minister getting in his ear about a particularly embarrassing moment in Cabinet – before stumbling onto the dance floor for a late-night embrace with a Liberal staffer that threatened to get out of control.

But while the night had been spirited, Dunkley's mind had been focused on something more tantalising than a night in bed with a political starlet – the scent of a cracking yarn.

The phone call had come a few days earlier, in the middle of a particularly rowdy Question Time, as a hunted Prime Minister tried to fend off some well-aimed darts from a baying Opposition. Dunkley was only half-interested in the staged pantomime when his phone rang, its face illuminating with a distinctive Canberra number: 6261-1111. The Department of Foreign Affairs and Trade – DFAT – full of diplomats and policy wonks, many with multiple foreign languages under their university-educated belts.

Fuck, what does DFAT want? Dunkley wondered. He turned the volume down on his flat-screen TV, anticipating a routine blast from one of DFAT's media nazis.

'Harry Dunkley? You don't know me, and you don't need to

know my name — yet — but I have something for you, if you're interested.' The voice was cultured, with an accent polished, Dunkley suspected, by a life serving successive Australian governments in various exotic locations and shitholes around the globe. There was enough in those few words to prick Dunkley's interest.

And so now, as most of Canberra's population snuggled under their doonas, Dunkley idled his LandCruiser down a narrow dirt track off Lady Denman Drive. His destination: Yarramundi Reach, a lonely clip of land tucked away at the north-western end of Lake Burley Griffin.

He had barely ever ventured to this part of the lake, which, like much of the capital, had been designed by bureaucrats paid to suck the marrow from the city's soul.

Yarramundi Reach had been chosen by Paul Keating as the original site for the National Museum in 1993, back when the Labor Party was filled with men and women of substance and steel; not the current mob of shallow careerists whose sole ambition was chasing power at any cost — before pissing off to a nice offshore sinecure.

In recent times, Yarramundi Reach had become a well-known gay beat for those who liked it rough and discreet. Word around Parliament was that a small cabal of MPs, including at least one Shadow Minister, the flamboyant Eddy Sully, had been spotted picking up late-night trade, but Dunkley, like most in the press gallery, really didn't give a toss. 'Each to their own, mate,' he'd told a member of the ALP dirt unit, when he'd come knocking with salacious details of Sully's fetishes.

Now, in the early shadows of the day, nothing much stirred. Through a thin mist, a four-man rowing crew was slicing through the lake, their oars in rhythmic harmony. Further across the water, somewhere near the imperious High Court, several hot-air balloons climbed effortlessly, languid in their skyward arc, carried away on the whim of an early morning current.

Dunkley slowed the LandCruiser to a crawl and wondered, what next? The instructions had been specific: drive past the timber toilet block to a small clearing near the lake's fringe; be there at 6.45 a.m. But who was he meeting?

Unusually for Dunkley, he was on time; in fact, he was a few minutes early. I've beaten the deadline, he chuckled, but it was too cold for grinning. He stepped out of the car's warmth, his feet stamping a mark on the frosted ground.

The sun still barely mattered, its tepid rays too weak to pierce the gloom. He was in the dark, in more ways than one. Suddenly he heard the thud of a car door, maybe fifty metres away on the other side of a small grove of eucalypts near the shoreline. Dunkley curled his fists into a ball, close to his mouth and blew some warmth on them. 'Okay, time for action, let's meet this joker.'

He walked in the direction of the sound; steady, not too fast. Through the trees he caught sight of a late-model dark-coloured European sedan – a Mercedes, he guessed. It started reversing and then accelerated down a dirt track in the direction of Lady Denman. 'What the …' Dunkley said and scrambled towards the departing vehicle, wondering whether he'd been tricked. He managed to glimpse its rear numberplate: blue with a distinctive DC stamp. A member of the diplomatic corps.

Close to the point the vehicle had driven off from, propped up on a small picnic table so he could not miss it, was an A3-sized manila envelope. It bore a single marking – 'Embassy of Taiwan'.

From a safe distance, they appeared like a fast-moving caterpillar, strung out for fifty metres or so, all blinking lights and lycra. Canberra's notorious early-morning cyclists were well versed in the art of riding two abreast and getting right up the noses of motorists. Dunkley eased off the throttle, uncertain about overtaking even though the road was near to empty. 'C'mon, boys, get a move on ...'

Despite having the best off-road cycle paths in the country, the capital's cyclists seemed determined to hog the tarmac and slow the traffic to a crawl. It was no surprise that the odd scuffle had broken out as impatient drivers grew fed up with kamikaze riders, one hoon landing an Olympic hopeful in hospital for a week. 'Spoke-Rage', the *Canberra Times* had called it.

Dunkley cast a sideways glance at the A3 envelope, anxious to prise open its secrets. He was five minutes from a cheerful joint in Yarralumla that served a decent latte and Spanish omelette. Most importantly, at this time of day, Beess & Co Cafe would be near-deserted, perhaps hosting just a few hardy souls who'd ventured out to pick up the papers or get an early gym fix.

Pulling into the car park, Dunkley could see Julie, his favourite waitress, setting up outside tables. Surely you jest, he thought, given the freezing temperature.

In the corner near the window, at a table for one, Dunkley poured a glass of water and scanned a menu absently, even though he knew what he wanted and was impatient to order so he could turn to the business at hand, without interruption.

'Morning, Harry, the usual?' Julie knew better than to interrogate her best customers and, even though the hour was early, she sensed the urgency in his manner.

Dunkley unwrapped one of the morning papers he'd brought with him, glancing at its headlines and waiting until he was sure it was safe. Eventually, his fingers stopped drumming the table and opened the envelope.

Three faces stared at him in glossy black-and-white. Two were Asian – Chinese, he guessed, given the Mao caps – and the other belonged to a Caucasian man in his early twenties with long sideburns and thick wavy hair. From the generous lapels on the man's open-necked shirt, Dunkley reckoned the photo dated back to the late 1970s, when Malcolm Fraser was in the Lodge; those years before the former Liberal PM began courting the urban elites, pretending that he had a conscience.

Despite the time that had passed there was no mistaking that face with its trademark toothy smirk. 'Bruce fucking Paxton.' Dunkley took a swig of his double-shot latte and turned the photo over, seeking confirmation. There was none.

But he was sure the young face gazing up at him belonged to the man who had improbably risen through the Labor ranks to be crowned Minister for Defence.

Bruce Leonard Paxton. A former poster boy for one of Australia's biggest blue-collar unions – the Construction, Forestry, Mining and Energy Union – Paxton was in his mid-fifties and had been the Member for Brand, a Labor seat on

Perth's southern flank, for the past fifteen years. It wasn't listed on his CV, but he was also the least educated man ever to have been sworn in by the Governor-General as the Minister for Australia's proud defence services.

The appointment had brought jeers from the Opposition, and with some justification. Paxton was the epitome of the Labor career man, a former union heavy who had been a fearsome figure in the Wild West, cutting his teeth as a paid thug with the notorious Building Workers Industrial Union. He had left school at fifteen, the moment he was legal, and through a family contact landed a job almost immediately in the building sites around Perth, shovelling sand and shit, and learning to talk fast.

After a few years labouring and doing odd jobs for men who worked hard and drank wildly, he'd joined up with the local ALP – or, more correctly, the BWIU had paid his dues and directed him to the Rockingham branch.

His career had really taken off though when he'd switched allegiances and risen to become State Secretary of the United Mineworkers Federation, then in the process of wielding its muscle across the State, particularly in the Pilbara, where the first riches of the mining boom were being exploited by hungry entrepreneurs. In the early 1990s the UMF merged with the BWIU to become a more potent force – the CFMEU.

Paxton and another union thug, Doug Turner, had forged a tag team that ran amok, taking on bosses and union rivals alike. (They once planted several kilos of explosives in the ceiling of a union rat's home before calling in the cops.)

It was during one of these escapades that Paxton mysteriously lost his left hand, claiming to be the victim of an industrial accident. 'Fucking drop saw took it clean off,' he would say over an ale, seeking to impress whoever cared to listen.

Instead of getting the prosthesis recommended by a team of specialists, he had a hook fitted in place of his missing hand. He famously paraded it on the front page of the *West Australian*, grinning maniacally beneath the cheeky headline 'Hook or Crook?'. He was dubbed 'Captain' by adoring building unionists and the unique look only served to build on the already menacing Paxton mystique.

After a decade and a half of union power, Paxton was persuaded to move into Federal Parliament. A safe seat was found, the Labor incumbent bought off with a promise of a diplomatic posting to the Holy See. Paxton came to Canberra masquerading as a workers' hero – 'Hawkie without the charisma', was the view of more than a few Labor colleagues – and set about using the skills he'd honed during his union career to build support within the parliamentary caucus.

He was forced to cool his heels during the long years in opposition, finding the travel between the West and Canberra a burden on his family life, an argument he used to justify the occasional dalliance with one of his female staffers. 'Well, we do support fucking affirmative action,' he joked, when quizzed by his colleagues on his unusually high female-to-male staff ratio.

In Canberra he toned down his wild man image by replacing the hook with a black-gloved prosthesis. But he kept the hook in his office and was rumoured to put it on behind closed doors whenever he faced a particularly tough meeting.

Now Harry Dunkley stared at the youthful facsimile of the Minister. A single photo, with no obvious inscription to identify it. Someone was trying to damage Paxton, of that he was sure. But who? And about what?

'Another coffee, Harry?'

'Yes thanks, Julie. Single shot, though, otherwise I'll be walking on the ceiling.'

Just then he noticed a small marking along the top right-hand edge of the photo, faded slightly, hard to see except in a certain light. 'Acacia.' The name meant nothing to Dunkley but he was sure it carried some significance. He shuffled a few papers, put the photo back into its envelope and then into a leather shoulder bag, a gift from his daughter, Gaby. His hangover had receded, the caffeine jazz had taken hold.

Dunkley was ready to look the world in the eye, to take on the latest political travesty. As for the photo of Bruce Paxton, he had no idea what it meant – but he knew who to ask to find out.

June 16, 2011

Catriona Bailey peered into the dark barrel of the television camera and felt a trickle of sweat forming on her upper lip. She was beginning to feel the strain and hated herself for it.

The Foreign Minister had slept fitfully, catching not much more than an hour's rest between two and three, which wasn't enough, even for her. She usually lived on four hours a night, finding it sufficient to keep up her inhuman work pace.

But two days ago a magnitude-eight earthquake had struck north-west China, killing hundreds and injuring thousands. That alone was enough to spark media interest, but the fact that a small number of Australians were missing – including a child – meant the domestic media was in hyper-drive.

And that was a great opportunity.

The Department of Foreign Affairs and Trade had set up a crisis centre and a hotline, and the Minister was where she felt most comfortable: feeding the 24/7 news cycle. But keeping pace with the news had eaten into the few hours a day she normally set aside for rest.

In truth, DFAT wouldn't usually establish a crisis centre when so few Australians were at risk, but Bailey, typically, had demanded it. She also demanded half-hourly updates on any progress local consular officials were making, hourly briefings on the Chinese and international reaction, telephone calls with every Chinese official imaginable, and regular contact with her former academic colleagues to practise tricky local pronunciations.

She then regurgitated this information in dozens of interviews on every radio and TV program in the land. No audience was too small; no request went unanswered.

Bailey had parked herself in Canberra for one very good reason: every network has a studio in the press gallery. She could talk to Australia from 6 a.m. until midnight and only have to walk a dozen metres of carpet between interviews. Most of the real work fell to the staff updating the blizzard of briefing papers that she demanded, queried, annotated, recited – and then discarded.

In an earlier life Bailey had been a gifted Chinese scholar, fluent in Mandarin, and one of the youngest people ever appointed a professor at the Australian National University. She had a work ethic that bordered on the demented, burning through staff and earning the sobriquet 'Attila the Hen' from one office refugee.

She was also utterly awkward – 'socially autistic', her colleagues would say – and seemed unable to settle on a private or public persona. So she approached life as a chameleon, trying to tailor her language to the temper of her audience. And that was a problem because she had absolutely no empathy and often misjudged her cues, leading to some spectacularly awful public performances.

Worst of all, she felt most comfortable speaking 'academese' and loved parading her intellect. So the simplest question to her would be met with a wall of sound littered with incomprehensible words.

Recognising this as a problem, she had worked hard at contriving a common touch. 'Call me Cate,' she implored everyone she met. In casual conversation she would deploy words she imagined were in routine public use; unfortunately, since everything she learned came from books, much of her information was dated and she fell into a unique argot that one wit dubbed 'wonk-strine'.

It led to famously weird constructions like, 'Come on, cobber, that's a bodgie piece of analysis. I am fully seized of the need for China to engage with the councils of the world and, in due season, it will.'

One colleague mocked her as a 'human metaphor for the chasm between knowledge and wisdom'.

A long-time member of the Labor Party, Bailey had ditched academia in the '90s to have a tilt at a seat in Sydney's west. Once elected, her relentless work ethic and fixation with being in the media every single day saw her rise further and faster than anyone had imagined possible, especially given few in Labor's ranks liked her.

'She is in the party but not of it,' critics would say.

But the public loved her, every card seemed to fall her way and, eleven years after entering Parliament, she became the country's first female Prime Minister.

As PM, she was Australia's equivalent of Princess Di, feted like a rock star, every women's glossy clamouring to dress her for their cover, a one-woman political phenomenon whose approval ratings soared into the stratosphere. For a while, at least.

The descent was just as swift. A little over two years later her party abandoned her. She suffered the indignity of being the first Prime Minister to be dumped without being given the opportunity of recontesting an election. And that burned still, deep within. She became driven by revenge.

Now she was Foreign Minister and believed she could climb back to the top … eventually. She would do it the way she did it the first time: bypassing the party and talking directly to the people – her people – every hour of every day. And she would not stop, no matter who stood in her way.

It was 10.30 p.m. and, though she would have denied it, all the tiredness was catching up with Catriona Bailey. She had known it would be a gruelling media round and, the night before, had escaped the Midwinter Ball early, mercifully avoiding the Prime Minister's attempts at humour.

Her day had begun with a 6.30 a.m. interview on Sydney radio station 2GB, moving on to News Radio and a quick ABC News 24 spot, back to commercial TV, then an appearance on Sky. And now, a dozen interviews later, she was fronting up to *Lateline*.

Curiously, she wasn't feeling her usual level of total control, and that was upsetting. She had found the last interview on *PM* a trial and had rare trouble concentrating. She'd spilled a glass of water while being made up and had a headache from hell. This made it difficult to concentrate and write notes on her briefing papers. Naturally, she pressed on, and now was being beamed live across Australia.

TONY JONES: Foreign Minister, what can you tell us about the missing Australians?

CATRIONA BAILEY: Well, Tony, minutes before this interview I got off the phone to our Ambassador in Beijing who informed me that we have four embassy staff on the ground in Qinghai province. You will be aware that the epicentre of the quake was in Yushu, which is about 772 kilometres from the provincial capital, Xining. Which is about 2000 kilometres by rail from Beijing. So let's be frank: it's a long way, cobber, that's just a fact. And the infrastructure and communications are badly damaged, so we haven't yet been able to ascertain the whereabouts of the four Australians, but I can assure you we are sparing no effort.

Bailey began to feel light-headed and her left arm was weirdly heavy. Maybe she should have had lunch, or dinner. She had to work hard to stay focused, and she feared tripping over some of the regional details.

JONES: So you don't have any new information?

Bailey hated to admit that she didn't – and wasn't about to.

> BAILEY: Now, Tony, I said we are doing everything we can, employing every resource. I have demanded that the Chinese spare no effort in assisting us to locate our citizens.

As soon as the words left her tongue, which now felt thick in her mouth, Bailey realised her mistake.

> JONES: You demanded? Foreign Minister, the Chinese have 400 confirmed dead, 10,000 injured, hundreds of thousands homeless. And you are demanding that they look for a few Australians?
> BAILEY: I mean ... I said ... I have asked, of course ... but I ...

The television lights started to swirl before Bailey's eyes and then everything went black. She fell face-down on the gleaming white oval-shaped desk.

> JONES: Minister? Minister? For God's sake, someone at the Canberra end give her a hand!

June 16, 2011

Brendan Ryan's plump figure lay propped up in bed with the remnants of a light snack scattered across his blanket – an empty Coke bottle, a packet of chips and three chocolate bar wrappers. The dietary habits of the Labor power-broker were as slothful as his brain was sharp.

While most of Canberra's population was relaxing in front of the television or reading steamy novels, Ryan had spent the last hour studying a photograph of the familiar hole in the Pentagon wall. It was there, according to the mainstream media, that American Airlines Flight 77 crashed on September 11, 2001. But Ryan was not convinced.

'How does a plane 125 feet wide and 155 feet long fit into a hole that is only 60 feet across,' he muttered aloud, echoing the words of one of his favourite books, *9/11: The Big Lie*. 'What were our friends thinking?'

Ryan possessed one of the finest minds in politics and was

considered the best Labor strategist in a generation. At thirty-eight he was already the party's most powerful factional warlord and a grateful new Prime Minister had appointed him a junior Minister with some Defence responsibilities. But his immersion in the darkest arts of politics had triggered a strong fascination with conspiracies – JFK, the moon landing, the death of Elvis …

Unlike most conspiracy theorists, attracted to the fringes of politics, Ryan was a Centre-Left patriot. The only place he loved as much as Australia was the United States. So the Americans must have had a good reason for allowing, or causing, the carnage of 9/11. But what was it? The only logical conclusion was an excuse to wage war in Afghanistan and then Iraq. But that jarred with his strategist's brain.

'Afghanistan, sure, but Iraq, for fuck's sake … the enemy is Iran.'

Ryan had always opposed the invasion of Iraq. First, because he predicted it would distract the West from the job in Afghanistan, but also because it would provide an opening for Iran to spread its malign influence through the region. Whatever you thought of Iraq, it acted as a brake on Iranian power. He didn't much care how many Iraqis Saddam Hussein had killed because he'd killed a whole lot more Iranians. Not enough, mind, but more.

The phone broke his train of thought.

'Freak Show's had a heart attack.'

'What?'

'Freak Show … Bailey … The bitch just seized up on *Lateline*, halfway through an interview … it was brilliant. Turn on the television.'

It was the familiar voice of Sam Buharia, the Don of the New South Wales Right, a fellow Senator who played politics with all the sublety of a Somalian warlord.

Ryan reached for the remote, and flicked on the ABC.

Tony Jones was scarlet-faced, reliving the moments before the Foreign Minister's collapse. And then the ABC replayed her seizure.

'Jesus,' Ryan muttered as he watched the Minister slump forward. 'I'll call you back,' he told Buharia, not waiting for a response. He dropped the phone onto the bed.

Would Catriona Bailey die and finish the work that Ryan had started more than a year ago when he'd decided to kill her off as Prime Minister?

'Please, God, be merciful, let the bitch die quickly,' he entreated. He had long since lost any respect for the former leader who had all but destroyed the party he loved through her self-centred and anarchic use of power.

Ryan had been instrumental in her downfall, just months before a general election. And she had not had the decency to go quietly, instead making a public show of recontesting and winning her seat.

Thanks to Bailey's shenanigans, their election campaign had been a debacle. In the end, the major parties had been locked on the same number of seats and Labor only clawed its way back into office by stitching together a shaky alliance of independents and Greens. With Parliament so finely balanced every vote was vital and Bailey had forced the Prime Minister to give her Foreign Affairs, threatening to sit as an independent if he refused.

Ever since, she had used Australian foreign policy as a vehicle to promote herself, looking for high-profile crises to exploit, parading on the world stage and making statements without consultation – some as baffling as they were damaging to Australia's international standing. She was a lone wolf, only interested in her own status; a publicity-seeking missile despised by her colleagues but still liked by the public.

'I call it the Bailey paradox,' Ryan would say. 'The further you get from the cow the more you like her.' Ryan's capacity for hate was legendary, and Bailey rated top of the pops on his list of foes.

Well, hopefully it would all be over soon. He began to ponder possible candidates to fill the inevitable Foreign Ministry vacancy. 'Me, maybe.'

Then his blood ran cold as a single word ricocheted through his brain: by-election!

June 17, 2011

Harry Dunkley rifled through his leather bag for his faded parliamentary pass, twisting it around his wrist as he swiped the security scanner and offered a cursory 'G'day' to the two uniformed attendants. He was in no mood for socialising.

He considered it indecent for a journalist to be anywhere near a newsroom before ten. And yet on this Friday morning at the fag end of a long and eventful week, he was dragging himself into the office and it was barely 9 a.m.

Dunkley had no choice this morning, though. He'd been on the receiving end of a vibrant phone call from the *Australian*'s chief of staff and told to haul his arse into work. A big political yarn was running and he was trailing the pack. Catriona Bailey had nearly snuffed it on national television the night before and the media had gone into overdrive. Everyone but Dunkley, who had gone to bed early and then slept in, switching his BlackBerry to silent as he tried to shake off an exhausting week.

There used to be an unwritten political armistice about reporting national politics – Fridays would be light duties only, with most senior gallery hands retiring to the better restaurants of Canberra for a lunch that often stretched into the weekend.

Those days were a distant dream. The rise of online technology and social media was changing the very fabric of journalism. Dunkley's great love – print – was on the guillotine. Today's media was full of bits and bytes of bulldust, digital opinion stretching as far as the eye could see. Decent long-range reporting had given way to instant, shrill sensationalism, while newsrooms – roaring on the high octane needs of a 24/7 product – were demanding more and more from their best reporters. The daily news now had no beginning and no end, just one continuous loop with every last gram of information shovelled into the machine.

Christ, even Laurie Oakes and Michelle Grattan were on Twitter, feeding short missives to their followers.

Dunkley could sympathise with politicians who grumbled about the incessant demands from the rapacious media. But he had no idea what to do about it, any more than they did. 'Mate, there are no virgins in this, we're all part of the one long daisy chain,' he'd told a Minister who'd complained about rougher than usual treatment from the press gallery.

Arriving at his desk, he punched the four-digit speed dial to the Sydney conference room of the *Australian*, located on level two of News Limited's Holt Street head office. 'Hate media central' the Greens called it.

A gruff voice answered. 'Who's that?' It was the familiar bark of editor-in-chief Deb Snowdon.

Harry tried to respond in a more moderate tone. 'Dunkley.'

'Oh, I'm so glad that our esteemed political editor could join us this morning. Just where have you been for the last eleven hours while our competitors towelled us with the story of the year? Even the ABC's dopey political editor managed to file something before midnight.'

'I turned off my phone. I missed it. So can we quickly dispense with the ritual flogging and get on with today?'

Snowdon, the first woman to storm and then command the male citadel of the national broadsheet, wouldn't let it go easily, but after a few more insults the conference call got back to business and the team hammered out a plan of attack. After a ten-minute discussion, Dunkley was given his marching orders. He didn't bother to mention the potential story about Paxton. After all, he had little to go on – just a single black-and-white pic. With the Bailey story occupying everyone's attention, the Paxton lead would be filed in the to-do list. Dunkley sensed it was a bigger story than that, but it demanded time. Plenty of it, and that, for now, was in short supply.

June 17, 2011

'I don't care what you say, I am not fucking going!'

Martin Toohey's voice – agitated and defiant – could be clearly heard by staff in the corridor outside his office. By contrast, the response from his chief of staff was muted, but stern.

'Prime Minister, this government hangs by a thread and a by-election loss to the Coalition would see it fall. I agree Bailey is a complete bitch who almost single-handedly destroyed our party when *you* let her run it. She then pissed all over our election campaign and all but handed power to our opponents. But we survived. That is our one piece of luck and genius. We survived by swallowing our pride and giving Bailey the ministry she wanted. We survived by putting together an alliance of Greens and independents to keep our fingernail grip on power. And if we survive another two years we might just win government in our own right again. For reasons best known to the sad bastards in Bailey's electorate, she is still popular there. If we are to survive we must win that by-election. Which means you must visit Catriona Bailey in hospital.'

Martin Toohey hated arguing with George Papadakis because he so often lost. The two men stared at each other as their wrestle for control fell into a silent battle of wills.

The Prime Minister and his chief of staff had been friends for more than thirty years, harking back to their student politics days at the Royal Melbourne Institute of Technology.

Toohey would readily admit that Papadakis outgunned him, and most people, intellectually. The first-generation son of Greek immigrants, Papadakis had toiled in the family's grocery shop while he blitzed his way through school.

He left RMIT to specialise in economics and public policy at the Australian National University. Entering Treasury as a graduate he had marched through the ranks to first assistant secretary level before leaving to become chief of staff to a newly elected Victorian Labor Premier.

There he had helped replant Labor's economic credentials in the wasteland of the Cain–Kirner era, and developed an unrivalled reputation for having that rarest combination of gifts: the ability to devise good public policy and the political nous to implement it. He had returned to Canberra, as a deputy secretary in Treasury, when Labor won its first Federal election in twelve years. It was his dream job. The hardest thing he had ever done was abandon it to guide the campaign of his old friend. And he did it for one reason only: because the party he loved stood on the precipice of electoral annihilation.

Of medium height, Papadakis had begun to go bald early and now sported just a half-crescent of short black-grey hair. He was round-faced and his body was heading in the same direction, thanks to a love of fine food and wine, and a grim determination never to exercise. 'God gave us brains so we could make and take the lift,' he would say.

Although not physically imposing, Ministers quailed when he summoned them. His authority was unquestioned and his mission was simple: to protect the Prime Minister and drag Labor back from the abyss.

He was acutely aware that sometimes in politics the best you could do was hold on, and he saw his party's current circumstances in classical terms.

'We're standing in the pass at Thermopylae. In front of us are the countless Persian hordes and we are just 300. If they win then everything behind us, the society we built and nurtured to be one of the best and most decent in the world, will be levelled. We must fight here because we have no other choice. We cannot run, we cannot hide and we cannot advance. So we must stand and fight. We might all die here but we cannot let them pass. The Spartans hung on for three days; that was enough. They lost the battle but Greece won the war. We have to hang on for three years. If we can do that then I believe we can win this war. But we cannot make any more mistakes.'

The Prime Minister knew Papadakis was right about visiting Bailey, but every now and then he had to make a stand just to remind himself that he was running the country. Though he lacked Papadakis's intellectual firepower he knew his political instincts were often better and he loved nothing more than those rare times he was proven right at the expense of his friend.

Toohey was tall, handsome and looked younger than his fifty-four years. He still had a hint of athleticism about him from his brief stint as a ruckman for Geelong West in the Victorian Football Association. He had learned to use his height and his deep baritone voice to great effect and was a passably good public speaker. He was no fool and knew his political strength lay in his union power base and his ability to get across a brief and sell it in the public market.

Toohey's path to power had been more politics than policy. He had followed the well-worn track from university politics to union organiser and then swiftly risen through the ranks to lead the oldest right-wing union in the country: the Australian Workers' Union.

Pre-selection for a safe Labor seat followed, but as he neared the top he was forced to make a dreadful choice: continue to support a good mate as Labor leader, and undoubtedly be led to defeat again; or throw in his lot with Catriona Bailey and possibly win office.

Bailey did not have the Caucus base to take the leadership on her own and neither did Toohey. What galled Toohey was that he had more support than Bailey, but she was far more popular where it counted – in the electorate.

There is an old saying in Australian politics: the very worst day in government is better than the very best in opposition. So Toohey backed Bailey, destroyed his old friend, and won government.

For a while, despite Bailey's astonishing personal weirdness, Toohey actually believed she might just be a political genius and that they could be a formidable tag team, making the kind of changes that would lift them into the same Labor pantheon as Hawke and Keating. But after just a few months in power, he began to see how bad his judgement had been.

Bailey was chaos. She could not focus on one idea at a time and, with every finger-snap announcement, entire tracts of the public service would have to scramble to try and make policy sense of it. As PM, she tended to make grand pronouncements in public which then had to be retro-fitted behind closed doors. Her advisers were too young and too green to corral her and to correct her mistakes. And her determination to micro-manage meant she got buried in the weeds and lost sight of the big picture. 'She is like a lighthouse and a microscope,' one Minister complained. 'Endlessly sweeping the horizon and then focusing for a millisecond on some trivial detail.'

Bailey's language was absolute, allowing no easy path for retreat when things went pear-shaped.

The bureaucracy – which initially hailed a Labor Prime Minister after what many saw as the dark years of the Howard era – quickly grew to despise her and dubbed her TB, which, handily, stood for both a virulent disease and 'The Bitch'.

But the bureaucratic disdain was trumped by the hatred she engendered in her Cabinet and Caucus. They were sidelined and routinely subjected to the sharp edge of Bailey's tongue. She abused and ridiculed those who dared question her, and her colleagues began to dream of her demise. But while her poll numbers remained sky-high that day seemed a long way off.

For two years, the public had remained her best friend, despite increasing whispers of Napoleonic behaviour. Like the time a departmental head had been ordered to return from a summer holiday in the US because the PM had demanded a brief on her desk 'within a week', only for it to sit, untouched, in Bailey's in-tray for a month. Or when a senior Bailey adviser spent a frustrating day chasing the PM around Australia seeking a meeting, eventually ending up in Darwin, close to midnight, without even a toothbrush, and the PM still refusing to speak with her.

For a time, Bailey's constant stream of reviews and announcements gave the impression of a dynamic government, but the smokescreen would eventually blow away to reveal an empress without clothes.

Six months before the election, Bailey's poll numbers collapsed and Labor hardheads feared they would become the first government in eighty years to be turfed out after just one term.

Martin Toohey, the loyal deputy, began to contemplate the unthinkable – capping the PM.

When the execution came, it was over in a heartbeat. Once the possibility of knifing Bailey became a reality, almost the entire Labor Caucus wanted to get its hands on the blade – she was gone in less than twenty-four hours.

But she wasn't really gone, winning her western Sydney seat of Lindsay comfortably and demanding the Foreign Affairs portfolio as her compensation.

Oh, and hadn't she enjoyed giving the 'up yours' to the colleagues who had torn her down.

Toohey despised Bailey. But he was trapped. He knew it and Papadakis knew it.

He finally broke the silence.

'Okay, I'll go,' he seethed. 'But I'm not taking flowers.'

'That's fine, I will,' said Papadakis.

And he swept out of the room, victorious.

February 16, 2011

In the dim glow of a Beijing night, scented candles dancing light across her silhouette, Weng Meihui brushed back her long black hair and glanced at her delicate features in the mirror, wondering, 'Will he remember me? Remember us?'

The distant hum of traffic was a constant reminder of the restlessness of Beijing, a city always on the move, in thrall to the dictates of its masters.

She pulled her silk robe tighter and wondered what he was like now and whether she would have the same old feelings. Or had too much changed?

She used to tease him when they were locked in each other's embrace, whispering in his ear, *'Dà Xióng Mao.'* My giant panda. He had loved it. She recalled how it would titillate him and spur him to greater heights of passion.

They used to joke about how they were bridging the East-

West divide, forging closer diplomatic ties, working together for global peace.

He had trusted her — he was so foolish and naive.

When had they first met? Was it 1979 or 1980? Perhaps as he strolled through the Forbidden City as she relayed facts to tourists about the history of the Imperial Palace, or on a walk around Tiananmen Square. Those years had blurred into one, back when the People's Republic was emerging from decades of darkness, from the bloodied cloak the Gang of Four had bound tightly around its citizens. The first flush of Deng Xiaoping's reforms was just taking hold, giving hope to a nation that had endured the iron-fist rule of its Communist dictators for thirty years.

For the first time since the Kuomintang had been swept from power, China had been open to foreign investment, eager for hard currency, and the West had responded with lust, sending delegations to size up the business opportunities in a land of almost one billion people. Diplomatic relations were being restored with Western powers — the United States and Britain — with Australia, too, coming along for the ride.

Those first delegations experienced a country that preached socialist equality but in reality had stagnated economically, many of its people too hungry and too scared to protest against the ruling clique. But these intrepid Western explorers also sniffed the huge opportunities that lay ahead, as an emerging middle class grew in a marketplace the likes of which the world had never known.

And they were introduced to razor-sharp young Chinese officials like Weng Meihui. Tibetan by birth, Weng's parents had turned their backs on their country and cast their lot with the Chinese after the 1950 'liberation'. Her father rose to become assistant governor, earning the wrath of the global 'Free Tibet' movement which dubbed him the 'Puppet of Beijing'. He was rewarded with a plum job in the Communist capital and broke the final link with his homeland by changing his family name.

Weng Meihui was recruited as soon as she'd graduated from Peking University with a double major in international relations and classic Chinese literature. Her handlers would joke among themselves that she was perfectly suited to the tasks they had in mind for her, because 'betrayal ran in the blood' of her family.

She was sent straight to the Ministry of Culture – a prized posting – as one of a small group of multilingual officers who would act as unofficial escorts for the growing numbers of Westerners eager to sample the delights of the East.

She was clever and confident, recruited as much for her sexy good looks as for her brains – not to mention her willingness to do whatever was required by her superiors to satisfy their convictions of loose Western morals and loose Western lips.

It was in this crucible of capitalism, communism, opportunism and sin that their sweet, sexy, impossible relationship had been forged. A meeting of minds as much as of bodies – an implicit understanding by both parties that each could only give so much; no more. Now, reminiscing in the soft candlelight as she dressed for dinner, Weng Meihui wondered just how mutual that understanding had really been.

A little while later, still tangled in reverie, she stepped delicately from the car, the door held open for her by the restaurant's attentive concierge. Almost absentmindedly, she entered the fashionable establishment – and pulled up short. There he was. A little older, a little more padding, but he still took her breath away. A giddy cocktail of lust, affection and regret surged to her head and heart, forcing her to stare at the floor for a long moment while she regained her composure. By the time she steeled herself to raise her eyes, he had discovered her. Pretending a cool she did not possess, Weng Meihui took her seat across the table from him, and so began a long, slow, painfully erotic dinner flirtation, destined to end only one way.

The black limo pulled up outside the St Regis, still Beijing's best hotel, he believed. It was a little after 11.30 p.m., the Chinese capital slowly emerging from its deep winter, the heaving smog of so many millions wrapping around him like a thin layer of clothing. He stretched and stifled a yawn as he wandered through the lobby towards his fifth-floor room, glad to be alone and rid of the minders who usually accompanied him.

It had been a wonderful evening, the formal dinner giving way to a few hours of honest intimacy, just the two of them, alone, again.

He had surprised himself over dinner with a steady seduction, using his toes to first stroke, then part, her slim legs, then to tease her to distraction, all the while carrying on a diplomatic discussion with a level head. He had learned a thing or two since those young, impetuous days. But, as the seemingly interminable formalities had finally plodded to their unhurried conclusion, he'd felt the old habits of subterfuge stir. Negotiating wordlessly, they'd arrived separately at her room.

She had changed into her silk robe, opening the door to him silently. He quietly closed it behind him, then pressed her against the wall, holding her hands above her head as he leaned in and kissed her – at first gently, then, as his blood rose, with increasing passion. She submitted to his touch, met his flicking tongue with her own and arched forward to press her breasts against him as he teased her by holding himself back just a little.

Her robe fell open and he gently slid his hand inside, sweeping her still-taut torso from hip to breast. She gasped as he squeezed her nipple. '*Dà Xióng Mao*,' she groaned – and that undid him. With urgency now, he pulled the robe from her shoulders, leaving her small hairless body completely exposed, her nipples straining towards him. Still dressed in his expensive suit, he felt a surge of power as he drove her towards the king-sized bed. She lay on the covers and smiled, pointing her delicate feet towards him and slowly stroking the inside of his thighs in a teasing echo of his dinner-time antics. He wrenched off his jacket and tie, throwing them in a heap on the floor, and fumbled with his shirt buttons. Finally freed of his clothing, he dipped his head and hands to the bed, sliding slowly up the length of her body, tasting the familiar tang of her. He used his tongue and fingers in the way she had always loved, teasing her until her body bucked and arched so hard in ecstasy that, panting, she begged him to stop.

She had kept some of her old habits too, straddling his prone body and moving oh-so-slowly as she drew him into her, raising and lowering herself in the way she knew would drive him crazy, leading him ever so delicately to that delicious, shuddering conclusion.

Three times over two-and-a-half hours she had brought him to climax – not bad for a bloke of my vintage, he had thought. It reminded him of the restless energy of his teen years: running on the beach, swimming until he could barely move then backing up for a hard game the same afternoon, coming in off the bench to throw all he had at the last half of a match. She made him feel so alive, so vital.

Lying alone now on his anonymous hotel bed, he allowed his eyes to shut, weariness overtaking his body as he mentally flicked through his marathon twenty-four hours – a long flight and a day full of meetings, then that dinner that would have been deadly dull but for the fact that she was there, seated across the table and looking like heaven. He drifted off with a slight, unconscious grin – she really had made it all worthwhile, every moment of it.

June 17, 2011

Draped in a lush fur stole that hung theatrically over a clinging black evening gown, Ben Gordon was impossible to miss.

An imposing six feet and two inches, he perched at the bar of the Atlantic, sipping a messy-looking cocktail and flicking through a glossy magazine peddling real estate dreams off the plan. Gordon had retained the Nordic good looks of his youth and his body had not yet succumbed to the middle-aged spread of so many his age. But he resembled nothing so much as a character from *Priscilla, Queen of the Desert*, Dunkley thought, and was perhaps the least convincing transvestite in Australia. Although, given Dunkley's experience with transvestites was limited, it was possible there was a cross-dressing man in a bar somewhere who looked less like a woman than Ben.

But he doubted it.

As Dunkley approached, Gordon looked up and smiled through several layers of carefully applied hooker-red lipstick.

The rest of his face was buried behind a thick layer of make-up, a crimson rouge giving extra texture to his angled features.

'Dunkie!' he squealed, a tad too loudly, as he rose to meet his friend. Every eye in the darkened room locked on the pair.

Dunkley stood uncomfortably, not sure whether to respond to the greeting with a hug, or a kiss, or a simple manly handshake.

Gordon tottered across to him, his size eleven feet crammed into black Jimmy Choos that added several inches to his frame. A Gucci handbag the size of a rucksack was slung over his right forearm.

He planted a kiss, and about a centimetre of lipstick, on Dunkley's cheek.

'Hi, Ben.'

'Dunkie, you know better, it's Kimberley,' Gordon chided before launching into a monologue that Dunkley knew would have to be endured for ten or so minutes before sensible conversation could begin.

'You never call. It's been what, two months? And don't tell me you're busy because you can always make time for your very best friends …'

The drone gave Dunkley time to reflect on their friendship. They had first met thirty years ago at Sydney University's rugby club, Dunkley a handy fly-half and Gordon the kind of hard-hitting line-out-jumping lock that coaches dream of. Both could have played in the top grades but they instead plumped for the more leisurely status of fourth grade, where serious training gave way to serious drinking.

While Dunkley was enrolled in the soft-ply humanities – majoring in politics and English – Gordon was immersed in pure mathematics and linguistics. He passed with honours. But work was scarce and he'd racked up thirty job applications before he finally landed a position as an analyst with the nation's domestic spy agency, the Australian Security Intelligence Organisation. After several years compiling files on mostly harmless citizens who had strayed into ASIO's orbit, he'd transferred into the bowels of the most secretive building in Canberra: the Defence Signals Directorate.

Nestled on the western end of the Defence precinct at Russell Hill, DSD stands out from the rest of the Lego blocks dumped on the hillside by virtue of its menacing hi-tech perimeter fence. Inside, it is Australia's listening post. The nation's electronic eavesdropping is deposited there. And it is where senior bureaucrats and Ministers go when they want to have secure video-link conversations with their counterparts in the US and UK.

Gordon was the best analyst in the DSD. He made sense of raw data and had specialised first in Indonesia and later engaged with the emerging giant of China. He was fascinated by the mega-nation of 1.3 billion people, millions of them in rural ghettos, thousands in prisons for not much more than the crime of questioning Beijing's iron-fisted rule. He was particularly interested in China's push into the Asia–Pacific neighbourhood, where it was buying favour with nations small and large.

Outsiders might wonder how Ben managed to hold one of the highest level security clearances – AUSTEO: Australian Eyes Only – given his unusual lifestyle choices.

For Ben the answer was easy.

'The security clearance tries to uncover areas where you might be compromised, some weakness that might leave you exposed to being blackmailed,' he said. 'How can someone blackmail me for being a trannie if I dress like this in the cafeteria every day?' It was a compelling argument.

'So, what do you really want?' The change of tone shook Dunkley out of his mental meandering.

'I've got a photo we need to talk about. I don't know what it means.'

Gordon's eyes narrowed. 'Well, we're not discussing it here. You have a look that tells me this is serious. I do my best serious business at Caph's in Manuka. Table at the back facing the entrance. Meet me in twenty minutes … I'll leave first.'

And with that, Gordon finished his cocktail and strode out, all purpose and intent, albeit in a pair of killer high heels.

Caph's, a downbeat joint in the cafe district of nearby Manuka, was unusually empty for this time of night, with just a few lonely souls scattered among its numerous tables. Ben Gordon, though, was taking no chances.

'Take the battery out of your BlackBerry.'

Dunkley followed the command, knowing that Gordon's knowledge of electronics and espionage left little room for argument. Ben had told him that an everyday mobile phone could be turned into a listening and tracking device, without much effort. And in Canberra, with its endless conspiracies and political intrigues, it paid to be ultra-cautious. Besides, Dunkley needed the advice of his long-time friend. The black-and-white photo was starting to trouble him. Bruce Paxton was easy, but who were the two Asian men?

Dunkley carefully eased the photo out of its envelope, discreetly placing it in front of Gordon as the two contemplated a menu they had little interest in ordering from.

Gordon studied the photo for a moment or two then carefully lifted his gaze to that of his friend.

'Jesus, Harry, where did you get this?'

Before Dunkley had a chance to answer, Gordon started again. 'Acacia ... you have no idea, do you?'

Dunkley stared at him blankly.

'It's the top-secret marking for ASIS, our international spooks. Jesus ... You are sitting on something potentially dynamite. Oh, and you are also in serious breach of the "Official Secrets" component of the Crimes Act – a crime, my friend, that could land you in jail.'

Gordon looked down at the photo again. He seemed slightly shocked, Dunkley thought. And worried. The reaction heightened Dunkley's excitement. Somewhere in this photo was a cracker of a yarn.

'Zhou Dejiang! My, you have snared a big one.'

'Zhou who?'

'Zhou Dejiang ... yes, I'm sure it's Mr Zhou. He doesn't look all that different today, either.'

'And just who is Zhou Dejiang?'

'Harry, I thought a political junkie like you would have known of our Chinese friend. He's one of the bigwigs in the current Politburo, the head of China's Ministry for State Security. Their top spy.

He was at one stage considered a potential candidate to become President, but there was some falling-out a few years ago, some mini-scandal that the Chinese were desperately keen to cover up. He may have got too close to the Americans ... or the Taiwanese ... anyway, his career path stalled for a while but in the past few years he's been placed in charge of ensuring the Chinese population plays within the rules – the rules that its leaders decide upon, of course.'

Gordon stared at the photo a moment longer. Dunkley could see it was triggering a grim series of connections in his friend's mind.

'Remember that unrest in Tibet a year or two ago? How the Chinese responded? We believe maybe forty or fifty monks were killed, rounded up like dogs and ... well ... even we don't know exactly what happened after that. We also heard reports of one isolated monastery being raided by Chinese soldiers who proceeded to cut out the eyes of several monks they believed were orchestrating protests against Beijing. Your friend Mr Zhou was in charge of all that.

'Harry, you are not playing with a nice guy. Zhou Dejiang is a nasty piece of work, even by the standards of the goons who've made their way up to the higher ranks of the Communist Party. So, what can you tell me?'

Dunkley fiddled with a beer that had lost its froth, tracking finger patterns in its cold glass rim, mentally preparing his notes so he could bring Ben Gordon in on this story.

'Last Tuesday, around 3 p.m., I got a phone call from someone in DFAT; they wouldn't identify themselves but the voice sounded like that of a diplomat. He wanted to meet with me, alone, said he had something of interest. We met at sparrows, the morning after the Midwinter Ball … believe me, Ben, I was in no shape for it. The rendezvous point was down by the lake at Yarramundi Reach. Six forty-five and freezing, half-light, no one around, could have been a scene out of a le Carré novel.'

Dunkley stopped briefly to take a swig of his Grolsch.

'Anyway, this car with DC plates speeds off when I approach it; I couldn't quite get the full numberplate. On a picnic table I find an Embassy of Taiwan envelope with this photo in it. No other identifying marks. That's it, that's the full story. So – now we have two out of three. Bruce Paxton and Zhou Dejiang. What do you reckon?'

Gordon adjusted his posture and took a sip of the house white. Gone was his flirtatious manner; he was now deadly serious. 'Firstly, that phone call from DFAT could have come from anywhere. I could make that number flash on your phone with fifteen dollars worth of kit from Tandy Electronics. I wouldn't say that it's not our friends in Foreign Affairs, but you … we … can't be certain that it is. It could have been ASIS, ONA, it could even be Defence intel – there are plenty of boffins in my agency who could probably masquerade as an intern at the White House if they wanted to. And, of course, it could always be a spook attached to a foreign embassy.

'I don't know about the links between Bruce Paxton and Zhou Dejiang, I'll have to sniff around on that. But I do know that Paxton is hated by the military top brass and he, in turn, is paranoid about being spied on.' Gordon paused, instinctively scanned the room, and continued.

'Paxton thinks there are forces inside his Department determined to bring him down. Remember, he's the first Defence Minister in a long time prepared to stand up to the hierarchy and call their bluff on their demands for more and more billions of dollars to waste on the latest hi-tech gear from France or the States. He's been on a one-man waste-watch campaign and the CDF and his sidekicks don't like it one little bit. The shouting matches, I am reliably informed, have been doozies.

'As for the third gentleman in your photo ... he has a passing resemblance to Xiu Jeng, the former Chinese Ambassador to Washington ... but I would have to check that one more thoroughly.'

Dunkley was perplexed, but tried not to show it. He had been hoping Gordon would provide the missing pieces, but now he could see that the jigsaw was much bigger than he'd thought, and even more intriguing.

Gordon halted and locked eyes with Dunkley in a way that said he meant business. 'Look, Harry, I don't know exactly what you've got – hell, we don't even know who gave you the Paxton photo ... but, believe me, there's a rich history there. Our Defence Minister friend is in the sights of quite a few players in this city, make no mistake about it. And if some of the bigwigs around town catch up with him, he could be toast.'

'What do you mean, toast?' Dunkley was sceptical. Paxton might be a professional scumbag, but he was no fool. He had outwitted many people over the years to advance his career and given the finger to all those who'd deemed him too thick to make it in the caged ring of Federal politics. Dunkley had spent too many years up close and personal with some of the most conniving minds in the business to ever doubt Paxton's ability to survive.

'Harry, you haven't lost your cynicism, I see. Fair enough, doubt me if you like, but Mr Paxton, as this photo suggests, is in the sights of some very powerful people. And the fact that you have it means they want him gone. We need to find out who we're playing with. You mind if I borrow it for a few days?'

'No worries,' Dunkley nodded. 'I've already scanned it into our system and I was going to ask you to keep it in your safe.'

'Sure.'

Dunkley felt the tingle of excitement that always came when he was on to a big yarn. And having Ben's help was a godsend. After all, if he couldn't trust Ben Gordon – aka Kimberley – a friend he'd known for nearly thirty years, and a man who wore the sharpest dresses in Australian intelligence, well, then who could he trust?

June 18, 2011

The morning sun was just visible through a thick fog as the prime ministerial car – C1 – approached the main entrance of Canberra's public hospital, the vanguard of a small procession that included two Parliamentary Secretaries and a clutch of advisers. Despite the hour, a gaggle of journalists was on hand to form a loose guard of honour.

The bulletproof glass distorted the outside world but Martin Toohey recognised several straightaway. 'Christ, those bloodsuckers …'

Across from the main entrance, a half-dozen satellite trucks were parked on the hospital grounds, beaming live footage of the Prime Minister's arrival to a national audience. Although it was Saturday, the networks had been broadcasting since 6 a.m. and would carry on for hours yet, trying to turn a moment of hard news into a continuous reel of infotainment.

The problem, as always, was pictures. Before the PM's arrival there was nothing to actually see, except the network talking heads and people coming and going from the hospital.

The crews had been told that Toohey would have nothing to say either on the way in or the way out. What they would get in several hours of broadcasting was one shot, endlessly repeated, of several white cars pulling up and the prime ministerial entourage solemnly proceeding into the hospital, ignoring the media demands.

But that was not the point. In the world of twenty-four-hour news, what was happening was often secondary to 'being there'. Each of the three networks and two twenty-four-hour news channels had their best-known anchors perched on stools or standing outside the hospital. In a country where not much happens, the near death of a Foreign Minister – and former national leader – was show-stopping stuff, even for a public that mainly despised politicians. Catriona Bailey was a celebrity and Australia had all too few.

'The carrion crows,' Toohey muttered as they approached. 'Just what do these jokers find to talk about for hours on end? And why does anyone listen?'

Mostly they talked to themselves and the public lapped it up. The semi-famous anchors in the studio would cross to the really famous anchors in front of the hospital and they would reminisce and speculate. About every half-hour they would replay the final moments of Bailey's fateful *Lateline* interview, now an internet sensation. In between they would host guests who had some level of expertise in politics or health or, even better, some personal association with the stricken Foreign Minister.

The ABC went for foreign-policy wonks and academics, while Sky plumped for political insiders and journalists from the *Australian*. But it was the commercial stations that, as always, showed real enterprise. Already this morning, an executive producer at Nine had sacked one of his underlings because Seven's *Morning Glory* had beaten his *Wakey Wakey* to Bailey's primary-school teacher.

Felicity Emerson had appeared on a stool next to the king of morning television, Peter Thompson, or, as he was affectionately known nationwide, Thommo. She had regaled the audience with a heart-warming story about how a poor but socially aware six-year-old Bailey had offered her battered teddy to the Red Shield Appeal in place of money she didn't have.

'So she always had a deep social conscience,' Thommo prompted Emerson.

'Oh yes,' Emerson beamed, warming to the task of embroidering the past, 'and I remember saying at the time, that girl will do great things.'

Nine was already starting a long way behind Seven in this story because the nation knew that Thommo and Bailey shared a special friendship, struck years before she had become Prime Minister.

Together they had dived the Barrier Reef to highlight the threat of global warming and had shamed the former Coalition Government into spending more money on cancer research. Bailey was an official member of the exclusive *Morning Glory* family.

Now, about fifty metres from the media melee, Toohey got a text message.

Mate, consider it personal favour if U stop 4 a chat,
Thommo

'Fuck,' seethed Toohey. 'The bastard will make me pay if I don't talk to him and everyone else will crucify me if I do.'

'So what are you going to do?'

Dylan Blair was twenty-five, good-looking, and had a way with the girls. But when it came to the media, he had no practical experience in it and no idea how it worked. Yet for reasons no one could fathom, he was senior media adviser to the Prime Minister, a title that allowed him to throw his weight around – a task he enjoyed immensely.

'We plough through the pack and deal with the consequences later,' Toohey said. 'We've got the reasonable defence that this is too solemn a moment for us to be doing doorstops.'

A wall of light and sound – the flash of cameras, the shouts of reporters, the whirr of motor drives – bombarded them as they emerged from their car.

'Prime Minister, a moment …'

'How are you feeling today, PM?'

'Do you regret knifing her?' came Thommo's familiar voice. A question designed to provoke a reaction.

Toohey didn't blink. His face was grim determination as he walked through the hospital doors, leaving the baying crews in his wake.

Moments later an awkward group formed around Bailey's bed. She lay still, pale, a drip in her arm, a monitor measuring out the slow beat of her heart.

Toohey asked the obligatory question of her specialist. 'How's she doing?'

'Not good. It will be touch and go.'

Toohey surprised his colleagues with his response: 'Can you please give me a moment alone with her?'

Confused looks were exchanged, but everyone was quietly relieved to be able to leave the room.

As the group moved out of earshot, Toohey looked down on his fallen colleague.

'You selfish bitch.'

June 19, 2011

When the Argyle Apartments were first sold off the plan to eager Canberra buyers, they were touted as a 'delightful retreat in the Paris end of Kingston'. The marketing whiz who came up with that beguiling description was later jailed for false and misleading conduct.

The final effect was more Cold War East Berlin than Boulevard Saint-Germain.

Still, the Argyle Apartments had been snapped up by hungry investors who sought the charm of inner-city living without the traffic snarls of Sydney or Melbourne. An architectural travesty on the outside, they were, however, tastefully finished with modern European appliances and smart concrete floors. All in all, they had much appeal in an upmarket suburb favoured by professionals, well-paid bureaucrats and those parliamentarians with enough cash – and confidence – to buy investment properties.

Unit Six was a stand-out, gorgeously furnished with a blend of imported lounges and tables, its walls lined with an impressive collection of indigenous Australian art.

Ben Gordon had bought the two-level townhouse four years ago, regretting none of the $850,000 he'd spent. Enterprising agents would regularly tell him that he could sell for a handsome mark-up – close to one million, according to one blond-streaked prince who'd said all the right things ... up to a point. But Gordon was having none of it. He needed some stability in his private life, which had swung between disaster and catastrophe for much of the past twenty-five years since he'd left Sydney.

He'd arrived in the national capital in late 1985, on a windswept Sunday after a four-hour drive down the Hume, negotiating two rainstorms and the treachery of a single-lane highway that snaked around Lake George.

He'd gone straight to work in ASIO, surprised and delighted that his peculiar blend of talents and obsessions could be put to good use in the national interest.

On this late Sunday morning, the apartment filled with the scent of fresh lilies and long-stemmed roses from the nearby Bus Depot markets, Gordon poured a black coffee from his Diadema espresso machine before firing up his impressive network of computers.

'Thunderbirds are go,' he said quietly to himself.

Despite owning one of the most expansive private databases and most secure networks of computers in Canberra, the task seemed daunting. He was starting with just two names – Bruce Paxton and Zhou Dejiang – a mystery third man and the Acacia marking. It was an intriguing cocktail, one that had immediately captured his imagination, and one that would have been far easier to understand if he could have accessed the DSD's vast data banks. But working on a project like this at the directorate was a huge no-no – every keystroke was logged and employees who breached the strict security protocol would be quickly shown the door. Or worse.

Gordon had spent years building up his credentials and skills, proving to his superiors that he could be trusted with the nation's most sensitive matters, even while wearing the most revealing of dresses. He'd been a fastidious worker and was now far too valuable for DSD to let go, even when the top brass got wind of a trannie working in the senior ranks of intelligence.

Like all computer junkies Gordon spent hours each day working with random data that meant absolutely nothing to most normal people. What set him apart from the scores of other PC hacks was that his home, instead of being littered with empty pizza boxes and soft-drink bottles, was always spotlessly clean – and tastefully finished with *Vogue*-like touches.

First, Zhou Dejiang, Gordon thought. An impressive CV sprang to life, courtesy of his access to Chinese data and his fluency in Mandarin. Much of it was already known to him; he had memorised the names and spouses of most of the top ranks of the Chinese Politburo – the murderers and torturers who controlled the daily lives of the mighty nation's 1.3 billion folk.

Okay, thought Gordon, we know about his upbringing, his graduation from the University of Peking, a stint at London's

School of Economics – his first taste of the West – his return to Beijing and the long march to the upper levels of the Chinese Communist regime. But what was the photo trying to tell us? What were his links with Paxton? Where did they start and where did they lead?

Gordon punched in 'Bruce Paxton' to see what would emerge, and wasn't disappointed when a lengthy list was displayed on his main screen. Database One was doing its job, uploading line after line of useful information about Paxton's early career in the United Mineworkers, his elevation to the helm of the powerful union, his first taste of notoriety after a march on the West Australian Parliament got out of hand and Paxton and a few of his cronies ended up in the back of a paddy wagon on the way to an overnight stay in Perth Central.

Another coffee was needed, a caffeine hit to get the brain into gear. Even security analysts succumbed to the lazy tones of a Sunday afternoon. Gordon had made slow progress, but patience and diligence were the keys to good intelligence gathering. The most valuable breakthroughs rarely came without hour upon hour of often tedious research and mind-numbing checking. This task would be no different.

Zhou Dejiang and Bruce Paxton – what *was* the link? Was there a hidden meaning?

Gordon kept on searching, urging his machinery to spit out something that would offer a hint on a relationship that led – where?

And the mystery third face in the photo? That would need another kind of software: face recognition technology. Australia's intelligence community – flush with funds after 9/11 – had invested heavily in this software breakthrough. The Australian Federal Police, ASIS, ASIO and even some of the States had rolled it out. Gordon had been impressed when shown how it worked and had managed to persuade a contact at the AFP to 'lend' him a shadow program.

Now it was time to put this sucker into action. Harry Dunkley, he knew, had been making inquiries of his own about Zhou Dejiang, but the two had made little headway on the third face, and that was hurting like hell.

The original pic lay on the table before him. He scanned it and highlighted the face of the unknown third man, before revving up the application. The minutes ticked by, the software refusing to give up the man's identity.

'C'mon, my friend,' Gordon coaxed.

Yet another fill of coffee – and the screen had frozen on two images. The scan of the original photo and a match.

Zheng Wang. The name meant nothing to Gordon and, irritatingly, the program had spat out only those two words. He keyed them into another database, and an immediate jumble of information appeared. 'My God, there are a lot of you.'

He scrolled through page after page of Zheng Wangs, none with accompanying photos. After a fruitless thirty minutes, he made a note of the file before closing down his computer network.

He made for his hall cupboard, a splendid seventeenth-century French piece crafted from solid oak, to grab a scarf and his favourite cashmere jacket.

A walk in the brisk Canberra air was called for, to clear the head and get the circulation flowing in feet which had been cramped by a new pair of Tods.

He would deliver the name of the third man to Dunkley, let his friend take on the quest to find the meaning in that, while he focused on the more pressing task of chasing down the link between China's top spy and Australia's Defence Minister.

March 31, 2011

She had nipples like bullets and was not afraid to flaunt them.

Emily Brooks was a warrior of the hard-Right whose hatred of the Greens was surpassed only by the contempt she had for moderates in her own party. The self-appointed patron saint of the Liberal Party's 'harden-the-fuck-up' faction, Brooks was a disciple of Thatcher and Reagan. But when it came to the bedroom, she knew no ideology.

'So, how was your day, my little meister of spin?' she asked of tonight's conquest, a smallish man with an extended ego.

They had arrived separately at her mock-Tudor apartment – a five-minute drive from Parliament House – saying little before shaking off their clothing.

'Very productive, Emily. We managed to get the 6 p.m. yarn away in record time.' He poured another glass of pinot gris, studying her form in the semi-dark, seduced by her evil ways.

Brooks was nearly fifteen years his senior. But he cared not a jot. What she lacked in nubile touch, she more than made up for in guile and experience. And she brought plenty of experience with her.

They had made love on the rug in front of her fireplace, careful not to stain a lovely handwoven piece that had been transported back to Australia after one of her jaunts to the third world. It was now approaching 10.30, nearly time to turn on that communist broadcaster, the ABC, for the nightly dose of *Lateline*.

Brooks nonchalantly checked her Cartier watch. 'I had a productive day too. That leader of mine, what a wonderful political talent she is, don't you think?'

Her words dripped with sarcasm. Brooks, a Queensland Senator, was known to bear a deep hatred of her leader, the very small-l Elizabeth Scott, who she considered had sold out the Liberal's 'tough love' philosophy for a limp-wristed pandering to inner-city elites. It was sending the party base feral – the Federal director had recently shown Brooks deeply distressing secret focus-group polling. In the minds of ordinary voters there was now little discernible difference between the government and the opposition.

Martin Toohey might be hanging on by a thread as Prime Minister but Scott was also failing to make any inroads with the swinging voters the Coalition needed if they wanted to feel the familiar touches of the executive ministerial suites. Something had to give and Brooks, arch-conservative and master plotter, had her sights on the weakest link. It was the Darwinian way, after all. But she needed a loyal lieutenant – or better still, a gullible member of the fourth estate – to carry out her dirty work.

Stretched out on her Assyrian rug, his fingers clasping the stem of an expensive wineglass, looking cute and too buff for his own good, Brooks' lover would come in handy, in more ways than one.

March 1, 2011

Forty-three pages of crap, every single fucking word. Bruce Paxton was furious with his top brass, incensed at being stuffed around by a Defence hierarchy that was used to getting its own way with Ministers too easily dazzled by expensive military toys.

Two weeks ago – just before jetting out of Australia – Paxton had given his Departmental Secretary, Hugh Trounson, strict instructions to prepare an interim savings plan for the coming Budget. He wanted fair dinkum cuts too, not the cosmetic bullshit that Defence was used to serving up. He had hoped the bureaucracy would play ball. He needed help to find the considerable reductions required to meet the government's strict fiscal targets. Its grim determination to return to surplus by 2013 was not negotiable.

There were just nine weeks till the Budget, and Paxton was preparing for a showdown. The Budget razor gang had given him an ultimatum: either come forward with $15 billion in savings over the next four years, or we'll do it for you.

And, for once, those fiscal goons in Treasury and Finance, those economic nazis who pranced around Canberra pretending they owned the place, were in the driver's seat – and they weren't about to take their foot off the brake.

All Ministers had been ordered to perform heroics with their portfolios. Savings, savings, savings – that was the mantra flowing through the bureaucracy as the Toohey Government tried to dig itself out of a big hole by preaching the virtue of economic responsibility. And the Greens and independents were letting all their newfound power go to their heads, telling the Prime Minister that he should wind back some of the extravagant spending in Defence, which had been off-limits since 9/11. 'Overblown balance-of-power shitheads,' Paxton liked to call them.

He leafed through the document again, took a gulp of his tea and grimaced, not for the first time today. Defence had shirked it, big time.

'Jesus, Rhys, this really is kindergarten stuff. Do those bastards think I'm going to buy it? And the Cabinet?'

Unlike his boss, Paxton's chief of staff, Rhys Smyth, combined street smarts with a tertiary education and had emerged as a valuable backroom operator in a portfolio that had chewed through eight Ministers in fifteen years.

If he wasn't careful, Smyth sometimes thought, Bruce Paxton would end up as number nine. Smyth had been with Paxton from the day he was sworn in as Defence Minister. He'd been brought in as a troubleshooter, at the direct request of the PM, to help out Paxton, who many thought was in over his head. Since then, Paxton and Smyth had forged a close and trusting relationship, Paxton surprising Smyth and other senior players in the government by getting on top of the tough portfolio. Together they'd seen through the military bullshit, even insisting that the Chief of the Defence Force, Air Chief Marshal Jack Webster, and his three-star companions revert to economy class for short-haul domestic flights. The brass had hated it. But this – this was their toughest fight yet.

A knock on the door interrupted the two men. 'Minister, the CDF and Secretary are here to see you.'

'Thanks, Sharon. Let them … ah … could you ask them to wait for a few minutes? I want to keep them on edge a little longer.' Paxton stood up from his desk and loosened his tie. He knew the next thirty minutes would be ugly, but he wanted to show the two men that he meant business.

Both would be dressed impeccably, Paxton knew, Webster in four-star military splendour and Trounson – well, he took his fashion advice from his former boss, Paul Keating, that poser from Sydney who now spent his time ripping into the party he had once led.

'Fuck 'em,' Paxton said with resolve. He removed his black-gloved prosthesis and pulled his favourite hook from the desk drawer.

More and more it was clear to him that the defence of Australia was not just about life and death or protecting the citizenry from hostile foreign forces … no, on many occasions, it seemed to be more about protecting a multi-billion-dollar industry that relied on gullible governments being sweet-talked into supporting massive projects and equipment deals. In the time he'd been in the portfolio, Paxton had marvelled at the ability of the military to sound convincing as they laid out their arguments on why the taxpayer must stump up for the latest hi-tech gadget, the latest weapon to kill. The two men about to enter his room were among the very best – true veterans who had been trained by some of the finest to either capture or destroy their Minister.

Paxton was fed up with the excuses from Defence on the latest cost blow-out, the latest equipment cock-up, the latest delay in rolling out some multi-billion-dollar program of marginal value to national security. It had to stop, not just because the razor gang was jabbing his arse searching for big savings to bring the Budget back into surplus, not just because the Greens were demanding a halt to the endless increases in military spending – someone had to stand up and declare 'enough is enough'. After all these years in the civility of Parliament, Paxton still felt the best way to negotiate came from his days as a union standover man – hit 'em hard from the opening bell, and don't relent until they are on the canvas begging for mercy. And when they start begging, start kicking.

The Defence regime had been out of control for years – Bruce Paxton was about to seize back the levers, for the sake of the Budget ... Jesus, for the good of Australia.

'Gentlemen, take a seat, let's get down to business.' Paxton's gleaming hook caught the light from the window as he beckoned them in.

The CDF and Secretary were quick to notice that the Minister had dispensed with the usual pleasantries, offering them the barest of greetings. It went downhill from there.

'I gave you firm orders to deliver a savings plan to me by the time I got back from OS – a serious savings plan outlining how Defence could deliver on the government's intention to shave half a per cent from Department outlays over the course of the next year. Simple, right? A down payment, gentlemen, on what will be a much bigger return to the taxpayer. I wanted real savings, a sign from you that Defence is serious in meeting what the government is demanding of all departments.

'Instead, you deliver this crock … well, I don't want to call it a pile of shit but it ain't much better …

'Am I filthy? Yep. Will I stand for it? NO. NO. NO. Do not underestimate my resolve to extract a great big dividend from the Defence Department. Do not, for one minute.'

Paxton slammed his hooked hand down on his desk, and a small chip of wood arced over the heads of his guests. He paused, picked up the Defence document and flung it across the room. The two Defence men sat poised, unflinching in the face of this ministerial tirade. Their expressions never faltered. Paxton was on the warpath and in a foul mood, as they had anticipated. They were copping plenty of flak but had expected that; as with most skirmishes, the enemy would soon run out of ammunition.

'I wanted more than a rehash of previously announced plans. Yes, I know that when Bailey was PM she led the charge for a big increase in military spending. Yes, I know the White Paper called for – what? – a $130 billion expansion of our military capability. But that was two years ago and you knew then – and I certainly know now – it was just bloody unrealistic.

'Gentlemen, we are in a new fiscal ball game. I was going to use "paradigm" but that word gives me the shits. I'm not going to let those bloodsuckers at Finance tell me where to find the savings in my own Department – that job is for you and me to deliver on. Understand? Rhys …'

Smyth rose and handed two short documents to the CDF and Secretary.

'Okay, fellas. Here's the plan …'

Air Chief Marshal Webster and Trounson read quietly and slowly, carefully avoiding any display of emotion. They were, after all, masters of the art of camouflage. But as they digested the words laid out in front of them, in twelve-point Verdana type, their internal thermometers rose towards boiling point.

What the Minister was proposing was preposterous, a major cutback to the $8 billion program to build three air-warfare destroyers and, even worse, the first serious hint of cuts to the $16 billion purchase of up to one hundred F-35s through the Joint Strike Fighter program.

Eventually they looked up, the CDF clearing his throat before carefully speaking his mind. 'Minister, you can't be serious. What you are proposing would, in my view – and I am sure Secretary Trounson would agree – it would compromise Australia's national security. And that, Minister – well, that is a very big call.'

'That's bullshit and you know it, Jack.' Paxton rarely called the CDF by his first name, but he was clearly fired up. 'The bottom line is this. Budget cuts are inevitable, you know that as well as I do. I was trying to get us – Defence – on the front foot, hoping you would see merit in laying out some strategic savings to appease those bastards in Treasury.

'Let's face it, you've had it too good for too long. The build-up of defence and security assets since 9/11 has been extraordinary, fuelled by that warmonger John Howard and those patsies who hung on his every word as if he was fucking God. Well, he wasn't – and I'm not fucking Satan. But I am about driving change in this arena, fellas, you'd better believe it.'

Trounson spoke up. 'Minister, what about the build-up by China of its military assets in the Pacific? It's off the charts. It will have three aircraft carrier groups by 2025. It will control our trade routes. And Beijing is ploughing billions into the region, buying favour, trying to act as a kind of pan-regional financier. We don't want to leave ourselves exposed. The Americans are nervous, as you know, and so should we be.'

Paxton fixed the Secretary with a hard stare. 'Why? Why should we be nervous? Maybe it's time for some … er … strategic realignment. China is our biggest trading partner now, or soon will be. It makes more motor cars in a day than our fucking industry makes in a whole year. It has a middle class of – what? – some 200 million people and they are growing like topsy.

'Our future lies far more with China, with those 1.3 billion people to our north, than it does with America and who it wants as its dancing partner.'

He was warming to a theme now. 'Perhaps the time is right for a subtle shift in our thinking about the Chinese. The Americans have their hands full with Afghanistan, and Obama, for all his rhetoric, has shown scant interest in the Pacific. The Stars and Stripes ain't what it used to be, fellas.

'What I'm suggesting makes not only good sense from a Budget point of view, it will also send a clear message to the region — particularly to Beijing — that Australia is no longer interested in playing the deputy sheriff to the US, to being its fucking lickspittle in the Pacific. Do you understand?'

Paxton waved his hooked left hand menacingly as his words ricocheted around the room, so extraordinary the CDF and Secretary could scarcely believe them. Was Paxton, Australia's Minister for Defence, really suggesting Canberra cosy up to Beijing at the expense of Washington? Was he suggesting ANZUS, that proud strategic compact that had served the Americans and its two south Pacific partners so well for sixty years, was reaching its use-by date? For nearly forty minutes, they listened as Paxton, their Minister, offered the first outline of a plan that, if it was allowed to proceed, would overturn Australia's military alignment.

Shaken, the two men rose from their seats and collected their briefcases. Paxton had offered a gruff farewell, but if he wanted to be rude, well, that was not the Defence style. They left the Minister's office, delivering a courteous nod to the receptionist on the way out. They were too professional to show emotion but both men were livid. They were used to the occasional dressing-down from a Minister but Paxton's diatribe had gone too far. This was, they both agreed, an unofficial declaration of war.

Their surprise at the bollocking gave way to something else — a firm resolve to save the realm, to stop that meddling Minister from destroying Defence. Most importantly, they would fight to protect the great US alliance.

If Bruce Paxton wanted a fight, they were holding pretty good artillery of their own. If he wanted a full-scale battle, well, that was fine too – the Minister would discover soon enough he was dealing with trained killers.

April 1, 2011

It was like writing a haiku.

Jonathan Robbie pondered his script. Every word had to count, and every word was counted. A small box at the top of the INews template on his computer screen remorselessly ticked off the seconds.

A word had to add something because it stole a fraction of a second. So none could be wasted, inappropriate or out of place. Those print profligates don't really appreciate words, Robbie thought; they have the luxury of too many of them.

Robbie worked in the most punishing place in media, as a senior political reporter for Channel Nine, one of Australia's three commercial TV news stations. The 6 p.m. bulletin was still where most Australians got their news and each night 1.2 million of them tuned to Nine. The competition was fierce; more so now that advertising dollars were hemorrhaging to cable TV, free digital stations and new media. Everyone's profits were down, nobody knew what the future held and so the pressure for an ever bigger, attention-grabbing splash grew.

'I don't care what the fuck you write,' Robbie's news director would say. 'Just don't bore me with pointy-headed policy. Politics is about conflict. Cover the fight. And cover it first.'

Each night, if he made the cut against fatal crashes, crime, fires and heart-rending animal stories, Robbie had just one minute and twenty seconds to make an impression. One minute and twenty seconds to grab the nation by the balls.

It had been a long road to this job and for the first time in his journalistic career he really felt the pressure of the daily demand for something dramatically new.

Robbie was a latecomer to journalism. He didn't fall into it until he was thirty, and was hired by the *Daily Telegraph* as probably the world's oldest cadet. He'd never looked back, and made his name covering lurid crimes on the Sydney tabloid's police beat.

Then came an unusual approach. With the pending retirement of press gallery legend Laurie Oakes, Channel Nine came knocking, even though Robbie had never worked in TV and knew nothing about politics. Desperate to maintain its dominance of the 6 p.m. bulletin on the east coast, Nine had poached Seven's news director, the ageing and irascible Paul Blackmore. He immediately sacked a host of people and reset Nine's news sensibilities to the shock and scandal end of the scale.

But politics still mattered and getting the Canberra bureau right was crucial. Blackmore wanted a presence. He wanted someone with flair, someone who could take the piss and who knew how to sell stories to punters. And that's what he liked about Robbie. Putting someone who had never written a TV story into such a tough gig was a risk. But Blackmore was a gambler.

It was a challenge Robbie would have found hard to resist at any price. But the price on offer was breathtaking.

Robbie was no Laurie Oakes. All he cared about was making a splash, not accuracy. He found the competition in the press gallery brutal, and making the contacts he needed to break news took time he didn't feel he had. He was prepared to cut corners to make an immediate impression. He was the press gallery version of a radio shock-jock.

Robbie never set out to make anything up – but near enough was always good enough. He would run on the mere sniff of a story, never waiting for a second source to confirm something that sounded good.

And tonight, ironically April Fools' Day, he had a yarn that would put a torpedo hole in the side of Opposition leader, Elizabeth Scott. He was about to break the news that a Canberra bureaucrat was a Liberal Party mole – leaking information to Scott to damage the Toohey Government.

And, for once, he was pretty sure it was true – because he'd received plenty of help from inside her tent.

June 22, 2011

The soft melody of Neil Young's 'After the Gold Rush' washed over him with its gentle three-chord arpeggio, a slow rhapsody in blue. Another Canadian songsmith, k.d. lang, had taken it to a higher place, caressed it with her rich chocolate lilt. Harry Dunkley loved the barefoot chanteuse and her ventures into the melancholy, a place he knew well. He was not about feeling sorry for himself but there were moments, quiet times like these, when he would reflect on what life had thrown up, the regrets that gnawed away. Now, with a glass of red in his hand, tired and frustrated after another day doing battle with a government intent on total control, it brought on memories he fought to forget.

Sydney's State Theatre – 1992? '93? They'd held hands tight, just the two of them, in love for the first time, or was it the last? He'd promised a lifetime of happiness as they'd taken the vows, a garden wedding with a celebrant, some distant relative with a trilling voice that had given them the giggles.

But Belle had left the national capital four years ago, for a new life away from politics and the wreckage of their marriage. She'd grown bored with Canberra, bored with him, sick of eating alone in their Red Hill home with its neat brick-and-tile symmetry, much like every other residence in the city's inner south.

After she'd fled he'd gone looking to fill the hole, testing other warm bodies against his own, but casual flings had never really satisfied him. Canberra was a city dedicated to the transient relationship, with its Parliament full of cheating hearts and daily lies. His brief loveless efforts to satisfy a yearning that could not be met had convinced him: he wanted none of it.

Besides, work had always been his deepest passion, his finest affair; the constant calls for 'the splash' from the news desk, the need to try and stay a step ahead of the competition. The press gallery had once soared with an esprit de corps born of a conviction that they were defending democracy, taking on the bastards, fulfilling an important role in a free country. But these days most of the bureaus resembled bank offices, with diligent tellers churning through work like automatons, counting the bucks, making it all tally, taking orders from the government of the day, waiting for the truck to back up.

Ah, he hated the soulless parade, the battery-hen mentality.

Feeling a little dirty for allowing himself to indulge in a silent rant against the decline of the free political press, Harry's melancholic nostalgia took a right-hand turn out of the gallery and up the highway to Sydney.

Gaby had left another message, this one a notch up on last week's. She needed his help with some university assignment and was unimpressed that he'd ignored her pleas, not for the first time. He made a mental note to call her in the morning, began practising an apology he'd learned so well. 'Sweetheart, sorry, so sorry ...'

Why did his interactions with her always make him feel like a lousy dad? He would lay down his life for her, his angel. She knew that. They shared a mutual talent for teasing each other, sensing each other's vulnerabilities and, occasionally, overstepping the mark. The flipside of that edgy intimacy was the joy of their cryptic calls, their secret word games. That intellectual connection with his daughter made him feel special. Protected. Alive. He loved her with all his flawed heart.

Dunkley's apartment, if it could be called that, was located at the back of a large blond-brick home in Canberra's inner south, owned by a retired couple, and a convenient drive to Parliament along the twisting maze of back roads.

It was comfortable enough, one decent-sized bedroom and another, smaller, that doubled as storage space, not that he had much of value to store. Belle had done well from the settlement, leaving him with a suitcase of regrets. He treasured an old Olivetti, a gift from his first boss, Peter Shaw, a true legend of old-school journalism. A cigar-chomping womanising free-wheeling rascal who drank himself to death, leaving a legacy of great writing and even grander tales that were still fondly recounted by the old-timers down at the Press Club.

The speakers had just finished their cello hum when the BlackBerry heralded a text message from Ben Gordon, snapping Dunkley from his reverie.

> This gets more interesting by the hour, my friend. Let's stay on it. Kimberley x

Dunkley refreshed his glass and yawned as he settled further into the stained armchair, familiar and comfortable as an old boot. 'We'll do that, Ben, we'll do that …'

June 23, 2011

Another day, another sordid chapter of the Bailey media circus. Each small change in her condition, no matter how tiny, was being regurgitated on an endless 24/7 media loop. All of Dunkley's print rivals were devoting copious column centimetres to the Foreign Minister's condition. Which meant that he was trapped into feeding the daily beast. Half-heartedly he put the finishing touches to another tedious fifty-centimetre piece on what it all meant for the future of the government, citing two constitutional experts and a former party hack.

He'd just filed the story when the phone rang, an immediately recognisable number lighting up the screen. Jesus, you again? he thought.

It was Mr DFAT, the same cultured voice from ten days earlier. 'Afternoon, Mr Dunkley, trust you are well and, ah, no doubt intrigued by my little present?'

Intrigued? That was an understatement. Everything about you, mate, even your phone number, could be a lie, Dunkley reflected.

Gordon had already delivered some solid intel about Zhou Dejiang and Bruce Paxton – dates of their first meeting together in Beijing, records of various times they had met since. On the third man they just had two words: Zheng Wang.

'Well, nice to hear your voice again, whoever you may be,' Dunkley said in a mocking tone. 'You wouldn't care to reveal yourself, by chance?'

'Not yet, Mr Dunkley. Some things are best done behind the cloak of anonymity. But I'm interested to find out if you've made any progress.'

What did Mr DFAT want? To damage the Minister? Destroy the government? Or, as had happened before, to set Dunkley up for a fall? Gordon's warning about the internal jihad against Paxton meant Dunkley needed to be cautious.

'Well, I was interested to receive a 25-year-old pic of our Defence Minister with a senior official from the Chinese Government … one Zhou Dejiang.'

'Very good, Mr Dunkley. You no doubt know then that our Mr Zhou is a real charmer.'

'Yeah, yeah, real nice guy – unless you're a Tibetan monk.'

'I see you have a good grasp of the region's geopolitics.'

'Well, I'm a journalist, and we're all bleeding hearts, aren't we?'

'In the eyes of some, perhaps. And the other face in the photo?'

'I'm still working on that.' Dunkley wanted to give no hint of Gordon's involvement.

'The past always points to the future, Mr Dunkley – this case is no exception.'

And with that little homily, Mr DFAT hung up.

Dunkley was puzzled by his mysterious informant. In his long experience he had never come across anything quite like this. He was always careful, but knew he had to proceed more cautiously than usual. He was part of someone's game, but then journalists always are. He just needed a clearer idea of who he was playing with. And what they wanted. He feared it was a deadly game and Dunkley didn't intend to appear on the casualty list.

Dunkley had suspected he would have to delve way back into Paxton's past if he wanted to solve this puzzle, and Mr DFAT had just confirmed it. Happily the looming five-week winter break meant he would have more time to pursue the Defence Minister. He was going to have to wear out some shoe leather – and he would take leave to do it. He would work in the old way, check every detail. This yarn was not grist for the 24/7 mill. He checked his watch: 3.13 p.m. That made it lunchtime in Perth.

2004-2007

Elizabeth Scott had not just broken the glass ceiling – she had destroyed it. Born into a wealthy family on Sydney's moneyed North Shore, she had the talent to make the most of her privilege and, by forty-two, had amassed a personal fortune topping $100 million. *Business Review Weekly* tagged her 'Australia's most formidable business figure' and splashed her arresting image across its cover, her athletic body wrapped in figure-hugging fencing gear. With her chestnut hair spilling to the shoulders of her white jacket she looked dazzling and dangerous.

The business world was staggered when, in 2004, she turned her hand to politics. Everyone immediately assumed she was on a relentless path to the Lodge.

A seat in Parliament did not come easy. She'd had to blast out a sitting member from the blue-ribbon electorate of Warringah on Sydney's northern beach strip. So by the time she arrived in Canberra, Scott already had more enemies than most.

It was in the spring of 2006, a year before his demise, that John Howard had elevated Scott to the newly created portfolio of Water and Climate Change, pleading with her: 'Elizabeth, just get me back in the environmental game.'

The nation was in the grip of a crippling drought, water restrictions bit deep into every bathroom and garden and the bushfires came savage and early. The steady pulse of suburbia quickened as fear grew that climate change posed a real and present danger. John Howard, tapped into the values and aspirations of middle Australia, recognised the political dangers of doing nothing. The doctors' wives were in revolt and he needed a safe pair of hands, a believer in climate science and, critically, someone the public would trust.

Elizabeth Scott fitted the mould perfectly. But the Libs were starting well behind Labor, and its crafty new leader, Catriona Bailey, was using climate change as a totemic part of her pitch for the future. She had handed responsibility for the portfolio to one of her best, Martin Toohey.

There are many quirky relationships in politics, none more so than those between Ministers and their shadows. One has all the resources of government at his or her disposal and their job is to manage a particular area of state. The other, with the aid of a handful of staffers, spends all their waking hours stalking and trying to destroy the Minister.

Yet the incestuous nature of politics means they spend a good deal of time in each other's company, attending the same events or trudging to the same dismal dinners in all parts of the country.

Toohey's close study of Scott's character convinced him that, despite her obvious brilliance, she would never cut it in politics. Her two fatal flaws were a lack of political judgement and impatience.

Their first meeting was at the reception desk of the Embassy Motel, in the inner-south Canberra suburb of Deakin. Scott could have easily afforded to buy a luxurious home, but instead preferred to let it be known that she stayed in cheap digs. But she had another, purely sentimental, reason for choosing the Embassy. She had once attended a dinner there hosted by Bruce Ruxton, the curmudgeonly head of the Victorian Returned Services League. After a word in his ear, she had been seated next to Dame Pattie Menzies, the widow of Australia's longest serving Prime Minister and the founder of the Liberal Party.

And what a night they'd had, the two women forging a close bond over an average three-course meal. Dame Pattie had delighted in recalling her role in lobbying her husband to ensure the capital got the attention it deserved. After struggling to push her granddaughter's pram over a dirt track from the Lodge to a nearby shopping centre, she'd greeted her husband's arrival home that evening with, 'Bob, you have to do something about this town.'

But of all the stories Dame Pattie told that night, the one that moved Scott was an anecdote about the former Labor Prime Minister Ben Chifley. Apparently, his direct phone line was once just one digit different from the butcher's at Manuka. Sometimes the phone would ring, the Prime Minister would answer and on the other end would be a woman with her order. Chifley would dutifully write it down and ring it through to the butcher.

It sounded like a beautiful piece of mythology but Scott wanted to believe it. The relationship between Chifley and Sir Robert was certainly no myth. Dame Pattie said they enjoyed a great friendship and would often meet for a chat behind the Speaker's chair during parliamentary sittings.

Dame Pattie grew wistful as she recalled the exact moment when Menzies was told of Chifley's death during a State Ball in the King's Hall of Old Parliament House. He had closed down the evening with a solemn declaration of loss for his old friend.

Years later and now working in government, Scott was musing that cross-party friendships were much rarer these days when she heard a familiar voice.

'Minister, you must be lost. The Hyatt is on the other side of Parliament House.'

Scott knew who Toohey was, of course. The tall Victorian had been a player in Federal politics for years. He had been a junior Minister in the Keating Government and had held a number of senior shadow ministries since. He was well liked and well regarded, considered a decent man by both sides of politics. But all agreed he lacked the venom needed to take leadership.

'Well, now it *is* clear that I'm slumming it,' Scott responded. 'But it's too late to move.'

'See you about.' And he sauntered off.

And see him about she did. The Embassy's staff played a long-running in-joke on them, rooming the two political up-and-comers next to each other whenever they were both in Canberra. Many a time, Scott would be fumbling with her room keys close to midnight when Toohey's familiar silhouette would come striding down the hall towards her.

'Night, Minister,' he would say. 'Hope that dreadful policy of yours doesn't keep you awake.'

Finally, forced to sit next to each other on a flight from Darwin to Melbourne, they started to chat properly. About the absurdity of the parliamentary lifestyle. About how much they missed their families. About the tribulations and humiliations of being a public figure.

In the final sitting week before the 2007 campaign was announced, Scott and Toohey had arrived at the Embassy at the same time.

'Well, it won't be long now; Howard has to announce soon,' Toohey said.

Scott agreed. 'Then it will be six weeks of hell before we're creamed.'

'Sounds like a reason to celebrate to me. How about a drink?'

Scott hesitated for a moment. 'Okay, but not here. And not somewhere we'll be seen.'

'I know a place in Woden,' said Toohey. 'Most Federal MPs wouldn't even know it's a Canberra suburb. But you're buying because you're loaded.'

'Lead on,' she said.

1982

A gentle rain tapped on her umbrella, the first sign of impending winter. It fell softly on the ocean of people silently sweeping by on their bicycles. Young, alone and giddy with excitement, her first venture onto the streets of Peking was a dream come true.

For as long as she could remember she had wanted to stand here, to soak up the history, to be part of this great nation with its flawed, intricately embroidered history. She couldn't think of a time when she wasn't attracted to all things Chinese.

Perhaps the spark had been the tiny Ming vase her mother had treasured. She'd marvelled at its delicate beauty, strictly off-limits to young, inquisitive hands. Much like China itself, a mystery of politics and geography during the long decades of diplomatic isolation until Nixon and Whitlam extended the Western hand of comradeship, just ten years ago.

China had been at the centre of the world for thousands of years. A civilisation making wonders like gunpowder while the

West fumbled in a more brutish age. That was why the recent decades of humiliation at the hands of the West had been so hard for it to bear. She understood that and was angered by the West's oafishness. She knew that when China woke, nations would shudder. And when it woke she wanted to be part of its journey back to its rightful place: the centre of the world.

'Hey, sweetie!' An Australian accent, harsh and unpleasant, broke her blissful peace.

'Remember me?' The man standing beside her was stocky, with thick wavy hair. 'Dinner last night … all that Chinese tucker and not a decent sweet-and-sour to be seen … Anyways,' he gestured to her camera, 'would you mind taking a snap of us?'

She noticed then the two Chinese men, both in their midtwenties, and somehow vaguely familiar. Had they been at the embassy as well? There was one other, a beautiful woman standing slightly apart from the others, but clearly attached to the group.

'Okay, smile for the camera.' She dutifully took the snap of the three men with the Kodak she'd bought in Hong Kong and promised to make a copy for the loud Australian.

And she did, plus another which she gave to a friend she'd made at the Australian embassy. A man who reminded her that while it was good to be friendly with the locals she should still be wary. That while China would rise, you needed to always remember that your first loyalty remained to your country.

It was sound advice, words she would heed. Up to a point.

2007

The Elbow Room had all the charm of a 1970s brothel, or at least what Elizabeth Scott imagined one would look like. It was not a place she would normally dream of visiting, nor did she think she would ever return.

The tawdry lace and satin lampshades ensured the dismal glow that escaped them stained the room rouge. The lounges were op-shop chic and so dilapidated she almost sank to the floor when she sat down.

'How in God's name did you ever discover this small corner of hell?' she asked.

'Yes, I like it too.' Martin Toohey, from habit, surveyed the room for familiar faces. 'It was owned by a mate I played footy with. But for some unfathomable reason he went broke. I come here because no one else in Parliament does. Also, they don't play music so loud that you have to yell to be heard. And, frankly, you can barely see your hand in front of your face in here, so being recognised isn't an issue.'

He stared at her through the scarlet haze. She looked good in any light but in here the small flaws of age were erased. It struck him, as if for the first time, that she was dangerously attractive: high cheekbones, chestnut hair, haunting grey-blue, deeply intelligent eyes. She was wearing a wraparound dress that clung to her tall, lithe athlete's frame. Add the magisterial grace of her movements and Toohey began to wonder at the wisdom of his 'let's have a drink' suggestion.

'I have a question.' He cleared his throat and shuffled deeper into the faux-leather chesterfield. 'You don't have to answer but I'm intrigued. Are you only in politics to be Prime Minister?'

'Okay. I'll tell you if you answer this: why didn't you push to be leader over Bailey? You had more support. Do you lack the ambition – or the guts – to lead?'

He bristled. 'Oh, this is the "Toohey's a weak bastard" editorial I read in the *Australian* once a month.'

'I didn't say that.'

'Yes, you did. And yes, I did have more support. But not enough. If we got locked in a stand-off then everyone would lose. I would like to be PM. I think I will be. One day. United we have a shot at winning government. If I'd held out, Labor would be the loser. I put my party first.'

'Sounds noble. Sounds like you have yourself convinced.'

'So you do think I'm weak. You, of course, the famously tough negotiator, would have held out for everything and won nothing. That's a terrorist's bargain.'

'I don't think you're weak.' Scott sipped a very ordinary red and shuddered. 'But I do think we're very different. Yes, you have to risk it all to win it all. And yes: I came here to be Prime Minister. Why would you be a politician if you didn't want that?'

'To do something for your country,' Toohey answered. 'To make a difference. To try and leave things a little better than you found them.'

'I want to do all those things. And I don't think you can do them in our system without being Prime Minister. And I wouldn't have budged with Bailey because I believe I would do a better job than her. Or you. In the end it's individuals who make a difference, not groups. History is made by the unreasonable man … or woman. I think Bailey understands that; she's certainly unreasonable.'

'No,' countered Toohey. 'Here, the mob counts. Your liberal individualism jars. You're like the First Fleet jailers: never comfortable in the land, always looking to the horizon and yearning to leave. Labor was made by the jailed. We pitched our tent here. And we understood that only by sticking together could people thrive. We are the unique Australian political project and we built the fairest society on earth, despite you.'

Scott always enjoyed a contest and Toohey was proving more interesting than she had imagined. She had thought him pleasant but glib. Good with a quick political line but without the depth to imagine the next sentence. Now she sensed another layer and, despite herself, felt a surge of excitement.

As he spoke, Toohey leaned across the too-small table and locked her in his gaze. He had gentle eyes. Hazel. Just a touch on the green side. Age had weathered him, but he wore it well. The lines around his eyes and mouth suggested he laughed a lot. If it was true that you got the face you deserved by fifty, then he was clearly decent, but sharpened by experience. As he became animated he emphasised points with his strong, finely shaped hands, and a faint hint of aftershave drifted across the table. It was a clean smell, like fresh linen. She was drawn into his eyes and, for almost the first time since she was a teenager, Scott felt her body contract with desire.

It startled her and she realised he had stopped talking and she had paused a heartbeat too long. In fencing, the error would have been fatal. This game was getting dangerous, and she loved dangerous games.

'Do you lot ever tire of reinventing the past?' She recovered like a champion. 'It's a fine speech for the True Believers, but please don't delude yourself. This nation is as much a product of my political ancestors as yours. Labor opposed Federation. And the social compact here is Liberal, built on individual rights. A party that genuinely understands that respects everyone, no matter what their race, colour or creed.'

Toohey was revelling in the contest. He hadn't had this debate in years. The pub and the argument reminded him of late nights at uni. And there was that other intoxicant of youth he realised he had been missing for a long time – the company of a beautiful woman.

As his eyes adjusted to the light he began to see the care that had gone into Scott's make-up. Above her eyes was a subtle mix of two shades of shadow and, below, the finest touch of liner.

There was just the hint of blush on her cheeks and her lips glowed an expensive shade of burgundy.

He cleared his throat, again, and tried to clear his head.

'Australia proved the value of the group. Here the land was hard and settlers had to band together to survive. Here workers had to fight for every single right. We learned through bitter struggle that solidarity was our most powerful weapon. The group makes the weak powerful. And it makes the powerful tremble.'

Scott gave up on the red and leaned into the argument, and Toohey.

'You can murder millions in the name of the group, Martin. Hitler, Stalin, Mao, all of them championed the many over the individual. The bedrock of the West is the truly revolutionary idea of a personal, individual relationship with God. Our law is built on it. Erase it and everything is negotiable. Yet demolishing our Christian keystone has been the Left's great project for over a century. Congratulations! You succeeded. And put nothing tangible in its place. Is it any wonder we are morally adrift?'

'Don't pull the cheap debating trick of hitching me to the Left's worst ideas, Elizabeth. Nice sermon but your party uses its precious heritage to justify hoarding the wealth of many in the hands of a few. Mine understands that individual rights have to be balanced with the common good. And I know the Church, I was part of it once. Religion is the best and worst of us. At its worst it has slaughtered legions of innocents across every generation.'

'It wasn't the Church that was responsible for the mass slaughter of the twentieth century, Martin,' Scott smiled. 'It was the Messianic state.'

Toohey paused. This was too much fun.

'If I might offer one gratuitous piece of political advice,' he said. 'Your impatience to lead and determination to dominate will tear your party apart.'

'Clearly I don't agree with you – again.'

'Or me with you. But if there has to be a Liberal Party and someone has to lead it … then it might as well be you.'

'Thanks … And I think you would have been a much better Labor leader than Bailey. That woman is certifiable, Martin, and I'm afraid you will live to regret not manning up on that one.'

'You don't think I'm tough enough.'

'I didn't say that. I think … I think you're … surprising.'

Toohey reached across the table and cupped her cheek in his hand. It was an impulse. She could have resisted, but she didn't. She leaned forward and kissed him gently, her tongue flirting with his lips as she slowly pulled away. The cheap wine tasted intoxicatingly better on him.

She was breathless. Her entire body tingled, her head felt light and the rouge-tinted room swirled for a moment. She wanted more, but knew she couldn't have it. She stepped back from the edge and grabbed the lifeline.

'I'm married,' she said, holding up her left hand in evidence.

'Me too.'

'Pity.'

'Yep.'

They stared at each other through the gloom for a few breathless moments.

'It's late,' he said. 'Let's go.'

July 11, 2011

It was just over three hundred paces from the press gallery lair of Harry Dunkley to the office of Terry Burden, the Clerk of the House of Representatives. A quiet and fastidious man who had given thirty years loyal service to the Parliament, Burden carried more secrets than a Catholic priest.

He was scrupulously non-partisan, a trusted soul whose counselling was frequently sought by politicians of all stripes. He sometimes joked that he was a cross between Lifeline and Legal Aid. He was part historian, part psychologist … and keeper of one of the most sensitive documents in the House, the Register of Members' Interests.

The bound volumes, maintained in neat alphabetical order, contained vast reams of information about every member elected to the House of Representatives. No one, not even the Prime Minister or his retinue of Ministers, was exempt. And every MP was required to regularly update her or his pecuniary interests, providing details of hospitality received, family trusts liquidated and shares bought and sold. For any journalist prepared to sift through a mountain of information, it was a potential goldmine. And Dunkley was prepared to do the hard yards.

It was a Monday morning and Parliament had finally taken its winter break, so things had quietened a fair bit. Even the initial fuss about Catriona Bailey's collapse had died down now she had been in hospital for some weeks with no change. Finally Harry could focus on the Paxton mystery.

He had made the requisite appointment to pore over the register. And he'd asked for a specific folio from a specific date – the N-O-P-Q folio from 1996. He had a hunch, but he needed some proof. It was too soon to start making calls that would only set hares running.

Burden's assistant, a nosey parker known ironically as Susie the Discreet, carried the bound material out to the Clerk's anteroom, where Dunkley was waiting. Five minutes was all it should take, he hoped. Leafing through the fifteen-year-old document, he quickly found the entry he was seeking, a few lines that gave some credence to his embryonic theory.

The property had been sold just after Bruce Paxton had entered Parliament, as Dunkley had expected. Now he needed to find out where the money had come from to buy it. And that would take time even the reduced daily grind of work wouldn't allow. So, after he knocked off the Newspoll splash for tomorrow's paper, he was taking four weeks leave.

July 11, 2011

As regular as a metronome, Justin Greenwich would wake early every second Monday with a knot deep in the pit of his stomach.

The Opposition leader's press secretary knew that, later that day, a short walk from his Parliament House office, the *Australian*'s political editor, Harry Dunkley, would receive several pages of raw data that could make or break political careers. Eventually, Dunkley would call Greenwich to give him a heads-up on the numbers. Then it was Greenwich's grim duty to relay them to Scott. And she didn't take bad news well.

For two months, Newspoll had been a horror story for Elizabeth Scott and the Coalition she led. The slide had begun after a disastrous overreach by Scott. A Channel Nine story by Jonathan Robbie had shattered her credibility, revealing she had groomed a Finance Department official, Michael Hamilton, to give damaging evidence against the government at parliamentary hearings.

Hamilton was a Liberal mole who had been funnelling information to the Opposition for years. But, typically, an impatient Scott had pushed him hard and Hamilton grew reckless, handing over highly sensitive material on a financial rescue package for building societies in the wake of the global meltdown.

An internal investigation flagged Hamilton to the Australian Federal Police. While they watched he continued to shovel out information to Scott. But it got worse when, in his eagerness to please, Hamilton fabricated some facts to implicate the Prime Minister in dubious dealings with a building society based in Toohey's electorate of Corio.

In what Greenwich saw as a cruel twist, Robbie broke the Scott–Hamilton link on April Fools' Day. It caused a sensation.

Scott wasn't responsible for the fraud, but it didn't matter. Perceptions are everything in politics. The media crucified her and the story refused to die. The Coalition had been ahead of the Government in the polls but its primary vote dropped five points after the story aired. That was nothing compared to what happened to Scott's personal rating – it plummeted twenty points in a fortnight.

One thing that had surprised Greenwich at the time the story broke was how Scott had insisted on seeing the Prime Minister to personally apologise. Greenwich had gone with her but all staff were banished from the room. He didn't have to cool his heels in enemy territory long because the meeting was over in less than five minutes. Scott had been visibly upset when she emerged from Toohey's office.

Greenwich's BlackBerry rang.

'How bad?'

'Depends.' Dunkley's voice was friendly and Greenwich knew he was trying to soften the blow. 'The primary vote is basically stable on 39. But of course that still gives Labor a lead on two-party preferred, 52–48.'

'Don't toy with me, Harry,' Greenwich's voice quavered. 'You know there's only one thing she cares about. How is she tracking on personal satisfaction?'

'Ummm … satisfied, 21 per cent; dissatisfied, 62 per cent.'

Greenwich's hands were sweating so much he could barely write and his brain struggled to digest the figures.

'Jesus wept. What? Down four points on last fortnight?'

'Yes.'

'Down four points on what you said was the lowest rating of any Opposition leader in Newspoll history?'

'Yes, it's bad.'

'What's the splash?'

'Well, the splash is something else. But on Scott we have a breakout reviving the famous *Bulletin* front page on Howard.'

'What … "Why does this man bother?".'

'Well, to be accurate: "Why does this woman bother?".'

'Harry …'

'Yes, Justin?'

'I hope you die a lonely, slow and painful death.'

'You have a good night too, mate. See you about.'

The sweat from Greenwich's palms had made a small damp spot on his pad, smudging some of the figures. But he could not erase the horror of what they meant.

With the right leader the Opposition should be well ahead of the weak Toohey Government. But these numbers held only one message: Elizabeth Scott wasn't that leader.

Scott was in the adjoining office, waiting for her press secretary to deliver the numbers. He looked at his pad again and picked up his mobile. His fingers fumbled with the tiny keyboard as he punched out a text message. Then he grabbed his bag, hitting 'send' as he scurried for the door.

He was in the corridor when a familiar voice echoed down the hallway.

'You are JOKING! Justin, get in here. NOW!'

And for the first time in many years, Greenwich broke into a sprint as he made for the exit.

June 6, 2011

The two-car convoy, sleek BMWs with darkened windows and reinforced exteriors, snaked up the steep driveway. It approached the circular drive with military precision, coming to a halt just a few steps from an imposing front entrance. Three men wearing dark suits and even darker don't-fuck-with-me stares quickly stepped out of the vehicles.

It was Rambo-style, over-the-top, and Brent Moreton, the newly arrived United States Ambassador to Australia, loved every GI minute of it. He checked his Seiko Velatura – a personal gift from the President – and stepped out into the brisk Canberra air. 'Good evening, sir.' The concierge at the Commonwealth Club was unerringly polite.

It was a Monday night, June 6, and Moreton was meeting with the Alliance for the first time.

Ambassador to Australia was a mid-level posting by Washington standards, a chance for Moreton to work with one of

America's closest and most trusted allies – even if it was a country that most Americans had never visited and knew little about. Moreton had accepted the job with little hesitation, viewing it as a stepping stone to a more exciting and important posting – or possibly as an entree to a seat in Congress.

He'd struck up a firm friendship with the British High Commissioner and found the work satisfying but hardly intoxicating. Relations between the superpower and its Pacific cousin were in good shape, despite the occasional flare-up over trade and business issues. Until now.

Moreton walked briskly along a thickly carpeted corridor before entering a discreetly luxurious sitting room overlooking the club's garden, with views through to the lake. Three men were waiting, one in military regalia, the other two in crisp business suits, each of them cradling a beer or glass of wine.

'Ambassador, so very nice of you to come to our little gathering.' Jack Webster, Chief of the Defence Force, ushered Moreton into the private room and offered him a drink. Air Chief Marshal Webster, a thirty-year veteran of Defence, had met the Ambassador a number of times over the years, mostly in Washington where the two would sometimes cross paths during the Australian–American Leadership Dialogue and other bilateral talkfests.

They were both men of patrician bearing who shared a mutual love for their flags; both were dyed-in-the-wool patriots for the cause.

'Ambassador, I think you know Tom …'

Thomas Heggarty, Director-General of the Australian

Secret Intelligence Service, offered an outstretched hand. 'Good evening, Ambassador, glad you could make it.'

'Hello, Tom, you're looking prosperous as always.'

The two men smiled, as if sharing a private joke.

David Joyce, Secretary of the Department of Foreign Affairs, stepped forward. 'Mr Ambassador, you look well, this Canberra climate is obviously agreeing with you.'

'I don't mind these sub-zero temperatures, David, although Janet is finding it tough to maintain her Texan tan.' There were laughs all round.

'Okay, let's get down to business.' Webster spoke firmly. 'I'll call Fred and we'll get the dinner orders happening; after all, we don't want to be disturbed too often.'

'Correction, Jack, we don't want to be disturbed at all.'

The Ambassador fixed the three men with a look so serious, he could have been announcing a death in the family.

The four men took their seats, brushing away a waiter. Moreton clasped his hands and studied them, confident they could be trusted with the intel he was about to deliver.

Webster, Heggarty and Joyce had started meeting regularly at the Commonwealth Club some five years ago, drawn together by a common desire to protect – indeed nurture – the relationship with the United States amid a worrying trend on both sides of politics to forge ever-closer ties with China. Within the senior ranks of the Commonwealth public service, they were known as the most strident supporters of the US relationship and had dubbed themselves 'the Alliance' as a nod to this.

The Alliance's meetings were shrouded in Freemason-like secrecy. They told no one, not even their wives, of the gatherings, but the serving US ambassador had a standing invitation to attend.

With its lush two acres of gardens and old worldly atmospherics, the Commonwealth Club offered the perfect sanctuary. Sure, it was frequented by other senior members of the public service, but discretion was always honoured and private meetings could take place in its myriad of rooms.

Several days ago, Ambassador Moreton had contacted Webster on his secure private phone line, seeking an urgent meeting with the Alliance. He wouldn't give the reason over the phone, except to say it was of the utmost importance.

Now Moreton began. 'Gentlemen, we need to establish some ground rules before we start. What I am about to tell you remains within these four walls. It has to be strictly between us four – understood?'

No one demurred.

'Two weeks ago, I was summoned to DC for what I imagined would be a routine debrief on my first few months in Canberra, the kind of thing that could have been done over a secure line. It was far from it ...

'When I arrived at the State Department, I was whisked through security and taken directly to Assistant Secretary Robert Hinds' office; as you know he's one of Hillary's confidants.

'Guys, this is where it gets real touchy. Your Defence Minister, Mr Paxton ...'

Moreton's voice trailed off as he considered how best to phrase the coming bombshell. He trained his eye on Webster, and cleared his throat.

'Our government, at the very highest level, fears Mr Paxton is way too close to the Chinese. Given that we share our intelligence with you, this jeopardises us as much as it does you. I have been sent with a very specific message. Fix it or … or your access to our intel ends.'

The three mandarins sat stunned. The Defence Minister was treading all over his Department, trying to make absurd cuts – but Bruce Paxton, a traitor? It defied belief.

And the US was threatening to end what the Australian defence and intelligence agencies treasured above all else: access to the best intel money could buy. Thousands of spies and analysts and a spy satellite network that could read your newspaper from space.

It was one of the lasting legacies of the close friendship between John Howard and George W Bush. At Howard's insistence, in July 2004, Bush had signed a one-page presidential directive to the US Defense Department and the Central Intelligence Agency ordering them to allow Australia access to the Secret Internet Protocol Router Network (**SIPRNET**) used by the military to store information about intelligence, operations orders and technical data. Until then **SIPRNET** had a **NOFORN** ('no foreign eyes') classification, and that included the British and the Australians.

The US intelligence establishment was flabbergasted and pushed back, refusing to implement the directive for years. In

2006 Howard called his friend again and went public with his complaint, attacking the Pentagon for ignoring a presidential directive.

The barrier was lifted and Australia got access to what was described by former Defence Minister Robert Hill as 'the greatest repository of information that exists'.

Webster finally spoke. 'You can't be serious! Paxton's an amateur, out of his depth, but he's not a security risk. What evidence do you have?'

The Ambassador narrowed his gaze. 'It seems the Secretary of State heard it direct … from your Foreign Minister. Check his past. Fix this. You've got two months or the pipeline will be switched off.'

June 19, 2011

As she'd prepared for her *Lateline* interview, Catriona Bailey had carried the worrying signs of an impending stroke. All the things she'd put down to tiredness would have disturbed a trained eye: dropping the glass, the dizziness, the trouble she had understanding questions, the headache, the difficulty she had writing.

It was her addiction to galloping about the world to insert herself in the news cycle that was at the root of the problem. A punishing series of jaunts saw her more rundown than usual and she had picked up the flu on her way back to Canberra. Typically defying orders to rest she'd ploughed on until a fever forced her to bed. The flu is much more dangerous than many appreciate and Bailey's heart was damaged by it. Her fever broke but a blood clot had formed in her heart and was pumped out and up a vertebral artery that emerges at the base of the brain and merges with another to form the basilar artery.

Here the clot lodged. It cut the flow of oxygen-rich blood to the brain's junction box, the pons, which suffered catastrophic damage.

And so Bailey collapsed and appeared to be unconscious and unreachable. But she was not. She had suffered a very particular type of stroke and the effect was coma-like, but not a coma.

What Bailey was experiencing was locked-in syndrome. She had been completely unconscious for over a day, but then she woke. She struggled to remember what had happened. She found she could hear and think clearly but was unable to move a single muscle in her body, even to open her eyes. And there was the problem. Others afflicted by locked-in syndrome could alert doctors to their fate by blinking responses. But Bailey's eyes remained firmly shut. In any case, her doctors were consumed by the task of simply keeping her alive. Even the most astute neurologist would have struggled to diagnose what was going on in Bailey's brain at this stage of her illness.

The first words she'd heard on waking came from a familiar voice.

'You selfish bitch.'

It was Martin Toohey, the bastard who had stolen the only thing that mattered to her: her job. The man she would never forgive.

And the man who didn't know that she had already laid a landmine that would destroy him and bring down his government full of traitors.

That thought of revenge empowered and sustained her. If she could have smiled, she would have.

May 16, 2011

For nearly a century, the Brookings Institution has been at the heart of every serious policy tussle in the US. A brisk ten-minute walk from the White House, it has also achieved the near impossible: in blindingly partisan Washington, it has the respect of both the Democrats and Republicans.

For Catriona Bailey, Brookings was as familiar and welcoming as the United Nations headquarters in New York. She had been a regular visitor for thirty years, using its global diaspora as her own kind of personal Wikipedia. She'd shifted, slightly, her view on the West Bank settlements after a series of animated discussions with a Jewish academic she'd met a decade before, and who was now courting trouble in Jerusalem with his pro-Palestinian views.

For as long as she could remember, Bailey had wanted to be a part of Brookings, to be endorsed by it, feted by it and ushered into its inner sanctum.

As a student in the 1970s, Bailey had courted contacts at Brookings as a hooker courts her clientele; her appointment as a non-resident senior fellow was one of the proudest days of her life. But not the proudest. That came in April 2008 when Bailey returned to Brookings as Prime Minister of Australia, making her first trip overseas aboard the Boeing 737 the Howards had ordered six years before. She had chosen Brookings as the venue for her first serious foreign policy speech, a statement that she was sure would resonate around the globe.

Bailey wanted to recast the relationship between the US and China, and saw herself as a kind of regional intermediary, the Kissinger-of-the-Pacific. Her speech – an opus stretching nearly fifty minutes – outlined her views on how to manage the rise of China and how to refashion the post World War II power settlements to ensure China was a stakeholder in all decisions affecting global security. She argued that conflict between the US and China was avoidable and the 'Pacific century' should be marked by a close working relationship between the Americans and Chinese.

It was a bold foray into global affairs, and well received by the policy wonks at Brookings, who were delighted to see one of their own elevated into a position of serious influence. Over morning tea, the Washington intelligentsia helped to fuel the notion that Cate Bailey was the woman the West needed at this vital hour, when the power balance was shifting East. Some said she could be the most important leader of her generation, the Thatcher of her time, a murmur Bailey did nothing to dispel with the travelling Australian media pack.

But it was a special meeting after the speech that helped lift that day into the stratosphere. The US presidential primaries were in full swing and Bailey's office, together with the Australian Ambassador, had called in every favour to try and get 'face-time' and, more importantly, picture opportunities, with each of the three key candidates: the Republican frontrunner John McCain and the two Democrats who were still locked in a bruising struggle, Barack Obama and Hillary Clinton.

In the end, Obama proved elusive, and Bailey had to settle for a thirty-minute phone conversation with the black superstar, something her staff later paid for dearly.

But Hillary – well, that was a different equation. Clinton was an old friend, a member of the sisterhood and a Brookings fellow traveller. She called in for a delightful forty-minute chat with Bailey after her 'rise of China' speech.

So chuffed was Bailey by Clinton's show of support that she made a minor faux pas during the photo opportunity when the obvious question was asked: 'So, are you backing Mrs Clinton for President?'

Bailey got that goofy look on her face that always emerged when she knew she was cornered. Clinton had done her an enormous favour, but ... how could a new Australian PM express a preference in US domestic politics?

'Well, you know me ... we girls have got to stick together.'

Clinton beamed, taking it as an endorsement – a sentiment shared by the travelling media pack. The PM's media minders were forced to spend hours hosing it down, claiming it was nothing more than an expression of friendship, not a signal of preference over Obama.

Three years after she had delivered that brilliant speech, Bailey was back and so much had changed. Officially, Bailey was in DC as the Foreign Minister to hear Clinton, as Secretary of State, address Brookings on what the Arab Spring meant for US relations in the Middle East.

Unofficially, she had a very specific message she intended to deliver.

After Clinton's speech the two old friends sat down in the same room where, in 2008, they had met in such different roles. The irony was not lost on either of them.

'Things didn't exactly turn out the way we expected,' quipped Clinton.

'No,' said Bailey. 'I certainly didn't see it coming, did you?'

'For a long time Bill was convinced that we would win, and so was everyone else who mattered ... But what can you do? It's history; Obama has been surprisingly gracious and ... well, this is a great job.'

'So is mine,' Bailey lied. Just the memory of being Prime Minister was enough to make her wince. And she suspected Clinton felt the same about missing out on becoming the leader of the Free World.

'There's something we're concerned about, Cate.' Clinton seamlessly switched to business. 'We hear from our embassy that your Defence Minister is considering making big cuts. Our people are keen to ensure your commitment to the Joint Strike Fighter is rock solid.'

'Hillary, you know that's sacrosanct,' Bailey said. 'I made it a priority when I was Prime Minister and Toohey has publicly backed it.'

'We aren't concerned about you or Toohey. We're concerned about Paxton. Is he committed to the Alliance? His public remarks are quite pro-China.'

'Paxton's from Western Australia. They all love China because it's making them rich. I'm sure his past ... dalliances ... were, well, meaningless.'

'Dalliances?' The alarm in Clinton's voice was obvious, and Bailey closed the net.

'It was a long time ago. He was just a union official on one of those visits the Labor Left used to make to China. It was the first time I met him. He was introduced to a young Tibetan woman, Weng Meihui. She turned out to be working for their intelligence service.'

'And the nature of this relationship?' Clinton leaned closer.

'Well, she was very ... persuasive.'

'You're telling me that Australia's Defence Minister had a sexual relationship with a Chinese spy?'

'He wasn't Defence Minister then. And he hadn't seen her for years ...'

'Hadn't?'

'Until three months ago. February. They met again over dinner.'

'Are you sure? How do you know?'

'Because, Hillary, I hosted it.'

Bailey paused to allow her friend to fully absorb the revelation before continuing. 'Look, Hillary, I'm sure it isn't serious.'

'Cate, I'm not so sure.'

'Hillary, no …' For the next ten minutes, Bailey launched a strident defence of Paxton. For the record. But, as she left, she knew the damage had been done. The clock was now ticking.

A smile creased her face.

July 12, 2011

'Those bastards, those grubby, calculating fucking bastards.'

Each word was spat out by Sam Buharia, who sat with a neat espresso, dumbfounded by the front page of the *Australian*.

He both hated the national broadsheet for its relentless campaigning against Labor, and admired it for its audacious use of power. But this morning, Rupert's flagship had gone too far.

BAILEY IN COMA OUT-POLLS TOOHEY

In an act of rat-cunning Sussex Street would have been proud of, the *Oz* had included Bailey in its fortnightly Newspoll. Oh, and just to ram home the point, the paper had splashed it all over page one. Gleefully.

Catriona Bailey was ten points ahead of Martin Toohey as preferred Prime Minister – even more so with Labor voters – and twenty points in front of Opposition leader Elizabeth Scott.

The imagery was devastating, Buharia thought. A half-dead politician out-polling the PM screamed that Toohey was a dead man walking. The only good news, if any could be extracted from this stinking turd of a front page, was that the dropkick of an Opposition leader was stone motherless dead. If she was leading Labor, he would have capped her months ago.

Killing off leaders was something of a sport for Buharia. He was the one who signed the death warrant, leaving his loyal lieutenants to push the bodies down the elevator shaft. He'd had a hand in putting down two New South Wales Premiers and one Prime Minister, a record unique in Australian politics. Unfortunately he didn't seem to equate semi-regular assassination with long-term brand damage.

He was almost single-handedly responsible for what people dubbed the New South Wales disease: the poll-driven approach to politics that focused on spin, and had wrung the last juices of idealism out of Labor's marrow. What was left were the dry bones of a once great party.

Buharia was obsessed with polling, particularly the focus groups of six to eight people who were gathered as litmus tests of community sentiment. He did not understand that, properly used, the idea was to lead that sentiment, not follow it. Buharia's favourite saying after any focus group was, 'The punters hate it, mate.' One negative focus group on an issue was enough for him to start demanding that the government abandon multi-million-dollar projects. Several months of bad results saw him orchestrating Cabinet reshuffles.

He had coveted power from an early age and graduated from

playground racketeering to Labor politics with ease. He had a gift for arithmetic and soon discovered that a man who could deliver numbers in Labor was a man to be reckoned with. He cultivated ethnic community leaders who could swing large groups of their people into ALP branches at a moment's notice. These flying squads would arrive at a branch en masse, sign up as members and then vote whichever way Buharia wanted.

And so Buharia had risen through the ranks of his party to be New South Wales Secretary by the age of thirty, continuing the tradition of colourful characters who had littered Labor's past all the way back to its 1891 origins. But he lacked subtlety and foresight. He failed to see that just winning power was not enough to sustain a government, or a party. In the end you have to stand for something.

Watching appalled from Victoria, Brendan Ryan would note, 'Buharia thinks a year is 365 contests for the 6 p.m. news. He's all tactics and no strategy. And what he's done is lose us his State for a generation.'

Buharia quit his role as Secretary for the sinecure of the Senate before the full horror of his work in New South Wales was apparent. There he could enjoy a long career in relative anonymity. And continue to pull strings behind the scenes.

After about two minutes of absorbing the Bailey headline – a reasonably in-depth study by his standards – Buharia picked up his mobile and hit autodial 1.

'Cunts,' the current New South Wales State Secretary spat as he picked up.

'Yes mate, but what do we do about it?'

1980-2011

Ben Gordon had difficulty remembering the first time he'd felt different. He had wrestled with his gender and the key role this confusion played in his life for more than two decades. He often confided in Harry Dunkley, even though his old friend was clearly uncomfortable talking about it. 'Ben, you live your life to the fullest, mate, and I'll lead mine,' Dunkley would say.

Gordon was the product of a safe middle-class upbringing – he'd attended a GPS school, enjoyed strong academic results, had an excellent sporting record and an inquiring mind. Then, in his mid twenties, he'd felt a yearning to feminise his life. At his core he knew that his internal wiring didn't match his exterior. Dunkley would console him by saying, 'Everyone wonders who they are, mate; it's just that, for you, the question is more profound.'

He'd bottled these feelings up upon his arrival in Canberra, conforming to the regimented life of a bureaucrat, unwilling to stand out in a city that did everything in its power to fade into the landscape. And he did not want to cruel his chances of promotion. He spent eight years in the Defence Signals Directorate, working for one of the best analysts the agency had produced, Trevor Harris, before he'd worked up the guts to reveal all.

Unfortunately his timing was bad. Trev was working flat chat on a Friday evening to finish a top-secret briefing for the Prime Minister on an operation gone wrong in Iraq, when Gordon bowled up and burst out with, 'Trev, I'm going to change my name and identity—'

'Yeah, sure,' Trevor said, waving a hand to indicate he was busy.

Gordon had considered a full sex change and done the research on what was required; he had even chosen a pretty name – Kimberley. But he'd decided against meddling with nature and instead opted for the less extreme life of a transvestite. He'd be a cross-dressing transformer working in one of the most secretive and paranoid arms of government – all six feet two inches of him … er, her.

When Gordon arrived at the DSD office the Monday following his announcement to Trevor, the first hurdle he confronted was security – they wouldn't let him in. Trevor fielded an irate call from the chief guard.

'Trev, we have someone down here who claims to be Ben Gordon.'

'And?' said Trevor.

'He's a she.'

'Oh fuck …'

'That's what I said.'

'I'll be down in a minute.'

At this point Trev realised he should have paid more attention to Ben's change-of-identity announcement.

But Trev went into bat for him, extolling his analytical skills as some of the best in the business. The security clearance had then been routine, less trouble than Gordon expected. Reluctantly, the DSD hierarchy had given its blessing.

Trev's only request was for Ben to be discreet when he was at meetings with other sections of the intelligence community. 'No flirting,' he had insisted.

That wasn't an issue. However, Ben's insistence on using the female bathroom had caused a near meltdown.

Fifteen years later and Ben Gordon's cross-dressing lifestyle was now as routine as Friday night drinks. The women had even accepted him using their bathroom (but were quietly thankful when the agency installed a 'gender neutral' toilet).

From his kitchen, a kettle whistle sang, stirring Gordon from his thoughts. There is work to be done, Ms Analyst, he said quietly to himself. He had been putting in long hours at DSD and there'd been precious little time to pick up his 'project' with Dunkley. He'd finally squeezed a half-day off.

Dressed in a casual outfit he referred to as 'Target Chic', he was preparing to spend the next few hours immersed in what he imagined would be largely historical trivia. With just a few computers and a cup of steaming chai for company.

Whenever Ben hit a dead end in analysis his routine was to radically shift thinking. What made him the best in his trade was his ability to imagine another path. In his experience, too much focus on minutiae meant you could miss the big picture. The photo was a tiny part of the huge story that was Australia–China relations. So he would set it and his secret databases aside. Ben would now tackle the problem by using 'open source' material. And he would start with the woman charged with leading Australia's side of the relationship.

'Catriona Bailey, Catriona Bailey, Catriona Bailey.' Line after mind-numbing line of information about Ms Bailey consumed the 27-inch computer screen, mostly mundane facts about the Foreign Minister's early years in politics, her rise to the highest office in the land – and then her quick demise.

He was more intrigued by several pages of information that outlined Bailey's trajectory as an academic at the Australian National University. She had built such an impressive list of achievements before choosing a life in the helter-skelter of politics.

But nearly hidden among the reams of facts and figures was a nugget so golden it could have been sold then and there for a high price.

Gordon leaned forward, eyes trained on a single line. Bailey had been in Beijing for three months in the early 1980s. Wasn't that about the same time that Paxton had visited the Chinese capital?

The small gem, until now, had escaped both Gordon and Dunkley. Something inside the analyst's razor-sharp mind sensed it could be significant.

It would mean a short drive across the lake to the ANU. But that would have to wait. Gordon's real job beckoned. And the skills of a professional voyeur had never been more in demand.

July 13, 2011

George Papadakis scanned the small room and called the meeting to order. He felt like a Soviet general at Stalingrad, hoping to survive the latest setback in a long siege.

He had assembled his best war Cabinet to map out a strategy on what he called the Bailey Affair.

In the room were the convenor of the Victorian Right, Brendan Ryan; his NSW counterpart, Sam Buharia; National Secretary, Alistair Cook; and constitutional wizard Dr Sarah Franklin.

Franklin was there because Bailey's staunch refusal to die meant that they were now in uncharted waters. The Foreign Minister had been in a coma for several weeks now and while she thankfully hadn't woken up, she also didn't appear to be going away.

'Sarah, how long do we have to wait before we can declare Bailey's seat vacant?' Papadakis asked.

'That depends,' replied Franklin.

'On what?'

'On the question.'

Franklin loved knowing more than anyone else and Papadakis feared this was going to take a long time.

'Sarah, assume for a moment that I don't really care about the health of the member in question and might, if I let my dark side dominate, be wishing her a swift and not entirely pain-free death. Given she, typically, stubbornly refuses to die, what I want to know is how long it will take to kill her politically and have a by-election.'

'Unfortunately, given the circumstances, the Constitution isn't clear on this,' Franklin said. 'Nor is precedent much guide. The Constitution says she has to sign a letter of resignation to the Speaker of the House of Representatives.'

'For Christ's sake, she can't sign, she's a veggie,' roared Buharia, who was getting cranky surprisingly early in the conversation.

'If she can't sign we can get someone to act as her agent,' Franklin said. 'But we need to be able to establish that we have her permission. That is, we need to prove that she wants to resign.'

Brendan Ryan weighed in. 'In case my colleague didn't make himself clear, she has been on life support for weeks now. She's in intensive care and not expected to recover.'

'And you are certain she's incapable of understanding what's going on?' Franklin asked.

'Let's assume she's plant life.' Ryan confirmed Buharia's assessment.

'Well, if she's absent from Parliament for more than two months, the Speaker can declare her position vacant. But let's be very clear on this. In the one hundred and eleven years of Federal Parliament in this country no member's position has ever been declared vacant because he or she was absent without leave. Only one has ever been expelled. That was Hugh McMahon, the member for Kalgoorlie, on 11 November 1920, for making seditious statements against the Crown. And, by the way, changes to the rules since then mean that can't ever happen again.'

'Jesus, there must be some sort of time limit on how long you can represent a seat without showing up in Parliament,' moaned Buharia.

'Not really.' Franklin warmed to her task; she had spent a week buried in the finer points of procedure and practice. 'The longest leave of absence on record is Adair Blain, an independent member for the Northern Territory. And this might shed a bit of chilly light on the current state of affairs: he was captured by the Japanese at the fall of Singapore in 1942, and then re-elected unopposed in 1943, while he was a prisoner of war. When he finally walked into Parliament on 26 September 1945, wearing his uniform, after two years as a POW, he received a standing ovation. He was then granted another two months leave to recover in hospital.'

A shudder went through the room. This was stupidly harder than anyone anticipated, but it was par for the course when dealing with anything to do with Bailey.

'I swear this woman is like some kind of medieval curse on the party,' muttered Ryan, neatly summarising the feeling of the room.

'Indeed, but if there is no precedent, we will have to make one,' Papadakis said. 'Her specialists tell me there is no likelihood of recovery. We need to get that in writing, then we need to write to the Speaker asking that her seat be declared vacant. And the Speaker needs to say yes.'

'What if the House intervenes?' said Franklin. 'What if the independents, the Greens and the Coalition refuse to countenance the removal of a member at the behest of a party?'

'She was elected as a member of this party,' raged Buharia. 'She can't do her job from intensive care. We have a right to replace her.'

'You have no right to do anything of the sort,' snapped Franklin, irritated by the routine ignorance of the law she so often found in the Senators and MPs who were charged with making it. 'There is no mention of political parties in the Constitution. There is no mention of the Prime Minister or Cabinet. The law puts great weight on the people's right to elect their representatives and on the right of those representatives to hold their place in Parliament until the people remove them.'

'That may be so,' said Ryan, 'but I think that we should proceed as George advises. We should wait a decent amount of time, say a couple of weeks, and then put the advice of the specialists to the Speaker and encourage him to make the call, no matter how the House feels about it. He is, after all, supposed to be one of us. And we should begin planning for a by-election now, which, God knows, is going to be almost impossible to win.'

'And while the Constitution might make no mention of the Prime Minister or Cabinet, they both exist,' said Papadakis. 'And, after a decent amount of time, the Prime Minister will announce that his Foreign Minister is incapacitated and incapable and we will have a Cabinet reshuffle. Alistair, get a team together to prepare for a by-election in Bailey's seat. I'll be fucked if I'm leaving that in the hands of that dropkick Secretary of the New South Wales branch.'

Papadakis turned his attention to Buharia. He loathed the Senator from New South Wales and rarely deigned to speak to him directly.

'And, finally, Sam, is there anyone left in that festering cesspool you preside over who's not currently facing some kind of charge and is capable of actually winning a by-election?'

'I don't like your tone,' said Buharia.

'I don't like you. I don't like your branch. I don't like what you've done to our party. So we all have our crosses to bear,' snapped Papadakis. 'You were the clown who foisted Bailey on us in the first place. You backed her long after it was clear she was barking mad. You are the architect of this crisis and you would not be drawing breath if I had anything to do with it.'

'I didn't hear you complaining when we won the election, or for the two years she was untouchable in the polls. It's easy to be wise after the event, soft-cock.'

Ryan didn't like Buharia either but he needed a working relationship.

He intervened. 'Everybody take a powder. We all need to work on this together. It's going to be tough enough without squabbling among ourselves. Let's do the research, find a candidate, and see if there's a single positive we can massage into a message.

'And let's look on the bright side. Bailey might die any day now.'

July 15, 2011

It was a small obituary, tucked away on page 22 of *The Age*, a quarter-page of copy that most readers would ignore on their way to the crossword or TV guide.

Lifted from the *New York Times*, it was a perfunctory 350-word opus on Walter Chang, known to his Communist mates as 'Wally'. The reclusive industrialist had survived the brutal crackdown against capitalists at the height of the Cultural Revolution, later emerging as a central player in China's economic awakening from the late 1970s.

CHINA'S 'RED CAPITALIST' DEAD AT 93

Born in 1918, Walter Chang had a privileged upbringing, living in a luxurious mansion and driving an American-made sports car. On the eve of the 1949 Communist revolution, he took over the family's business, which by then consisted of more than twenty flour and textile mills with some 65,000 employees. But the Chang business empire was effectively shackled by the Communists in the 1950s as the State shut down large swathes of privately run firms, replacing them with centrally controlled mega-sectors. Despite losing much of his fortune, the diminutive Chang would later become one of Deng Xiaoping's most trusted advisers. He provided valuable guidance to the newly appointed leader as he encouraged like-minded entrepreneurs to attach their capitalist flag to the Communist mast. Chang took full advantage of his status, and played a key role in spearheading the first wave of Chinese mining investment to Canada and Australia through the State-owned investment vehicle, China International Trust and Investment Corp—

Dunkley pulled up suddenly, mid-sentence, doing his best not to spill coffee on a just-ironed business shirt. He reread the lines before reaching into his shoulder bag for the file he had already compiled on Paxton, a collection of notes and photocopies of documents and old press clippings.

And there it was. An article from the early 1980s taken from the business pages of the *West Australian*. Paxton and his UMF mates were running riot on building sites in what was then the very wild West. But a single line had struck Dunkley as odd the first time he'd read it.

Union Secretary Mr Bruce Paxton congratulated Guangzhou Mining for being a model employer in the WA mining sector.

And underneath it said:

> Guangzhou is a subsidiary of China's State-owned investment arm, CITIC, which is understood to be exploring offshore opportunities in Australia, as well as the US and Canada. Its chairman is Mr Zheng Tian, also known as Wally Chang, who has handed responsibility for the Australian venture to his son, Zheng Wang …

And now here, next to the obituary, was a photograph of the Red Capitalist and his son, Wang – the very same man from the black-and-white photo.

'Jesus, the third man is the son of the Red Capitalist … where is this going?' Dunkley said to himself.

He recalled the lines that Mr DFAT, his anonymous Deep Throat, had uttered during their most recent phone conversation: 'The past always points to the future.'

Now, after weeks of often fruitless searching, another piece of the jigsaw had fallen into place.

Dunkley knew that he needed to do a heap more digging, but it wasn't iron ore, gold or nickel he was mining for. It was something much more valuable. Something, he knew, that could not be found on the east coast.

July 15, 2011

Catriona Bailey lay stricken on her hospital bed, her life measured by a battery of medical machinery. To the untrained eye she was beyond resurrection. But Amy McCallum's eye saw things that escaped everyone else.

Regarded as one of the nation's best neurologists, she had been called in from Melbourne to examine the Foreign Minister. Bailey had been unresponsive for weeks now and the Canberra medical team had exhausted all possibilities. It seemed Bailey would never recover. But McCallum knew from long experience never to take appearances for granted.

She sat on Bailey's bed and began the ritual. She always assumed her patient could hear her.

'Hi, Ms Bailey, I'm Amy, a neurologist,' she started. 'You are in intensive care in Canberra Hospital. You have been here for a month after suffering a serious stroke. You are on life support. You were unconscious on arrival and showed no response to any stimulus. Your eyes have been closed the whole time and recently they have been taped down. I am just going to open your eyes now. It shouldn't hurt.'

McCallum gently removed the tape, wiped the outside of Bailey's eyes and opened them.

'Okay, I want you to do something for me. Look left.'

And Bailey's eyes moved left. The nurse standing next to the bed gasped.

'Look right,' said McCallum.

Bailey's eyes moved right.

'Jesus,' whispered the nurse.

'Blink if you can hear me clearly and understand what I am saying.'

Bailey blinked.

'That's excellent, Ms Bailey. Let's try something else. I am going to get the nurse to hold your feet. Can you move your toes?'

Nothing. The nurse shook her head.

'All right. I am going to put my finger in your hand. Can you squeeze it?'

Nothing.

'Okay, I am going to touch your arm. I want you to blink once if you can feel it or twice if you cannot.'

Bailey blinked once.

'I'm going to touch your leg now; can you feel it?'

Bailey confirmed she could.

'Ms Bailey, I think I know what's happened. You have suffered a rare kind of stroke. The lower part of your brain has been damaged and that means you have no control over any part of your body, save your eyes. In fact your eye movement is very good. And because your pathways have not been damaged you can still feel your body, which is one of the many aspects of this condition which makes it so distressing.

'It might be a long time before you can move.'

Here McCallum wasn't entirely forthcoming; she knew it was highly unlikely Bailey would ever move again. She knew that people with locked-in syndrome usually died within four months. But she saw no need to dwell on that now as there were things that could be done, miraculous things. And some patients lived for years.

'Your upper brain has not been damaged and that means you have had no loss of brain function. That's a start. And since you can move your eyes you can talk to us and give us instructions. We just need you to learn a new language. Here's what I want you to do.'

July 15, 2011

The two men sat in the darkened corner of the cafe, quietly talking. The orders had come through from DC; the risk of doing nothing was too great. The operation had begun.

Preparations had been completed, as instructed. It was time now to flick the executioner's switch.

It would be the usual modus operandi: a strategic leak to the *New York Times* or the *Washington Post*. It wouldn't be front-page stuff, but a skilled mention in the world news pages was just as valuable. After all, the intended audience was very select.

The leak would come from 'senior Pentagon sources' and would point to the target's public statements that suggested a retreat from the commitment to buy stealth bombers. The quote would include a direct criticism of the Minister, something that was rare. The intelligence-sharing agreement would be raised. Those in the know in Canberra would be left in no doubt that Washington was not pleased.

They had tried to warn him, several times in fact. Don't meddle with the Alliance. But he'd ignored them, another cocky Minister who thought he could play God and to hell with the consequences.

He'd set his course, ordering the Department to begin the process of winding back the Joint Strike Fighter program, as if it was his decision alone to destroy what had taken years to construct. All those billions invested in the Alliance, strengthening the common bonds that had withstood so much over the years. And it was never more important than now, in the endless fight against global terror, against the spread of militant Islam, and the rise of the Asian superpower.

He was putting it all at risk, goddamn him. Didn't he know, didn't he care, about this war? It was no longer defined in the old paradigm of armies rolling across countries and invading neighbours. It was no longer a fight over territory alone. This war wasn't being fought so much with guns and bombs as with ideology; it was about the struggle to establish a dominant culture. It was about the existential threat posed by an inscrutable enemy targeting a weakening West.

And he wanted to put the Alliance at risk? Now?

Who did he think he was playing with here? Fucking amateurs?

They would teach him what it meant to question the value of shared beliefs, to be unpatriotic. The target would not know what had hit him; the pincer movement would be deadly and, they hoped, swift. They didn't like to see their victims squirm for any longer than necessary.

They were human, after all. Most of the time, anyway.

July 18, 2011

BAILEY'S AWAKE!

The headline screamed from the front of Melbourne's *Herald Sun*, the country's biggest selling paper. The 100-point font was usually reserved for the declaration of war – or an AFL drug scandal.

Typically, it had a red 'Exclusive' tag splashed above the byline. And this time, the scoop really was a game changer.

Brendan Ryan stared dumbly at the page. Even his huge intellect struggled to deal with the story.

It told the remarkable tale of a Foreign Minister trapped inside a broken body, but whose mind was as sharp as a tack.

Given its parochial nature, the *Herald Sun* had devoted an almost absurd amount of space to the brilliant Carlton-based neurologist who had diagnosed Bailey. And, as a bonus, her husband had once trialled for St Kilda.

Amy McCallum was teaching Bailey to blink out words one letter at a time. It was a technique first developed by the doctors who'd treated a French journalist suffering the same condition, with the almost tabloid name of 'locked-in syndrome'.

Ryan read that paragraph over and over to let it sink in. Bailey was aware. She could communicate. That meant they would need her permission to get her out of Parliament. Ryan didn't need words blinked out a letter at a time to tell him what the bitch would do.

'This woman is like the fucking Terminator,' he said out loud. 'Blow her fucking arms and legs off and her fucking eyes keep blinking.'

July 19, 2011

The gentle nod of academia greeted Ben Gordon as he arrived at the Australian National University a shade after 3 p.m. The ANU was home to some of the country's brightest minds and the Crawford School of Economics and Government was a standout among its faculties – a treasure chest of boffins, all experts in their field, and hardly a grey beard among them. Crawford had been lovingly nurtured over the years by university management, always doing well during fierce budgetary debates – even during the dreaded Howard years when the Tories had threatened to cut off funding to any university refusing to bow to their right-wing industrial mantra.

Gordon drove his fashionably black VW Polo into the School's car park, nestling the hatchback next to an ageing Volvo station wagon caked in a thin film of dirt and a clichéd pastiche of left-wing bumper stickers. He'd lined up a meeting with George Tiding, one of the best university historians in the country, a walking encyclopedia with an amazing capacity to delve into the ANU's vast archives.

Tiding could recite the Head of Faculty list for the past two decades, or detail the ANU alumni starring on the global stage. He could also deliver precious information on just about any student who had trundled through the university's hallowed corridors. He and Gordon had been friends for close to fifteen years, since discovering a Sydney family connection and sharing the odd dark secret that each preferred to keep off the street.

'Nice to see you, my friend. I have a few notes ready.' Tiding beckoned Gordon into his compact office, cluttered with the trappings of academia and looking as if it was in need of a decent clean-up.

'Thanks, George, appreciate it muchly. What can you tell me?'

'Well, she was seconded to the embassy in Beijing – or Peking, as it was known then – for just a few months; it was 1982, in fact. The notes suggest it was a short-term arrangement, probably at her insistence so she could practise her Mandarin.'

'Do you have the precise dates, George? That is really crucial.'

'I can get those for you. You wouldn't like to tell me why Ms Bailey's deep dark past is so important to you all of a sudden?'

'Let's just say she's come into my orbit. I'm chasing a hunch, as they say.'

'Okay, my friend, but you should know someone else is interested in Ms Bailey's past, someone with a distinct American accent.'

Gordon didn't flinch, instead displaying his best look of indifference. But his mind was ticking fast.

Someone else was trawling the same waters.

Bailey. Paxton. China. What was the connection?

July 19, 2011

Rarely had Canberra Hospital experienced such a media circus. News that Catriona Bailey had woken, like some modern-day Frankenstein, had sparked a frenzy usually reserved for Kylie or Shane or some shallow celebrity *du jour*.

Every network had sent every spare journo and cameraman to stake out all entrances, in case they missed an important visitor. It was causing mayhem with the routine arrivals of the injured and the sick, not to mention the comings and goings of patients' families and friends.

Once more, the fourth estate was busy disgracing itself, giving new meaning to the phrase 'a low act'. One enterprising reporter from the Ten Network had borrowed her mum's nursing uniform in an audacious attempt to locate the stricken Bailey. A screaming match had ensued between Ten's chief of staff and the hospital management. 'See if I fucking care …' had been the journalist's delightful sign-off.

Jill Everingham, the hospital's exasperated CEO, had already dismissed an intensive care nurse for leaking the news of Bailey's condition to the *Herald Sun*. Now she had called a press conference for 10 a.m. in a desperate bid to try and wrest back control of her hospital.

But as she stepped in front of the television lights in one of the hospital's conference rooms, she feared things were about to get worse.

'Ladies and gentlemen, thank you for coming.' (Everingham actually wished them all to hell.) 'We understand there is considerable public interest in the condition of the Foreign Minister and that is why I have invited her specialist, Dr Amy McCallum, to speak with you today. But before we begin, can I implore you to treat this hospital, and its patients, with the dignity it, and they, deserve.

'Now I will ask Dr McCallum to say a few words about Ms Bailey's condition and then answer your questions.'

A nervous McCallum stepped up to the podium and squinted through the lights at the packed room. She'd had no idea there would be so many journalists. And there seemed to be a lot more television cameras than she imagined were necessary, a phalanx of them on a riser at the back of the room and others roaming to her right and left, or squatting directly below her. There were also a half-dozen stills photographers rattling off shots.

'Good morning, I'm Amy McCallum, a Melbourne neurologist,' she said. 'First, may I say how disappointed I am that the privacy of my patient was violated by a health professional. That is unforgivable.

'Yet Ms Bailey has made it clear to me that she wants the public to understand her condition and she has only one request, which I will get to in a moment.'

McCallum outlined Bailey's locked-in syndrome and the blinking communication system devised by the French doctors of Jean-Dominique Bauby, who went on to dictate a book, *The Butterfly and the Diving Bell.*

'Unfortunately, the prognosis for Ms Bailey is not good,' she continued. 'It is rare for people with this condition to survive for long. In 90 per cent of cases people do not live beyond four months following the trauma.'

In Parliament House, Martin Toohey and some senior staffers were watching the press conference live. At the words 'rare for people with this condition to survive for long' Toohey caught Papadakis's eye and lifted his own eyebrows hopefully. It was a brief moment of optimism.

'But there are exceptions,' McCallum continued. 'Bauby lived fifteen months, long enough to see his book published.'

The media waited impatiently through the description of the disease. McCallum was telling a great yarn but most saw it as background that they could get later. She had lost them early with the words 'only has one request, which I will get to in a moment'.

The second McCallum paused and Jill Everingham said, 'Any questions?' the room exploded into a cacophony of: 'What did she say?'

'It was an unusual request,' McCallum responded. 'I checked it with her and then she refused to say anything else.'

'What was it?' bellowed the room.

'"I only want to talk to Thommo."'

Five kilometres away, the blasphemy of the Prime Minister reverberated through the corridors of Parliament.

July 20, 2011

'Ease up, turbo.' Harry Dunkley pulled back on the accelerator and cursed. Loudly. He'd been warned about Perth drivers, those foot-to-the-floor hoons who practised death-roll gymnastics on the ribbons of asphalt dissecting their city, ignoring the safety of others.

He'd arrived the night before, late, on a Qantas 737 from Canberra, the jet pitching madly in the cross-wind turbulence that turned the trip across the Nullarbor into a white-knuckle adventure. It had taken two whiskies and a small bottle of G & T to calm the nerves. Jesus, I hope this is worth it, he'd thought as the plane bucked like a frisky nag.

It had been a decade or so since he'd last travelled to the Wild West, ten years in which Australia's mining boom had transformed Perth into a city of millionaires. The capital's suburban wastelands were now teeming with shift workers who regularly took the two-hour flight north to the Pilbara, enticed by the lucrative rewards. An ordinary cleaner could clear $125k working on a rig, while a barely qualified tradie could ask for more than $175,000 and expect to receive it.

It was close to 11 a.m. and Dunkley, in a rented Corolla, compact and gutless, was trying to follow directions to Osborne Park, a semi-industrial suburb fifteen minutes out of the CBD. One wrong turn – he'd headed left instead of right – and he was shuffling along beside Kings Park, trying to read a street map while keeping a watch on the race track that passed for one of the main arterial roads.

Twenty minutes later, he arrived at Unit 4, 321 Selby Street North, Osborne Park. So this is where public servants come to die, he thought.

His appointment was with Deirdre Patch, whose email signature dubbed her Processing Officer, Consumer Protection Branch, WA Department of Commerce. A brisk-looking woman greeted him then led him to a windowless room with cluttered shelves, a small table and two chairs.

'Please take a seat, Mr Dunkley. We don't often get personal visits for files, particularly ones this old ...'

Patch had already placed the file in question on the table, a dull green folder with a faded white label in the top right-hand corner. Six words stood out in clear font: 'United Mineworkers Federation – Workplace Reform Association'. Dunkley felt a slight tremble in his stomach.

'I'll give you some time; be back in ten if that suits.'

'Yeah, that'd be great. Cheers.'

Inside he found a handful of faded papers, A4 size, several stapled together in a timeline of sorts. The association had been incorporated in Perth on 15 March 1984 by a Tom Darcey from Slater & Gordon, that well-known Labor law firm. The name meant nothing to Dunkley but he took notes, determined to track down Mr Darcey.

He leafed through the papers until he found what he was looking for, a single sheet of white paper titled 'Form 1 – Associations Incorporation Act 1977 (Section 5(1)). Application for Incorporation of Association'.

To the average Joe it meant bugger all, but to Dunkley it was pure gold.

The purpose of the association was 'development of a framework to achieve a safe workplace'. A noble aim, he thought.

And the two signatories to the account? The names were semi-scribbled and had faded with time, but they still stood out like the proverbial: Bruce Paxton and Doug Turner.

Dunkley rocked back in the chair and heaved a deep sigh. The flight across Australia, that five-hour journey into the vast nothingness, had been worth it.

The voice on the end of the line grated, a cross between a fishwife and a bikie's moll. Jennifer Turner was a woman who'd clearly lived a hard life, and her voice held no expectation that it was about to get any easier. Dunkley had found her address and phone number with the help of a mate back in Canberra who was able to access even the most private of telephone numbers. Turner's had been listed 'silent' for some years.

Clearly, she instinctively mistrusted strangers, and Dunkley's introduction was hardly reassuring.

'Hi, Mrs Turner, I'm a reporter from Canberra. I'm trying to track down your husband.'

'Ex-husband,' she shot back. 'What do you want with that useless slimebag?'

'I'm working on a profile on Bruce Paxton … you know, the Federal Defence—'

'I know all about Paxton. As I suspect my ex-husband does … but as to his whereabouts, well, the last time I heard, he was somewhere in the wilds of Asia, probably rooting his silly arse off.'

'Would you know where in Asia?'

'No, I wouldn't, and even if I did I'm not sure I'd tell you anyway.'

Dunkley quietly sighed and turned to the oldest trick in the book – lay it on, with an extra dash of honey.

'Look, I really appreciate your time and I'm sorry to have disturbed you, but I've flown across from the east and I'm really hoping to … well, would you know who could help me find your ex?'

A pause. 'You could try Jimmy.'

'Jimmy?'

'Yeah, Jimmy Booth. He and Paxton and that scumbag ex of mine go back a long way … I think he's still working for the union, the Mineworkers or whatever they're called now.'

'Many thanks, Mrs Turner. Really appreciate it.'

'Okay. Oh and if you happen to find my former husband, tell him he's a fucking useless moron who owes the kids and me for a lifetime of strife.'

And with that, Jennifer Turner curtly hung up.

The building at 82 Royal Street, East Perth, was a pleasant-looking place, tastefully renovated with steel trim and a neat row of plants potted in terracotta placed out the front. It could have been the HQ for a medium-sized accounting or legal firm or some other paragon of corporate virtue. Instead it was home to one of the most notorious groups of union thugs ever to march across Australia's industrial landscape.

Dunkley, himself a keen member of the journo's union, was dressed in his best blue-collar chic, intent on trying to blend in with the bovver boys he was about to meet. He climbed an internal stairwell, passing a blue Eureka flag and a sign that screamed 'The workers united will never be defeated'. Ah, such magnificent cliché, he thought.

Jimmy Booth, all gruff-and-paunch, was in his mid to late fifties and dressed in a dark T-shirt and sleeveless CFMEU vest. He commanded a small office open to all, barking instructions to fellow organisers and secretarial help. Dunkley knew Booth had been on the union payroll for nearly thirty years, a hired goon who could be relied on to take it up to the bosses and coppers when the CFMEU needed a stink. He was a wild-eyed boy of the west and, in the eyes of Perth's establishment, pure evil.

Right then and there, though, he was Dunkley's best – perhaps only – hope of tracking down Doug Turner. That's if Booth gave a fuck, of course.

'Which paper did you say you worked for?'

'The *Australian*, Jimmy.'

'Ah, the fucking *Oz*, that right-wing shit sheet. They stitched me and the missus up good a few years back, claimed we were raking it in, living the high life on the Swan … Fucking Murdoch pricks.'

'Well, I … I cover politics out of Canberra, try not to get too involved in what happens over here. I'm sorry you had a bad experience with the *Oz* … Can I ask you a few questions perhaps about Doug Turner?'

'What, like what fucking size his coffin should be?'

'Do you know where he is? Somewhere in Asia, I'm told.'

'Don't know, mate, haven't spoken with the prick for years. Last time I heard he was working at a fish-and-chip place down on the coast, Cottesloe maybe … Why're you so interested in Dougie, anyway?'

'I'm trying to write a feature piece on Bruce Paxton. I thought Doug Turner might be able to help me piece a few things together.'

'Yeah, well he and Paxton were thick as thieves once, and I do mean thieves, mate. You could try one of those organisations set up by Vietnam Vets: Turner was in 'Nam for a couple of years, never quite got over it, either. Now, if you'll excuse me, mate, we have corporate dogs to take on …'

Jimmy Booth, 120 kilos of pure trouble, was on his feet and preparing to lead his stormtroopers once more into battle. For the benefit of the working man, of course.

July 26, 2011

It was the most powerful television network in the land, controlled by a small clique of ego-driven men. And one token woman. On this crisp Tuesday morning, the board of Network Seven was holding a special meeting in its Sydney boardroom, the chairman ringing in from Venice where he and wife number four were attending the Biennale.

It was the middle of the night in Europe but this hook-up was worth every lost minute of sleep and every euro. Seven was sitting on the biggest television scoop of the year, and it was determined to milk every last opportunity, and advertising dollar, from it.

A team of network specialists had been flown to Canberra from Sydney, taking over a half-dozen suites at the Hyatt. The bar tab alone would be enough to feed a small army. But this was of little concern as preparations began for the *Morning Glory* live broadcast from Catriona Bailey's hospital bed.

The first 'teaser' for the public was an appearance by Peter Thompson, the darling of breakfast television, making a pilgrimage to the hospital. They had filmed him standing solemnly beside Bailey's bed, patting her hand – the soft touch of a hardened professional.

'It's great to see you again,' he whispered. 'Blink if you're happy to see us.'

The camera was tight on Bailey's face. She blinked. The news that night showed what might have been a tear easing from the corner of Thommo's eye. He smiled and whispered: 'Thank you. The *Morning Glory* family is thinking of you and praying for you.'

It was pure TV gold and it ran, relentlessly, as a network promo.

Seven's ratings were piling ever higher as Thommo, working both ends of the day, reported every detail for the masses. The network's 6 p.m. numbers reached an unheard of two million by the end of the first week. Over at Ten and Nine, executives were having multiple seizures of their own.

John James, a private hospital, had agreed to the Seven Network's request to set up a room for the live broadcast after Canberra Hospital had said no. It was fitted out with the latest state-of-the-art medical equipment, overseen by the best medical staff money could buy. Seven spent an equally obscene amount fitting the room out as a television studio.

Friday night's news devoted several precious minutes to Bailey's transfer from Canberra Hospital to the more luxurious private suite a few kilometres away. But everything was being geared towards the live breakfast broadcast slated for Monday,

1 August. Entertainment pundits predicted an unprecedented audience when *Morning Glory* rose that day.

Medical, technical and computer experts had been hired by Seven to research and understand Bailey's condition, so that come the day of the program the best possible technology would be on hand to let Bailey communicate both with Thompson and, if possible, directly with the audience. The network's head of technology, a geeky spiv known as Spider, had even invented HospCam.

Part of the reason the network had delayed the interview was that Bailey had to be tutored in the use of a miraculous tool called Dasher, developed by David MacKay, a Professor of Physics at Cambridge, using probability to make a computer system that did away with the keyboard. Its humble looks belied its genius.

The Dasher screen showed a simple yellow page with colour-coded letters of the alphabet lined up on the right-hand side: 'A' at the top and 'Z' at the bottom. As the cursor moved towards a letter, the letter would begin to jostle forward, as if the cursor was a magnet attracting a pin.

Once the first letter was selected the program began to predict what would come next: combinations of letters would appear behind the first, with the most likely growing in size near the cursor. Once the first word was selected the combinations would grow to include whole words. So if you selected 'Hello', for instance, the words 'how' and 'are' and 'you' would start to pour from the right of the screen.

Given the program worked by slight movements of a cursor, it was not a huge leap to make it respond to eye movements.

But Bailey had more problems than most in mastering the technology because her vocabulary was so eclectic and her style so verbose. She was a diligent student, though, and after five painstaking days she could write 140 characters a minute.

And then it struck one of the Seven producers. That was enough to Twitter!

July 27, 2011

It is the dead hour, the time when everything finally rests. Between 3 and 4 a.m. most of those who inhabit the night have gone home and those who begin early are yet to rise. And those who lie awake fill the void with their hopes and fears.

Martin Toohey had few hopes and his many fears often kept him from sleep. So he was familiar with this dead spot in the Canberra night. He strained to hear a single note of human activity outside. But there was nothing: no cars on Adelaide Avenue, no voices in the distance, just the soft breathing of his wife beside him and the creaks of a Lodge that had seen many sleepless Prime Ministers.

Toohey stared across the room to the dim rectangle of light that sketched the bedroom door. He half-expected to see the silhouette of his dad, Alby: cigarette in mouth, holy water in hand, casting some drops towards his bed as spiritual armoury against the night.

Toohey had sometimes fought with his father but always loved him. He had envied Alby's unshakable faith, his sense of certainty about the way things were and the way a man should act. His unfettered belief in the power of his God, the love of his family, the might of his union and the right of his football team.

Alby was a painter, an organiser for the Operative Painters and Decorators Union of Australia and, to his core, Irish Catholic. He was appalled by the rise of Communism in the unions, so when the Labor split came in 1955 he cast his lot with the Democratic Labor Party. It divided Labor for a generation. Martin Toohey remembered leaving church, still dressed as an altar boy, to hand out DLP how-to-vote cards, and being spat on by the ALP faithful.

It was his father's faith that led Toohey to believe he was called to the priesthood. He left home for a Sydney seminary just months after graduating from high school. But, during sleepless nights out of Alby's orbit, Toohey began to doubt the God of his father: a God he couldn't see and didn't feel. In the dark, doubt gnawed at his soul.

It wasn't just by night that Toohey's faith began to take a different path to Alby's. A decade earlier the Catholic Church had been traumatised and revolutionised by the Second Vatican Council and the seminary Toohey joined had embraced the change.

So Toohey was exposed to the unorthodox ideas of Latin American Liberation theology. Priests like Gustavo Gutiérrez would help shape his attitude to how a Christian should act in the world. He became convinced that preaching salvation in the next life was meaningless without fighting for justice in this one. Had Alby known just what his son was learning at the seminary he would have been appalled by the Marxism at its core.

Happily, Alby didn't know and his pride in having a student priest for a son was unbounded. He adored his oldest boy and wanted the best for him, so he tried to mask the disappointment when, three years later, Toohey came home to Geelong and announced he was leaving the seminary.

Back home Toohey quickly converted to a different faith. At RMIT he immersed himself in Labor politics. The young man who wanted to build a better world found a different set of tools. And politics came easily to him. He had all the natural gifts – he was tall, good-looking, bright, passionate and articulate – and he made an impression early. Martin Toohey was marked for great things.

And he would achieve great things, but he swiftly discovered the original sin that stained his earthly faith was compromise. There was no purity in politics. Alby's faith could remain untainted; Martin Toohey's could not. But Toohey consoled himself that the compromises were small and convinced himself that when he was in a position to make real change he would.

But that day never came.

Toohey glanced at the bedside clock as it ticked off another minute of his existence: 3.35 a.m.

And the last twelve months, when he stood at the pinnacle of political success, had been the worst of all. He had not wanted to kill a Prime Minister to be Prime Minister and he feared the blood of Catriona Bailey would never wash from his hands. He knew the Australian people could never understand, or forgive, what seemed from afar to be an unprovoked act of political brutality.

The election had been a disaster, leaving him with a stench of illegitimacy he could not shake. And because every government decision had to be negotiated with the crossbench he looked weak. Worst of all, the deal he had signed with the Greens, against the advice of Papadakis, was turning into an unmitigated disaster: all upside for them, all downside for Labor. The only bright spot in the whole sorry mess was that the Opposition was hopelessly divided.

The office of Prime Minister had not hung so low in one hundred and ten years of Federation. The compromises Toohey had to make now were the most painful of his entire political life. And that destroyed his confidence and robbed him of his political gifts.

Some commentators now claimed Toohey was a more robotic and less effective communicator than the appalling Bailey. Worst of all, the party's pollsters had begun to worry aloud that people had stopped listening to him. If that was true, then there could be no coming back.

If the Opposition ever got its act together his government was dead. The only question was when it would be buried.

July 29, 2011

One clue, just a single clue. Harry Dunkley leaned back in his chair in his Perth hotel room, arms folded behind his head, and laughed. Heartily. It was so simple in the end. A throwaway line from Jimmy Booth, a man more used to industrial extortion than helping pesky journalists, and Dunkley had been able to track down Doug Turner, through Facebook, of all places.

The former union organiser had indeed been in Vietnam, serving with the 2nd Battalion Royal Australian Regiment in the Asian jungles during the latter half of 1967 and early '68.

Christ, he must have seen some shit, Dunkley thought.

He found five of Turner's Facebook 'friends' – none of the names familiar, but it was still his best chance of locating the elusive veteran. Three Google searches later and he'd tracked down 'Roy Shelley' to the Malaysian capital, Kuala Lumpur, where he was working as a consultant in IT.

Dunkley dialled the number into his BlackBerry. Six rings, and an Australian accent answered. 'Hello?'

'Mr Shelley?'

'Yep.'

'G'day, my name is Harry Dunkley, I'm a reporter with the *Australian* newspaper, out of Canberra. Sorry to disturb you but I'm trying to track down Doug Turner. Thought you may be able to help?'

'What do you want with Dougie?'

'I was hoping to speak with him about Bruce Paxton, the Defence Minister in the Toohey Government down here. They were close a number of years back.'

'Oh, is that so?' Roy Shelley sounded uninterested and none too trusting. Dunkley assumed Shelley was going to give him the old heave-ho, but instead he seemed willing to help, to some extent, anyway.

'Look, give me your contact numbers and email, and I'll pass them on to Doug, if I can find him.'

'You know where he is, then?'

'I think so, but Turner can be hard to track down, particularly if he's trying to dodge someone. You're a reporter, mate; he's likely to tell you to go to hell.'

And with that, Roy Shelley hung up, leaving Dunkley hoping that Doug Turner, Vietnam veteran and by all accounts a miserable low-life, could be coaxed out of whatever foxhole he was hiding in.

Four words that could last a lifetime: 'Give me a call.' It had taken five days for Doug Turner to make contact via email, but he was willing to chat, from the safe distance of overseas, anyway. Dunkley waited ten minutes and then punched in the number, hearing the familiar 'ping' of the international dial code. He was armed with a swag of papers: ASIC searches, file notes from his trip to the Association's register and a potted history of Turner's corporate exploits. There were plenty of missing pieces, but at least he would be able to ask some sensible questions.

'Well, hello Australia. Mr Dunkley, I presume?' Doug Turner sounded remarkably chirpy.

'Yeah, g'day Doug, nice to finally chat to you. Thanks for giving me your contact details.'

'No problem, my friend. So, tell me why you've gone to such trouble to find me.'

'Well, I'm a reporter with the *Australian* newspaper, as you know, and I've been working on a profile piece on Bruce Paxton – the two of you go back a way?'

'Yeah, you can say that again. I haven't seen or spoken to Bruce in, oh, ten or so years, maybe longer. What exactly did you want to know?'

'All about his past, how he got into politics, his early influences, those years the two of you were involved in the Mineworkers union together …' Dunkley left the words lingering, urging a response. An eternity seemed to pass before Turner spoke, this time in a more serious tone.

'Oh, I can tell you about those times, sure. The old UMF, yeah, we were quite a team. Had some fun, did some crazy things … some bad things too …'

'Like what?'

'Hmmmhhh, why should I tell you – a journalist, of all people? You guys never helped me in the past; why should I help you now? Besides, my life ain't as simple as you might think. You may be intrigued by the past and my very good friend Bruce Paxton, but I ain't sure there's a good enough reason to dredge all that shit up. Not now, not ever.'

There was a pause as though Turner were thinking about it, though. Dunkley let the moment hang.

'Tell you what … give me a few days to think this one over … There's something you may be able do for me … My research tells me you're a reporter of some note.'

With those cryptic words, Doug Turner disconnected. Alone and invisible in the wilds of Asia. Again.

August 1, 2011

Peter Thompson gathered his charges around him, like an experienced coach delivering a pep talk before a footy grand final. He felt on top of the world, and it was barely 4 a.m.

'We are making history, broadcasting history! I can almost sniff the Logie, fellas.'

The *Morning Glory* team was used to punishingly early starts but the pre-production for the Catriona Bailey shoot was more complex and gruelling than any before. It would be worth it, though. It was Monday morning, and at John James Hospital dozens of Seven technicians, producers and stars were gathering for the TV event of the year.

Thommo had spent the entire weekend working with Bailey and their encounters had been shot from multiple angles. Then they were edited down, to be rolled in once the show went live at 6 a.m. The best bits would be recycled several times during the morning. The relationship between Thommo and Bailey would be highlighted, as the program reclaimed the Foreign Minister as a much-loved member of the *Morning Glory* family.

The footage included a montage of happier times: Thommo and Bailey diving on the Barrier Reef, laughing at lame jokes, in serious discussions about the economy. The audience, of course, was part of the family. People would feel like they were at the hospital bed, wallowing in the emotion of the moment and flicking through the family album of mawkish, air-brushed memories. And they would be invited to join the conversation online, sending messages of support and asking Bailey questions.

Thommo's breakfast partner, Janelle 'Janny' Jeffries, was positioned in the freezing cold in the hospital car park, where a huge screen had been erected and the public invited to attend.

A deal had been cut with the News Limited tabloids, despite the reservations of some at Seven. The tabloids had been given Bailey's first words to run in their second editions, ensuring that as the nation awoke it could watch the seminal moment on TV and have it echoed in the most popular papers around the nation. It was a calculated risk. Some might see the paper before the show, but most wouldn't, and, anyway, Seven had much bigger surprises in store.

Seven had trawled the nation and the world, scooping up prerecorded messages of support from a bevy of politicians and celebrities. The coup would be a live cross to the US Secretary of State, Hillary Clinton, a long-time friend of Bailey's. There were also messages of support from the Prime Ministers of the United Kingdom, India, New Zealand, and the President of China.

Each stage of the three-hour show would be highly choreographed and dramatised. An enormous amount of effort had gone into staging the 'first words' Bailey blinked. This, of course, was utter nonsense given that Bailey had barely shut up since she had been taught to use the Dasher eye-movement word processor. She had been issuing a steady stream of instructions to everyone and had strong opinions on how the show should run and even where the lights should be.

The production was costing a bomb. The relatively small space of the hospital suite had to accommodate medical equipment and a mass of automatic and operator-controlled cameras. One camera was needed to get close-ups of Bailey's face and another to get a wider two-shot of Bailey and Thommo. A third was mounted on the ceiling to give an overview of the stricken Bailey on her bed with Thommo perched attentively alongside. Another was set up to show Bailey's words as they appeared on the Dasher computer screen. And positioning the computer monitor had caused all kinds of grief. It had to be close enough to pick up Bailey's eye movements but far enough away to allow the other cameras a clear shot of her face. A small camera was eventually set up on top of the monitor to shoot back at Bailey.

The show began at 6 a.m. with an establishing shot of Thommo outside John James Hospital.

'It's with a mixture of sorrow and joy that we join you this morning,' Thommo began.

Cut to the ceiling camera showing Bailey lying on her hospital bed, attached to all manner of medical machinery.

'Part of me is cut up at seeing our mate Cate trapped inside her own body, unable to move.'

The camera begins a slow zoom down towards Bailey's bed.

'But another part of me knows that her mind is still soaring like an eagle.'

Cut to a close-up of Bailey's face from the camera mounted on the Dasher monitor.

'She hasn't lost her great wit, her massive intellect or, most of all, her deep concern about us and this country.'

Cut to the wide two-shot of Thommo sitting beside Bailey's bed. (A miraculous feat of speed to get in from outside, but, hopefully, as with all great theatre, no one would wonder how he pulled that off.) The camera comes in for a mid-shot of Thommo.

'This morning, I guarantee you will shed a tear. But you will also laugh with and be inspired by Cate Bailey. It's been an extraordinary journey to this day ... but let's begin by remembering happier times.'

Cue the opening bars of 'You've Got to Have Friends' and the exquisitely edited footage of Cate rolls out into the lounge rooms of Australia.

The people who watch TV have no idea how labour intensive it is. The director in Channel Seven's outside broadcast van was a master of her craft and she oversaw a team of slick professionals. Everything had been timed to the second, with words and pictures married to tell a seamless story. By the time the montage was finished the ground was tilled for the first big bang.

'Cate, how do you feel?' whispered Thommo.

The director cut to a shot of Bailey's face, her eyes concentrating on the Dasher screen in front of her, urging the cursor to respond.

'B-o-n-z-e-r' was spelled out on the screen.

Outside, a small but growing band of hardy locals erupted in a spontaneous cheer. The broadcast cut to a shot of them and Janny leaping to her feet, clapping her mittened hands. 'Bonzer' was plastered across the giant plasma screen in front of them. The director cut straight back to a close-up of Thommo.

'That's our girl. That's our Cate,' he said, fighting back tears.

Days of effort had gone into considering that first question and Bailey had toyed with a number of responses. Most of them were ridiculously verbose and littered with medical terms she had imbibed from her specialist. She had been persuaded to keep the first message brief.

And then the single word had taken an hour to record, given Dasher was bewildered by the ancient ockerism.

The program's Twitter feed immediately spat out:

First words from hospital bed. Bailey says she's 'BONZER'.

It was re-tweeted by thousands and Bailey began trending around the nation. That chatter would be fed back into the program through the morning, amplifying the circular conversation.

The cynical and astute would note later that the headline 'BAILEY'S BONZER' was already splashed on tabloids across the nation, even though the papers must have been printed hours before, to be delivered to train and petrol stations, thrown onto lawns and unwrapped at breakfast tables. But they would be drowned out by a multitude who just wanted to believe.

The rest of the show was script-perfect.

The Chinese President announced that a panda cub born just a week before would be named 'Cate Cate' in honour of a much-loved, fallen friend of the People's Republic.

The half-hour set aside for direct audience questions to Bailey's Twitter account went off, despite the producers' fears it would be dreary TV. Thommo and Janny were at their nonstop chatty best while Bailey dutifully plugged out the answers.

A real highlight had been a question from a young cancer sufferer who asked: 'Are you still angry at the Prime Minister for taking your job?'

'N-o. T-h-i-s h-a-s s-h-o-w-n m-e t-h-a-t n-o-t-h-i-n-g i-s m-o-r-e i-m-p-o-r-t-a-n-t t-h-a-n y-o-u-r h-e-a-l-t-h.'

Hillary Clinton burst into tears at the end of her interview with Thommo when he told her that Bailey had been closely following her trip to South Korea and was impressed by her steely determination to bring the errant North to heel.

'You hang in there, girl!' urged Clinton.

'I w-i-l-l H-i-l-l-a-r-y,' Bailey said.

Outside, the crowd had grown steadily all morning to several hundred well-rugged enthusiasts. Across the nation the minute-by-minute breakdown of the ratings would show that the audience peaked at one million just after 7 a.m. and, more remarkably, stayed at that level until 9 a.m.

The show had been designed to end with a bombshell. As the clock ticked towards 9 a.m., Thommo leaned in towards Bailey.

'Cate, you've shown us this morning that you are as sharp and talented as you always were. What do you want to do now?'

'I w-a-n-t t-o g-o b-a-c-k t-o w-o-r-k.'

August 1, 2011

A light breeze filtered through Perth's CBD, taming the temperature that was nudging twenty-two despite the winter season. Office workers strode with purpose along streets that bore triumphal evidence of the State's economic boom – construction cranes thrusting silently to the sky.

Harry Dunkley checked his pocket map, turning left into Perth's main thoroughfare towards his destination. St George's Terrace was the epicentre of Perth's commercial district, littered with the head offices of the mega-corporates that were raking in the billions as they clawed ever deeper into the red soil of the Pilbara, hundreds of kilometres to the north.

Ah, the joys of rampant capitalism, Dunkley thought, as he listened for the ghosts of those crooks who had run riot in the '80s, aided and abetted by a WA Labor Government drunk on power and the proximity to great big chunks of cash. All those white-collar criminals – Bondy, Laurie Connell and their ilk –

who had ripped off gullible shareholders before the prosecutors reluctantly exposed their evil deeds. Now it was the mining giants that were scrabbling over indigenous land, reluctant to pay their fair share of tax and cashing in on the billions to be made from gouging precious minerals from the ancient landscape.

But it wasn't BHP or Rio Tinto or Xstrata that Dunkley was pursuing today. Entering the building's foyer, he scanned an index and quickly found his target, taking a lift to level three, before exiting opposite a prominent sign: the Australian Electoral Commission.

First established in 1902 as an arm of the then Department of Home Affairs, the AEC had evolved into a powerful bureaucracy in its own right, responsible for maintaining the electoral roll and ensuring that, roughly every three years, around eleven million voters exercised their democratic right to put either Labor or the Coalition in power.

While most of its records were now available online, the documents that Dunkley wanted – from the 1996 election – were still only accessible in hard copy.

Dunkley introduced himself to a smartly dressed AEC officer who had already done some preliminary work. He was led to a desk where a small pile of documents and files lay in wait.

'Cup of tea, Mr Dunkley?'

'No, thanks.'

'I'll leave you with these, then … yell if you need any help.'

The 1996 election had been a watershed. John Winston Howard, the man once about as popular as herpes, had surged into office, sweeping away Paul Keating and his dwindling band of True Believers. It was an emphatic victory, one that would usher in another long period of Coalition rule. Labor had lost a humiliating thirty-one seats on the back of a 6.17 per cent swing. But in a rare bright moment for the ALP, Bruce Leonard Paxton had fended off an enthusiastic Liberal candidate to take his seat in the House of Representatives, part of a Caucus reduced to a miserable forty-nine members of Parliament.

And while there had been whispers about the way Paxton had made it to Canberra – who he'd paid off, who he'd fucked over along the way – for the most part the current Defence Minister's past had been left alone.

Until now. Until Dunkley had decided the Minister's history was worthy of exhumation.

He started sifting through the electoral returns for 1995, trying to prise open the secrets of who was bankrolling Labor's WA branch. Nothing looked out of the ordinary: the pages were filled with blue-chip corporates who usually donated $50,000 or $100,000 every year to each of the major parties, seeking to remain scrupulously non-partisan. There were the standard big-ticket donations from the array of unions that stood to lose big time under a Howard Government, even though it was Keating and his sidekick Laurie Brereton who had taken on Labor's industrial wing, introducing enterprise bargaining.

The '95 returns gave way to 1996, a more solid-looking document reflecting the intensity of an election year. Both Labor and the Coalition had scored handsomely, Dunkley thought.

As he scanned page after page of mainly anodyne returns, a small item caught his eye. On 11 January 1996 – just weeks before Keating fired the election starter's gun – the CFMEU had made an $80,000 donation to the ALP. There was nothing sinister about that, but in brackets the words 'For the purpose of Bruce Paxton's campaign' had been added. And that, Dunkley knew, was highly unusual and needed further investigation.

August 1, 2011

In his plush Paddingon terrace, Jamie Santow sat entranced in front of his 50-inch plasma flat-screen for nearly two hours, digesting every minute of the *Morning Glory* broadcast. He had just one focused thought: how could *GetSet!* get aboard the Bailey Express?

The 24-year-old university whiz-kid (double major in public relations and sociology) was the master of seizing the moment to promote himself and his organisation by surfing waves of public emotion.

GetSet! was an online activist organisation. It rarely identified an original issue or put effort into a need that wasn't already on the political radar. No, that demanded spending real time and intellectual capital. It was best to leave that to the foot soldiers and just turn up with *GetSet!* banners as the wave began to crest and then claim the credit for any victory. Then you could chalk it up on the website as yours and move on to the next media event, leaving any unresolved issues for the worker bees in specialist lobbies and the public servants to sort out.

The beauty of Santow's progressive organisation was that it was virtual. Members could log into the state-of-the-art website, sign a petition on anything from live exports to climate change, watch their name and their issue appear on the front page, and then log off and get on with their day.

The protest movement was no longer about storming the barricades, making placards and singing the 'Internationale'. Activism and outrage now came free, with minimal effort and instantaneous gratification.

In a parody of Timothy Leary's famous '60s edict, the online protest anthem was now 'Dial-in, whine-on, log-out'. It was the perfect political forum for an increasingly self-obsessed world.

It was Bailey's return-to-work bombshell that gave Santow the idea he was looking for. He would use *GetSet!*'s considerable clout to lobby for Bailey to continue as the Foreign Minister, working from her hospital bed. She would become the pin-up girl – er, person – for the differently abled lobby. If Bailey could work as Foreign Minister then no one was barred from any job. She would inspire by example.

He assumed there might be a few practical difficulties for the government in having a Foreign Minister who could not travel, attend Cabinet, sit in Parliament or Caucus, or even make international calls. But that was not his problem. He would simply do what he always did: make an emotional appeal and portray any hesitation by the government as evidence of prejudice.

What he really needed was a slogan. After about ten minutes of doodling, he settled on 'Reinstate Cate'. It was easy to chant, would look good on the *GetSet!* website and fit nicely on T-shirts.

He picked up the phone to begin organising the first stunt. He knew Seven's commercial rivals would be loath to carry much of the *Morning Glory* broadcast, but neither could they ignore the huge political yarn. What they needed were fresh angles – and that was Santow's genius.

And what he really needed were some people in wheelchairs.

August 1, 2011

His voice was raspy, his breathing short and shallow, as if the mere act of speaking was sucking the life out of him. Doug Turner was back on the phone but it was difficult for Dunkley to reconcile the sickly-sounding man with the full-of-beans character of a few days ago. Something had changed.

They had played an email waltz, trying to line up a mutually convenient time to chat. Now Turner was offering the first tangible sign that he was willing to assist. There was, however, a catch.

From the get-go, Turner had made it plain that he wanted justice, and he saw Dunkley as the vehicle to achieve it. This was not going to be a straight ride to information, he'd written in one email. Four decades after serving in the shit and slime of Vietnam, Doug Turner was still seeking recognition for himself and his mates, those brave soldiers from 2RAR who'd carried out their orders diligently and had never wavered – even when the

Vietcong were threatening to turn them all into mincemeat and the body bags kept mounting up. No, the 2RAR kept its end of the bargain, fighting like mad men and defending the ANZAC honour, even when the Yanks had deserted them to their fate.

They'd been exposed to the worst excesses of the human spirit, seen enough senseless killing and brutality to make them question the essence of mankind, and lain awake wondering, 'Is this the night I die?' Yet when they returned to Australia, they were met by another vicious enemy: the cult of public opinion. At home they were treated like shit by anti-war bigots who'd lost faith in the campaign against Communism.

It was all too confusing for battle-hardened young men who'd expected sympathy and comfort, not the cold glare of an angry country at war with itself.

Doug Turner had tried to retreat into normality, moving to the west, where he scored work on the same Perth building sites as another tearaway, Bruce Paxton. The two had forged a close bond, chasing women around Perth's seedy nightspots and watching each other's backs when their wild ride threatened to spiral out of control.

And what a wild and exhilarating ride it had been! Paxton had looked after his mate as he climbed the greasy pole, securing Turner a junior organiser's role at the UMF while Paxton reached for the stars.

The work had been therapeutic, helping Turner cope during those long nights when he'd lie awake for hours, sweating blood and cursing, unable to shake off the memory of Vietnam and its deep unspoken terror. He knew he was suffering post-traumatic stress disorder but was equally keen to cover it up, afraid he would be deemed unfit for work. He'd descend on the weekends into a suburban funk, struggling to play out the role of loving husband and caring father.

He'd held it together as long as possible, even after Bruce Paxton announced that he – the union's great white hope – was being parachuted into a relatively safe Labor seat, bound for Canberra and a life of pampered civility. Their partnership, it seemed, was over.

The past decade had been particularly harsh. Turner had fallen out with his family after lapsing into routine depression mixed with alcohol-fuelled bouts of aggression, his torment not helped when he was sacked by the CFMEU for failing to turn up to work five days in a row.

And that prick Paxton? Why, he'd scooted off to Canberra with barely a farewell. Thanks-for-all-your-help-mate-now-fuck-off. A friendship sacrificed on the altar of one man's out-of-control ego. Well, Paxton could go and stick his political ambition where it fitted.

Turner had severed ties with Perth, escaping north to try and avoid prying eyes. He had tried to start afresh, working first on a pearl lugger in Broome, before drifting to the tourist-laden islands of south-east Indonesia, where he hoped to hustle a decent living.

But the torment of Vietnam – the memories of what he and his comrades endured – kept flooding back. The Department of Veterans Affairs had been miserly, offering him only a partial pension. The mere thought of those bureaucrats playing god with his life sent Turner into spasms of rage and alcohol abuse. After everything he'd done for this country …

He'd retreated into the semi-paranoid world of cyberspace, searching for similarly minded folk who'd been through hell. With a few mates found over the internet, Turner established Vets for Justice. The group had grown several hundred strong, a diaspora of fed-up Australian veterans who wanted nothing more than their dignity restored and their story heard.

They had delivered demands to successive governments in Canberra, always meeting the same response: 'Case closed. Next.'

'I tell you, Mr Dunkley, sometimes I get so mad, I want to take a plane ride down to Canberra and blow the place up, but then I figure I don't want to go down in history as Australia's Timothy McVeigh.'

'Very sensible too, Doug. I'm sorry to hear that you and your mates have been mucked around so badly. The disgrace of Vietnam … it's a sorry chapter in our history, I agree.'

'It is that, son. And as for Paxton … well, when he became Defence Minister, I finally thought, here's a bloke I can trust to set the past right, to look after those who've been fucked over. I sent him a long letter, you know, a few weeks after he was sworn in, congratulating him … and I meant it, too. Of course I mentioned the veterans' issue, asked him if he could personally intervene and help us out, give us some recognition, that sort of thing. You know what I received back from him? A fucking form letter sent by his chief of staff … not even a personal note. That's when I thought, mate, you'll get yours one day, you will get yours …

'So, let's cut to the chase. You want info about Paxton, right? Well, no one knows more about his past than me, I reckon. I played the loyal fucking lieutenant for him and that other pack of bastards in head office. Did everything they asked me to do, and then some. I can give you chapter and verse– but first there's a few things I need.'

'We aren't in the business of paying for stories, Doug.'

'Nah, I ain't talking about your money, son. I don't want Rupert's cash, although I reckon he'd have a few shekels to spare. There's something far more important to me, a job that you could do to bring our campaign into the public eye. Tell me, Harry, does the Battle of Nui Le mean anything to you?'

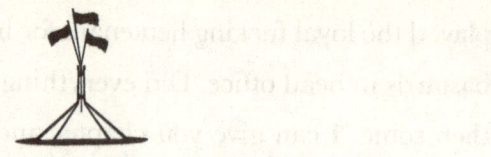

August 1, 2011

Jonathan Robbie stood by the window gazing out at Sydney's racing streets, a stiff whisky cupped in his left hand, the television remote dangling from his right. Oh shit, he thought.

The half-hour *Australian Story* profile on Opposition leader Elizabeth Scott had been as bloody as one of David Attenborough's wildlife documentaries.

Self-reflection wasn't a large part of Robbie's character, but he realised he had completely overplayed his hand in the gore-fest. What he'd assumed would be a cameo appearance instead came across as a narration – and a highly critical one.

The profile would have been sold to Scott as an in-your-own-words half-hour of soft-soap, a chance to humanise the Liberal leader and play down her image of immense privilege. Instead it had been a horror show. The first, and biggest, problem was timing. It had largely been shot during the Michael Hamilton 'Bank-gate' scandal. The producer had even been shooting in

Scott's office when Nine News went to air to reveal Hamilton's lies about the Prime Minister and his links to the Liberal Party.

Among many unfortunate moments immortalised on video was Scott's press secretary's priceless response to the news item. 'How the fuck did that shallow bastard Robbie find that out?' muttered Justin Greenwich. 'I'll bet my right ball there's a rat in our ranks.'

Robbie had no problem with that. It was his own reflection on the affair that was making him uneasy. He should have known better than to participate in anything to do with the bloody ABC. Those pinko bastards had flattered and beguiled him into doing an interview for the show, saying what a great job he had done in breaking the political story of the year when he'd first aired Hamilton's accusations.

He had learned a lot about the cost of making TV and never shot interviews that ran for more than six minutes. The *Australian Story* producer had asked him questions for an hour. And, towards the end, she'd invited him to comment on Scott's character. Finally he had offered that he thought Scott was 'heartless and cold-blooded' in her dealings with the deluded public servant Michael Hamilton.

Robbie had worried about that statement ever since and had even raised it once with Scott, asking whether she had considered what would happen to Hamilton. She had been adamant that he was a more than willing participant and she had seen him as a whistleblower on what she honestly believed was an enormous scandal. She had no sympathy for Hamilton and was enraged by the damage his lie had done to her. .

The call came at 8.34 p.m. Robbie knew without looking who was on the line. Elizabeth Scott. He was used to confrontations with politicians after his stories. But he suspected, after this one, that he was in for rougher than usual treatment.

'Okay,' he murmured to himself, 'she just needs a few minutes to calm down.' And he hit the red 'decline' button.

About thirty seconds later his mobile lit up again with a text: Call me ... NOW!

Robbie sat at the hotel desk and composed a few defensive notes. He needn't have bothered. Before he could say 'Elizabeth', the tirade began. She was calm at first, but there was a cold fury in her voice.

'Jonathan, you complete moron. You are such a moron it's hard to know where to begin. "Heartless? Cold-blooded? Expendable?" He came to us, you dumb bastard. He came to us. He was a suicide bomber.

'And I warned you. I told you there was more information to come. That when the police investigation was complete, the correspondence would show he was responsible for it all. That he alone fabricated information and wilfully misled me. He wanted to testify before the committee; it was his idea. I never forced him to do anything. He imagined himself a hero in a deluded fantasy he penned himself.

'And you, you dumb prick. You had to parade your so-called scoop. To stand in judgement of me and impugn my character and pretend you're something more than a third-rate hack who screwed his way into a yarn. Yes, Jonathan, I know. Don't think I'm blind to who's making the bullets you fire. Do you honestly believe that I think you're smart enough to have worked that story out for yourself? Or done some real journalism?

'It will all come out in time. And your judgement will be shown to be completely fucked. And it won't be a matter of opinion, it will be a matter of fact.'

And so it went for fifteen uninterrupted minutes as Scott unloaded. She worked herself into a rage and unpicked every element of his character with expletive-laced flourishes. Robbie could not help but be impressed. He had been on the receiving end of outrage before, but it was usually clumsy, like a drunk swinging at you in a pub: frightening, but as likely to miss the target as connect. This was different. Here was a great mind at work, someone who had identified all her opponent's weaknesses and then crafted arrows to hit every mark.

But as Scott's stream of invective began to run dry, she became introspective, mournful and self-pitying. Not knowing how to rebuild her shattered political capital was clearly tearing her apart.

'I don't know what to do. Why is the police investigation taking so long? Why don't they release some of the information they have? If people could only see it they'd realise I'm telling the truth, that *he* came to *us*. I've half a mind to hold a press conference and release the emails ... but then I'd probably be accused of interfering with a police investigation.'

Scott paused for the first time. 'What do you think I should do?' she said.

'Well, I wouldn't ask me,' Robbie spat back. 'Because some people think my judgement's pretty fucked.'

The phone went dead.

Scott dropped her BlackBerry on her kitchen table and stared blankly out the window, oblivious to the beauty of the ocean beyond it. Her thoughts were turned inwards.

For the first time she felt her life was beyond her control and it terrified her. Business success had come easily, but politics was an alien land full of unexpected dangers. Her mind wandered back over the horror of the past months, but her memories always ended at the same bitter encounter.

It was early April and she was standing in the Prime Minister's office in front of an enraged Martin Toohey.

'I respected you,' he said in a low and menacing tone.

'I never asked him to lie,' Scott said. 'He had good information about big problems in your bank finance scheme; you know he did because you've been trying to hide it. That's fair game.'

'We were trying to save an entire industry and hundreds of jobs threatened by a financial crisis,' Toohey said. 'Yes, it was flawed but there is no perfect solution. And you wine and dine this attention-seeking partisan. You flatter him. You get him to overwind his story and then he publicly accuses me of being corrupt.

'You know me. You know that's a lie. But you let it stand for three days before it was blown out of the water. Mud sticks. You know that.'

Scott's voice had a slight quaver. 'I didn't … know for sure. He said he had an email that would be a bombshell. And then … well. How could I be sure?'

'You knew. You saw advantage. You didn't care if it was true or not. And you were willing to let what little dignity I have left in public life be shredded because you saw a chance of charging back to an election.'

'Martin, I–'

'Get out. I am done talking with you. Anything I ever have to say to you again you can read about in the papers, watch on TV or cop in the parliamentary chamber.'

'I apologise.'

'Save it, you spoilt, selfish Tory bitch. Get out.'

Scott remembered being surprised as she turned to leave; she was used to confrontation but Toohey's words had cut deep.

Her personal standing in the polls had collapsed. And that meant that she was vulnerable. Her blood was in the water and the sharks were circling.

Now, four months later, on the back of the *Australian Story* profile that had been meant to save her, they looked set to feed.

August 6, 2011

Carved from solid oak, the Louis XVI table could extend up to three metres in length and was embossed with a four-leaf motif. On a quiet weekend with the sun streaming in, Ben Gordon loved to relax with a cloth and containers of polish and oil, smoothing the table's 1790s perfection and admiring the artisan toil that had transformed rough lengths of timber into a work of elegance and beauty. He liked to recall his favourite Keating story: the Labor PM would keep his Cabinet colleagues and advisers waiting for hours if he'd got into a groove with one of his Napoleonic artefacts. Ah, the sheer bloody indulgence of it all.

Gordon's table had cost a packet, but he considered it the soundest of investments. 'You don't put a price on something of exquisite beauty,' he would sniff to those friends who questioned the price.

The table served a practical purpose too, when he hosted dinner parties for his small coterie of friends. He loved whipping up culinary celebrations, experimenting with something he'd seen on *MasterChef*, with its marvellous tang of faux celebrity. But this Saturday afternoon, gourmet experiences were not on the menu. Instead, Gordon was seeking a breakthrough in an increasingly complex project.

Harry Dunkley had been in Perth working on a hunch that he hoped would deliver solid results. 'I'm making steady progress, I reckon,' he'd told Gordon, less than convincingly, the last time they'd spoken. The two friends had split the workload and while Dunkley was off chasing shadows in the west, Gordon was focusing on the links between Paxton and Catriona Bailey.

He'd arranged a series of papers on the table in careful order, short bios and other material he'd prepared on Paxton and the two Chinese men in the photo.

Somewhere in this jumbled maze were clues – but to what? He still wasn't sure.

Okay, he told himself, think logically. Bailey had been in Beijing at the same time as Paxton, perhaps when the Defence Minister had first met Zhou Dejiang. Was it a chance meeting? Unlikely. The Chinese were masters at placing the right person in the right place at the right time, hoping to trip up their international visitors. But the only clue was pictorial evidence from thirty-odd years ago. What was it about the past that was now shaking the present?

Just lately, the intelligence wires had been buzzing with news of a secret bust in Beijing – a woman named Lillian Chan had been recruited to entice Western diplomats into her lurid web, but instead was caught allegedly selling classified Chinese intel to the

West. She faced a lengthy stint in one of China's stinking rural gulags – a shameful end to what had been a promising career.

Had Paxton succumbed to the soft skin of some other Chinese temptress? There was nothing firm in the files that Gordon had seen, just the odd suggestion here and there of a man whose moral compass had been shipwrecked for many a year.

Gordon was tossing theories around but they all seemed to lead nowhere. His agile brain was blasting out a steady stream of possibilities, but just as quickly he was ruling them out, one by one. He'd come to a roadblock, the dreaded point that every security analyst feared. If Gordon was going to find out what it all meant, he would need help. And that raised an immediate problem.

He knew who to turn to – Charles Dancer, a senior DFAT official, the Department's under-the-radar troubleshooter with access to the very best in intelligence. Dancer was the complete professional and Ben knew him well. The problem? Perhaps Ben knew him a little too well …

It had started as a brief fumbling encounter, a Thursday night, late, at the National Press Club in the heart of Canberra's bureaucratic district. The regular blues crowd had shuffled in, joining a throng of public servants, to hear the Wah-Wahs, a decent outfit steeped in Buddy Guy licks, with a small but loyal following. Gordon had shown up around nine, hoping to meet up with some friends, including Annie the Trannie, who was as fond of people-spotting as she was of music. That night did not disappoint – a senior Liberal MP, an appalling man from

Queensland, appeared to be drunk in a corner, canoodling with a young male staffer in an embrace that Gordon suspected would find its way onto Facebook or YouTube within days. Or into that special file held by the Liberal Party Whip.

The NPC was rocking despite the lack of journalists – a fact that never ceased to amaze the management, who'd tried just about every trick imaginable to entice the press gallery into the club.

Three songs from the end, during a solid four-to-the-floor version of 'Little Queenie', Annie had grabbed Ben and marched him onto the dance floor and straight into the arms of Charles Dancer.

'Bugger you, Annie,' Gordon thought, though he was secretly pleased to have been introduced to the suave, older Dancer. Even though, despite his name, the man appeared to have two left feet.

A flirtatious relationship had ensued, the two bonded by their unusual lifestyles and penchant for French period furniture. But after a number of years the magic had died and they'd agreed to go their separate ways. There was no hostility, but the few times they had bumped into each other – once at the Dendy during Canberra's annual film festival and another time at the home of a mutual friend – they'd felt awkward.

Well, thought Gordon, he was just going to have to put that to one side. He was in need of a helping hand and Dancer was among the very best in the business.

He'd chosen the Chairman and Yip, a still fashionable place that had been serving excellent Asian-infused plates for nearly two decades. It was a little pricey but Albert, the Chairman's hunky manager, could be relied on to find a discreet table when asked.

The night air was brisk but bearable, and Gordon managed to snag a park almost opposite the restaurant. A good omen, he thought, as he spotted Albert through the window.

Dancer had beaten him by a few minutes and was already seated, glass in hand, when Gordon arrived at the table upstairs.

'Charles, you're looking well.'

'You too, Kimberley.'

A short silence ensued as they perused the menu and then ordered.

'So, Kimberley, why this great secrecy? That was a very cryptic phone message you left.'

'Yeah, sorry about that. Look, I want to ask a favour ... a purely professional favour,' Gordon added, a little clumsily.

Dancer's expression remained neutral. 'Go on.'

'Well, this has to remain hush-hush ...'

'Of course.'

'I am ... have been ... working with a friend on a certain project ... it's delicate and this is very much on the QT ...'

'Kimberley, you can trust me. You of all people should know that.'

Dancer's tone was reassuring and after a quick half-glass of riesling, Gordon felt relaxed enough to spill the beans.

'I'm working on Bruce Paxton ...' He halted, sensing a slight shift in Dancer's usually impassive gaze.

'Go on ...'

Gordon took another sip of wine, thinking that he should be reasonably restrained in what he said. 'Well, you know as well as I that Paxton has been stirring things up at Defence, particularly as he tries to slash spending. Then a colleague came across some material, old material, which suggests some links with the Chinese. Trouble is, there's precious little in the records to confirm any history between Paxton and our Asian friends, and my efforts to dig deep into his past have so far drawn a blank.'

Dancer waited till an approaching waiter had delivered plates of duck pancakes and steamed prawn dumplings before quietly speaking. 'Mr Paxton does indeed have an interesting past. In fact, I'm surprised that most of it remains hidden in the vault, so to speak.'

'What do you mean?'

'Let's just say he features in a few files that I'm aware of ... I presume you know what I'm talking about?'

'No, I honestly don't, Charles.'

'You've not heard about the ... Marmalade Files?'

'The what?' Gordon's surprised look left Dancer in little doubt that he really was in the dark.

'Heavens, Kimberley, I thought an experienced analyst like you would have known all about them.' Dancer's voice held a hint of mockery. 'As you know, in the mid-1980s, early '86 to be precise, I was given a special role in the Department, a job best described as Fix-it Man for our foreign service. I went largely undercover – an invisible diplomat, if you like.

'I was brought into a small team, just the three of us, reporting directly to the Department Secretary. We took our orders from him and no one else. We were given the task of cleaning up all our diplomatic messes – and Kimberley, as you well know, there have been more than a few. I'm not sure if you're aware of the incident back in 1996 when the Government of Thailand came very close to making an official complaint over the behaviour of David Bleasdale?'

Gordon shook his head as he bit into a dumpling.

'Mr Bleasdale spent his years in Bangkok indulging his penchant for underage boys. It had been tolerated at previous postings, but the Thai Government wanted to stamp out the growing number of paedophiles entering the country – and Mr Bleasdale; well, he was among the grubbiest of the lot.

'I had to hot-foot it to Bangkok, arriving in the nick of time to negotiate a truce. We had a fair bit on their envoy in Sydney, a man whose sexual fantasies would test even the most experienced of hookers. Let's just say the two countries called it a draw.

'It was during this time that I learned of this cache of top-secret files buried deep in the bowels of DFAT.

'They contain the secrets that our government doesn't want the public – or even you, Kimberley – to know about. These are not mere accidents, either; these are atrocities that plumb the depths. File after file of secret intelligence, some of it ours, some of it from our American or British friends. All of it highly, highly sensitive.

'You want another example? Years ago, one of our senior guys in Malaysia, a nasty little shit called Tim Hinton, went troppo. Succumbed to the flesh pots of Kuala Lumpur – not the first man to do so, but he had a tendency to mix violence with his carnal pleasures. Two women ended up in hospital, one needing some serious reconstruction work. He was "let go" after the Malaysians threatened violence of their own.

'You want to know about Mr Paxton, of course. Let me set the scene for you …'

Gordon already knew a fair chunk of the story but he was keen to hear it again, from an expert.

Paxton had first travelled to Beijing in 1980 as part of a Young Labor delegation, a regular trip for up-and-coming ALP stars. The delegations had become an annual event after Whitlam opened diplomatic ties with the Communist state in 1972. Daylong ventures to the Great Wall, evening drinking sessions with some of the Politburo's more promising cadres, and the chance to learn about China's rich history and forge closer ties despite the political differences. But for some members of the Labor family, the emergence of China from its economic slumber also represented a golden opportunity to do business in the way they liked best – corruptly.

On his second visit, in 1982, Paxton had met some young Communists keen to forge closer ties with the West and to learn more about Australia and its awaiting opportunities.

'Kimberley, Bruce Paxton is a nasty piece of work. He is also, in my view, completely devoid of moral scruples. He would sell his mother to make a profit. Over the years he has been tailed on his trips to China, and not just by us …'

Dancer's voice trailed off. He was willing Gordon to ask questions – clearly he didn't want this to be a one-way street.

'What sort of things did he get up to?'

'You name it. Paxton didn't mind experimenting. We followed him to Taipei a few times, kept track as he went from one brothel to another. The Chinese weren't dumb; we suspected they planted a few hookers of their own – Paxton obviously couldn't tell the difference between a communist and a capitalist between the sheets.'

Gordon was beguiled by the story, but there was still no loaded gun. He was hoping Dancer could open the door to more.

'Charles, that's quite a tale. I guess I have one burning question – who do you have to fuck to see these Marmalade Files?'

Dancer clasped his hands before his chest, like a priest in the confessional, and fixed Gordon with a seductive stare.

'I think I might be able to help you there.'

August 8, 2011

It was a small footnote in the history of the Vietnam War, but for Doug Turner and his brothers in arms it still carried a special significance – even forty years later.

On the morning of 21 September 1971, troops from Australia and New Zealand were combing the steaming jungles of Vietnam near the village of Nui Le, on high alert for their nimble enemy, when they stumbled into a Vietcong stronghold. Despite calling in US air power, a protracted battle resulted in the deaths of five Australian diggers. Three of those soldiers were left on the battleground for hours as their comrades fought a desperate hand-to-hand battle. They may well have been left behind for good but for the heroics of two New Zealand troopers who ignored the enemy fire to retrieve the bodies.

'They were fucking heroes and now both of them are dead. One of them passed away just a few weeks ago; I got word from his brother who also served in Vietnam. The other sadly took his own life in '95 – he'd suffered for years and eventually, well, he just couldn't go on ...'

Turner's voice was quivering, this emotional flight into the past clearly taking its toll. 'And you know what? They got diddly squat from their government, too. Sound familiar? Of course it does – those bastards across the ditch treated their vets just as shabbily as those pricks in Canberra.

'I reckon the Australian people should hear about these heroes, don't you, Harry? So here's the deal. You get your newspaper to write this up – and I'm not saying it has to be a long piece, just a good one – and I'll give you chapter and verse on my little mate ... what do you think?'

Dunkley needed little convincing, particularly as Turner held all the aces when it came to Paxton.

'Doug, I'm no expert on military matters but I reckon this is a story of real appeal, particularly for the national broadsheet. I'll need to get some contact details, see if we can speak to their relatives, that sort of thing. Are their wives still alive?'

'I can get you all of that.'

'Great, then I reckon we have a deal, mate.'

The story did have appeal. The *Australian* had been one of the few mastheads to campaign in favour of the Vietnam veterans when it seemed the nation was engaged in collectively snubbing their deeds, and the Defence editor loved the outline Dunkley sent, believing it would make a good Saturday read.

The die was now cast. All Dunkley had to do was conduct a few interviews over the phone, sketch out a 500-word colour piece and make sure the paper published it – hopefully in the first half-dozen or so pages, and preferably a right-hander.

The following Saturday, squeezed between a double-page spread on the current contagion felling global markets and a fluffy piece of nonsense on the latest marketing fad to target Gen Y's spending habits, a longish article was published on page 7. It was headed 'Forgotten Kiwi Heroes: The Vietnam Vets Who Risked All For Aussie Mates'.

A pictorial montage of the two men – taken several years ago, before their descent into ill-health – accompanied the story, which carried the byline Harry Dunkley. It was a long way from his usual sniping political fodder, but he suspected it might turn out to be one of the most important pieces he'd had published.

This morning he'd received a short email from Doug Turner.

> Harry, an outstanding piece. I got to tell you, it brought a tear to this old digger's eye – and I'm not sentimental. Okay, my friend, you kept your end of the bargain and I will keep mine. How soon can you hop on a plane to Asia?

August 8, 2011

Randal Wade rose from his seat with his hands parted in a priestly gesture, a political holy roller fuelled by the heady octane of the crowd. These are my people, he thought. Never before had *Q&A*'s live audience delivered a standing ovation and the young Greens leader felt an electric exhilaration as the love of the mob washed over him.

Wade was used to the adoration of the inner-city whingerati but tonight's response was extraordinary. But then so was his performance.

He was a regular on the *Q&A* panel and when the discussion turned to live animal exports, Wade knew he was on a winner. Even the beef farmers admitted the treatment of cattle in some Indonesian slaughterhouses was beyond the pale. But the shocking images of animal cruelty shown by *Four Corners* had traumatised city-dwellers already completely disconnected from their food sources.

A massive, well-coordinated cyber-cry had demanded an end to the trade and the weak Toohey Government had immediately capitulated, without thinking through what that meant for the diplomatic relationship with Indonesia and an industry that employed thousands in northern Australia.

The Greens had failed in a bid to have Parliament ban the trade for good and Wade had been discussing that when he received a question from an audience member.

'I applaud your plan to end live cattle exports, because it is as evil as the slave trade,' she said. 'But if exporting cattle to be butchered is wrong, why is it right here? Murder is murder. Isn't it time that we arrogant humans stopped treating other life forms as ours to exploit? Shouldn't we end animal cannibalism everywhere? And wouldn't that also cut greenhouse gas emissions?'

'You make two very good points,' Wade began. 'But we have to move a step at a time. Much of the rest of the community is not as enlightened as you and it will take years of careful and patient education before they see the truth in your words.

'But you pose a great moral question for all of us. And I intend to show leadership by rising to the challenge. From tonight I will never again eat the flesh of animals. I intend to become a vegan because it's the right thing to do: right for us; right for our planet; and right for our brother and sister tellurians.'

The crowd began applauding wildly and cheering. The passion even took Wade by surprise. As the audience rose to its feet he rose with it.

'We humans are guilty of terrible arrogance. We must change. We must de-industrialise and de-capitalise. We must start to right-think and right-act. All animals are equal and none more equal than others. We have fought to end racism and sexism. The next great challenge is anthropocentrism. Ending the enslavement of non-human animals is the next great liberation. We humans are only a small part of Gaia.'

The crowd was delirious and Wade ended with a Biblical flourish, a subliminal tilt at the obvious religious ardour on display.

'We must remember that we are no better than the dust that we walk on ... Join me. Join me now as we fight to get all animals to the front of the bus.'

It was an astonishing performance and a brilliant piece of political theatre. But political theatre was Wade's stock in trade. He never bored himself worrying about how his sweeping statements would work, and what the unintended consequences might be. That was the beauty of being a minor party: power without responsibility. What mattered was saying things that sounded good, because many of the people who voted for Wade just wanted to feel good about themselves.

And Wade knew how to make people feel good. He had been a brilliant young advertising executive who rose to public prominence through regular appearances on the ABC's *The Gruen Transfer*. There he quickly cast himself as the moral voice of advertising, even though he had made millions by conjuring catchy campaigns for junk-food giants. He always appeared wearing a T-shirt with a three- or four-word nod to the latest moral fad obsessing the moneyed, aware elite.

He joined the Greens and managed to win the Sydney seat of Wentworth on the retirement of a popular small-l liberal.

Wade's genius was an instinctive understanding of the market. He knew commitment to the environment rose in direct proportion to wealth. He understood that the rich loved to parade their concern for the environment because their other worldly worries were so well catered for. And, being wealthy, they wanted solutions they could buy, preferably cheaply and with a government subsidy.

The people of Wentworth wore their environmentalism like a high-visibility vest by covering the roofs of their vast estates with solar panels and plastering their massive four-wheel drives with bumper stickers supporting whales, forests and koalas.

Even with double-glazing and a liberal smattering of eco-cars, the denizens of Wentworth still had the largest carbon footprints in the country because, mostly, they projected their environmental concern outwards. Ending global warming meant ending the jobs of poor forest workers in Tasmania, or coal miners in Mackay, or power-station workers in Yallourn, or steel workers at Port Kembla.

If anyone raised doubts about the justice of that, the good citizens of Wentworth would repeat the mantra that thousands of new 'Green jobs' would arise miraculously as old industries were levelled. Trifles like how long the gap might be between the demise of a real dirty job and the emergence of a new clean one, or if the same people would get a job in the same place, did not concern them … because it wasn't their job.

Wade played Wentworth like a violin, championing the concerns of his constituents without demanding any real sacrifice from them. Better than that, he worked to ensure that the State and Federal governments supported feed-in tariffs for solar power – a policy that rewarded the rich and forced up the price of electricity so it was effectively subsidised by the poor.

His rise did not end there. On his arrival in Canberra he swiftly positioned himself for leadership as the ageing hero of the Green cause stepped aside for a new generation.

But, as the applause of the crowd died in the ABC's Ultimo studio, he did wonder if he might have bitten off more than he could chew. Because in the passion of the moment he had made one small but significant slip … he had meant to say 'vegetarian'.

And he was desperately trying to remember if vegans ate cheese.

August 11, 2011

Small waves danced on black volcanic sands as villagers fossicked for valuable stones rubbed smooth by time and tide. On a steaming Thursday, Harry Dunkley lugged a heavy overnight bag filled with clothes and his journalistic gear along a beach track, cursing his driver for the inconvenient drop-off.

Dunkley had done only preliminary research on Cucukan, a tiny village hidden away on Bali's east coast. He knew the local villagers numbered just 150, and eked out a modest living from fishing and small-scale farming. They also served the half-dozen expats who'd made this Balinese hideaway their home: two Americans, a retired Dutch lawyer, the odd blow-in from Britain – and Doug Turner, running from his past.

The Vietnam veteran had stumbled on Cucukan just over a year ago and had been captivated by its quaint nod to the past. He'd told Dunkley about the goose farmer who daily led his flock along dirt roads, the fishermen dragging in their nets of meagre catch, the traditional dances performed by young girls in ornate costume. He had also given Dunkley instructions on how to find the village.

It was close to 10 a.m. and already the wretched tropical heat was festering like a wet blanket of sweat. Just as Turner had said, there were a half-dozen villas, too luxurious for their own good, nestled close to the beach, with sweeping views across to distant shores.

Third from the left, as you look from the ocean, Turner had said. Dunkley set out along the top fringe of the glistening sands, politely declining the attention of several hawkers. It was only a five-minute stroll to Turner's white-walled two-storey villa with a roof of heavy clay tile, but in this climate it felt longer.

Okay, Dunkley thought. Time for rock'n'roll. He was closing in on this yarn, he knew, but it was still proving elusive. Doug Turner was the key; whether he was still willing to play ball would be settled soon enough. Dunkley felt the tingle down his spine he always experienced when a story – a big story – was within reach.

A paved walkway veered through heady jasmine vines, past a small over-chlorinated swimming pool with recliners scattered around its edge. An outdoor table suggested a late breakfast – several dishes with the oily remains of food, a plunger of coffee and a bowl of tropical fruit cluttered its surface.

And standing in the doorway, dressed in a silk robe, with thinning hair and a whitish goatee, was Doug Turner. He gave Dunkley an impish grin.

'Welcome to paradise, Harry Dunkley. Nice of you to drop in.'

August 11, 2011

It was dubbed 'Gareth's Gazebo', a sneering doff of the hat to Gareth Evans, the former Foreign Minister who reputedly packed two suitcases for his first trip to Canberra: one for his clothes, another for his ego.

Just a stone's throw from Parliament House, the headquarters of the Department of Foreign Affairs and Trade is officially known as the R.G. Casey Building. Its vast confines are home to more than a thousand of Canberra's most cunning bureaucrats – and some of Australia's best-kept secrets.

On the fourth-floor executive wing, where the Department's Secretary and his deputies have vast, palatial suites, is the Minister's office. Except very few Ministers have ever stepped inside it. Evans spent the occasional hour there between his tantrums on the hill, and Alexander Downer once poked his Tory nose inside. But otherwise it sits empty.

Nearby, in a small airtight room, lie hundreds of carefully bound and numbered files. The existence of this vast treasure of secret intelligence is known to only a handful of senior DFAT officers, along with the Foreign Minister of the day and his chief of staff.

These are the Marmalade Files.

Charles Dancer was one of the select few who knew about, and had access to, the files. After all, some of his best work had made its way into the archives. Now, with the bulk of DFAT's employees winding down after another crazy day of diplomacy and paper-shuffling, Dancer fondled the keypad that would allow him to enter the file room's secret confines. It was just after 6.30 p.m. and he had promised to update Ben Gordon later that night, over a quiet drink at the Realm. He did not want to disappoint.

He'd been in the room just a few weeks earlier, performing a specific research task delegated from the Secretary himself. That had been official business; this time he was working without the protection of the Secretary's authority. It was a calculated risk, one he considered worth taking.

A row of gleaming cabinets greeted him once he'd been approved by the special security screen, and within a minute he'd removed the file he wanted and placed it on a table to skim its contents. He planned to copy what was needed and then get the hell out.

'Lord, Mr Paxton, you have been a busy boy ...' He flicked through the rich history of a man who'd been tailed, spied on, tapped and surveilled – the very thought always sent a small chill down Dancer's spine.

His eyes fixed on a particularly juicy few pages, including several photographs that gave graphic meaning to the phrase 'compromised'. Nine pages in total, to be copied and then placed back into the file. Everything neat and in perfect order. After all, that was the goal of foreign diplomacy, wasn't it? To maintain the mirage of stability, to avoid the appearance of confrontation, even when things were turning to shit.

Charles Dancer, with his decades of hands-on experience, wasn't about to meddle with the DFAT golden rule. Not now, especially.

August 11, 2011

The bank of television screens in the Prime Minister's press office was blasting out a nonstop barrage of Bailey Mania – in the long winter break it was the only political story filling the void. Brendan Ryan and George Papadakis, two of the most powerful men in the country, stood impotent, shaking their heads in awe at the power of a political zombie who was tearing the heart out of their government. And at the ability of the media to keep talking about the same story for weeks.

Transfixed, they watched as a small demonstration outside John James Hospital was beamed on each of the four TV screens. A beautiful young girl in a wheelchair, wearing a *GetSet!* pullover, was demanding that Catriona Bailey be allowed to continue in her job.

'My name's Lydia Ainsworth and I know what it's like to have people discriminate against you because you are differently abled,' she said. 'I think the Toohey Government now has a great opportunity to show leadership. Catriona Bailey has clearly proven she is still capable and she can communicate. She should be allowed to stay on as Foreign Minister.'

'Won't that pose a few fairly significant practical difficulties?' asked an ABC journalist. 'I mean, she can't leave hospital. Which means she can't attend Parliament or Cabinet and can't travel.'

'That's old-think,' snapped Ainsworth. 'That's can't do. Technology is the great leveller. Cate can communicate. The world can come to her. She can be a symbol for all the differently abled: we can all aspire to the dignity of work, if we are only allowed to. And if Toohey won't let that happen then it is a second betrayal. A greater betrayal than when he backstabbed her so he could become Prime Minister. He would be betraying all of us as well.'

'Sweet Mother of Jesus take me now,' muttered Ryan. He turned to Papadakis but he was interrupted by an explosion of expletives from the next office.

'Fucking flaming bull's tits and rat's cocks!' The Prime Minister stormed though the door, incoherent with rage. 'Did you see that shit! If I sack her now it'll be like clubbing a one-flippered harp seal cub to death.'

'Or boiling a three-legged baby panda in tar,' Ryan offered.

'You're not helping!' roared Toohey. 'You two are supposed to be the geniuses – what do I do?'

Both Ryan and Papadakis were, for once, lost for words. The void was filled by the voice of *GetSet!*'s Jamie Santow, who had stepped up to the ABC microphone, exuding his all-too-familiar moral superiority.

'I think there is little left to say after those stirring words from Lydia,' he said, then continued for another twenty minutes.

'The gauntlet has been cast. Will Martin Toohey take up the challenge?'

'I fucking hate that opportunistic little prick.' Toohey was seething.

'Maybe we're looking at it the wrong way,' Papadakis said.

'There's another way of looking at this other than it being one of the largest shit sandwiches in Australian political history?' Toohey said.

'I'm with the PM,' Ryan shrugged. 'Except it isn't just a shit sandwich, it's a whole bain-marie full of turds.'

'We've been preparing for a by-election we probably can't win,' Papadakis said. 'If we lose it, we lose government. But if, out of the vast generosity of our spirit, we keep Bailey, then the weight is back on the Coalition. They have to offer her a pair and we keep our majority in Parliament. Imagine the outcry if they took advantage of Bailey's stroke to try and take control of the numbers in the House.'

'What if they say the country is ungovernable and they're doing it in the national interest?' Ryan said.

'Scott is a small-l liberal. She wouldn't do it. It would make her look like a monster and she's already got an image problem. It would kill her with her socially aware support base.'

'But what does it buy us?' Toohey seemed to have calmed down. 'We've already been compromised at every turn. This minority government is killing us. Everyone wins but us. All we get is three years of taking it up the arse followed by an eternity in Opposition. Why should we try and hold on?'

'It buys us time. We survive,' Papadakis said. 'Something will change.'

'It better,' said Ryan.

August 12, 2011

It held the same appeal as eating one's greens, attending Mass or getting the cane on a winter morning. Once a week, Martin Toohey was obliged to sit down with Randal Wade, all thanks to the accord he'd signed to keep his government afloat.

But it had quickly become the mark on his weekly calendar that he dreaded – the ordeal of having to endure lengthy sermons from a pretentious twat with a Messiah complex.

The PM believed that Wade and other moralising hypocrites had arrived in an era tailor-made for their brand of fast-food activism. Elizabeth Scott had been right; the demise of Christianity in the twentieth century meant the West was adrift. With no agreed set of values, it now ricocheted from one daft idea to the next, driven by the winds of emotion. Today, the only measure of what was good was what felt good.

The profound irony was that the Greens despised Christianity yet their brand of politics mimicked religion: their followers were the New Puritans, on a relentless quest to rid the West of its many vices. And, stripped to its core, their creed, like the Puritans' of old, was deeply misanthropic. In the end the Greens believed people were a pestilence on the face of the earth.

And, despite all their posturing as champions of the oppressed, the Greens represented the richest and whitest people in Australia. They hated everything about the working class: their jobs, cars, houses, choice of food, sports; their drinking, smoking and gambling. So the Greens determined to legislate these vices away, or make them really expensive.

Without the burden of having to run a country Wade could take the moral high ground in every argument. And he paraded his virtue on the platforms of the public broadcaster, particularly ABC local radio.

The PM was in the middle of writing himself a memo to 'call Mark Scott and threaten to cut ABC funding … again' when George Papadakis knocked.

'Mr Wade is here,' Papadakis said, with that cheese-eating grin he wore when he knew he'd spend the next thirty minutes watching his old friend being tortured.

'Martin!' Wade flounced across the room with his hand extended. 'I'm sure you look forward to our chats as much as I do. They are always so fruitful.'

'Sure,' Toohey said. 'Sit. What's on your mind?'

'Well, I don't need to tell you how upset the community is about the decision to restart live cattle exports, Martin. I have never seen so many emails.'

'I agree a lot of people are upset,' Toohey said, emotionless. 'But emails are no measure of how the community feels.'

'I don't believe what we saw in those Indonesian slaughterhouses was at all complex. It was clearly animal cruelty, and you obviously agreed because you shut the industry down. And I supported that.'

'We overreacted,' Toohey shot back. 'Our advice was to move slowly, to shut some abattoirs, not the lot. But, driven by you, and our own Left, we made a mistake … again.'

'And saved many animals from being treated cruelly, Martin. Your first call was right. Those cattle have feelings and desires. What really is the difference between them and us?'

'The fact that I can understand how stupid the statement you just made is, and a cow can't.'

Papadakis shifted in his seat, just enough for Toohey to recognise that his friend was sending him a 'calm down' message.

Wade was taken aback by a tone he had never heard from Toohey before and he dialled up his own passion. 'Some of us believe you restarted something as evil as the slave trade,' he said.

Toohey wrestled with his temper. 'Only someone who believes human and animal life are equivalent could say that. And to be consistent you would then have to demand an end to all slaughter of animals for food everywhere. So you want me to ban the eating of all meat, Randal?'

'Of course not. Don't be absurd.'

'I'm not being absurd. But, mark my words, once we close the door on live exports then the militant vegetarians behind that campaign will turn their attention to the domestic meat market. How's the new vegan regime going by the way?'

'Never felt better, you should try it. In time, I believe many more people will discover the benefits of not eating meat. And, no matter what your excuses, I am reintroducing my bill to ban live exports and I expect you to support it.'

'I won't be doing that. We've had this discussion; the matter is settled.' Toohey glanced at Papadakis. His expression did not change but his chief of staff got the message. Papadakis had often said that the Greens were never satisfied with compromise and always returned to the well for more.

'Well, perhaps you should reconsider,' Wade said. 'I know you have a big agenda when Parliament resumes. I know you need to deliver some big reforms to show you can govern. I'm sure you wouldn't want to see any of that jeopardised.'

'Are you threatening me, Randal?'

'Of course not. I'm just saying that this is a core issue for us and we want it fixed.'

'It wasn't even on your radar until the ABC covered it.'

'We are not kidding about this, Martin. This is deadly serious.'

Toohey locked Wade in his gaze and willed him dead. He thought of several bitter responses but, out of the corner of his eye, he could see Papadakis silently urging him to keep his cool. He took a deep breath.

'Too bad. We've already done this. You put up your bill and got to parade your concern. We opposed it and you had the pleasure of attacking us as heartless animal torturers. Go ahead.

Put your bill up again, but, mate, I am telling you now, we will never support it.'

'Then I will have to reconsider some of the other conversations we have had. My base is very angry about this. And I'm personally disappointed, Martin; I thought you'd see reason.'

There was a long pause as Wade left the room and closed the door. Papadakis broke the silence. 'Not exactly the way I'd hoped to end the week,' he said.

Toohey was in no mood for banter. He drummed his fingers on his notepad for a small eternity as he struggled to regain his composure.

It was time to fight back.

'George,' Toohey sighed, 'I have tried, God knows, to hold this circus together. But that's it. I'm done being the only one eating shit.' He picked up his mobile, scrolled through some names and dialled a man who made his skin crawl.

'Sam, it's Martin. I need your help.'

August 12, 2011

This was the moment of truth, a slug-'em-out showdown between two Liberal heavyweights, the female equivalent of Ali versus Foreman. And just like the rumble in the jungle, only one of them would triumph.

Emily Brooks and Elizabeth Scott sat a metre apart in a corner of the Opposition leader's office, a plunger of coffee and a tray of biscuits untouched between them. They were hardly friends at the best of times, but this afternoon, in an empty Parliament, the hatred was electric.

'I think you will agree it's time for a change of tactics, Liz.' Brooks found it difficult to maintain a façade of respect when she spoke with her leader. She despised Scott's soft-Left world view and saw it as a cancer on the party. (The only thing she hated more than Scott was the Welcome to Country, that politically correct nod to indigenous history that Catriona Bailey had foisted on Parliament.)

'How so?' Scott, typically, disagreed with Brooks. 'We went within one seat of winning an election against a first-term government. That's the first time that has happened in eighty years. Now the government is in disarray and we are well-placed.'

'True, but that was all their doing, not yours, Liz. Labor committed the greatest act of self-harm since Federation in killing a Prime Minister six weeks before the poll. And they still won. They formed government. Don't forget that. And don't forget that, since then, you have managed what I thought was impossible. Your approval rating is worse than that joke of a PM's. We should be untouchable, but we aren't.'

The blood rose in Scott's face. She had a quick temper and Brooks could see she had to fight to keep her emotions in check.

'I think we both know how Jon Robbie came by his story, Emily. Scoops are usually delivered in manila folders; you clearly prefer a box.'

'I don't know what you're talking about. And isn't your highly offensive accusation missing the point? You made a play against the Prime Minister that fell apart in three days. The leak wasn't the problem, wherever it came from.'

'Get to the point.'

'You're the problem – you. Your foolish attempt to try and blast out Toohey shattered your credibility. It called your political judgement into question, again. It reinforced all the hesitations that the electorate has about you. I don't know if you can recover.'

'Are you threatening me? Is this a challenge?'

'No, it's a warning. This is your last chance. I could get

the numbers tomorrow to spill your position; it's not as if our colleagues are that attached to you.'

Scott eyed Brooks carefully. 'What do you want?'

'I want you to refuse a pair for Catriona Bailey when Parliament returns.'

'You want me to deny a pair to a woman on life support?'

'Yes.'

'It's indecent. I can't do it. And I won't.'

'Do it, or I'll find someone who will.'

'I'll be murdered in the media. It's well known that I have a godchild with cerebral palsy. And I'm the first female leader of the Opposition. You know that I've made a stand to try and make politics more family friendly.'

'That's your problem.' Brooks stood up. 'I'll show myself out.'

That night Jonathan Robbie ran an 'exclusive' which foreshadowed plans for the Coalition to adopt an extreme position on pairs, which would include denying one to the now wildly popular, bedridden Foreign Minister. The story included the classic non-denial: 'A spokesman for the Opposition leader declined to comment.'

Within the hour Bailey had tweeted: 'Scott reaches a new low. This is the politics of the gutter and a direct attack on the disabled.'

Online polling ran at 90 per cent against the plan and by morning a *GetSet!* picket had formed outside Scott's electoral office.

The Liberal leader was trapped, faced with a diabolical choice – conscience or career.

August 13, 2011

The narrow streets were humming with madness. Sheer fucking madness. Sunburned tourists in white Bintang singlets; the flip-flop of a thousand marching thongs; street-stall hawkers seeking out the fat wallets of their prey; the din of a cheap loudspeaker – Hendrix in all his distorted glory.

Harry Dunkley gave a deft flick of the wrist and his Suzuki scooter immediately darted into the traffic.

The reporter had left Cucukan and Doug Turner behind, arriving in touristy Kuta earlier in the day, restless to get back to Australia. He'd hired a scooter for the ridiculously low sum of five dollars and set off, determined to follow the coast road as it snaked through Seminyak and the small coastal villages further north that still offered some remnants of the magic and beauty that had first enticed travellers to the island, back in the days before Mercure and Best Western had laid their foundation stones.

For several glorious hours he had sailed through small villages and past temples offering up their souls to their gods, with petite women guarding the sacrificial goods – fruits and nuts and other foods that Dunkley suspected would be better served lining some child's stomach rather than the footpaths of the city.

The first stain of the night sky was taking hold across Kuta, eager tourists drifting down bustling streets, the Hard Rock Cafe and other Western icons cheek by jowl with local shacks. He was close to the Sari Club site where Islamic terrorists had torn apart so many lives on that fateful night in 2002. Since then, Bali had managed to recover some of its former glory, the strong Aussie dollar and the cheap flights promoted by discount airlines proving an irresistible cocktail.

It was nearing 5.30 p.m. Legian Street was chockers as Dunkley navigated his way back to the Tanaya B&B, a mid-market hotel that offered a clean, pleasant functionality and was an easy walk to the main beach. He was choking on the smog of the city and loving every minute of it.

Pulling into the driveway of the Tanaya, Dunkley pressed the off button on his scooter, and dragged his helmet from his head before lifting his seat to take out a small rucksack. It contained several notepads and two voice recorders, one digital and one of those old-fashioned analog machines that used a cassette.

Their collective value, in hard currency, was not much more than a hundred dollars – but right now, alone in this thumping city, Dunkley thought they were the most valuable possessions imaginable.

August 14, 2011

The photo was postcard perfect, the couple was unmistakable. Ben Gordon exhaled, too loudly for his own liking, but this ... well, this was a remarkable sight. Bruce Paxton and his Chinese Mata Hari enjoying a quiet dinner at the Green Tea House in Beijing. The Defence Minister and his illicit maiden. What had he been thinking?

Gordon worked methodically through the pages Dancer had lifted from the Marmalade Files but their theme was clear after a few sentences. The man with one of the most sensitive portfolios in the Australian Government had revisited a dalliance with a woman as dangerous as a fresh drift of snow on a steep mountain cliff.

'Christ ...' No wonder Paxton was setting off alarm bells in Defence and beyond; the man had succumbed to the lures of one of China's best, a deadly assassin practised in the fine art of seduction. Weng Meihui was a real piece of work, a magnificent asset for her Communist masters. She had used her nubile charms, the intel suggested, to secure all sorts of secrets for the state.

She was programmed to lure men of power and dubious moral fibre to her lair, where they would fall for her beauty and charm, seduced by the prospect of an affair with an Asian princess. If only they knew.

Paxton and Weng had been first 'identified' as a couple in 1982, but the relationship caused few concerns for the Australian embassy – Paxton was just a union bovver boy with a healthy libido. Any nuggets of pillow-talk he was feeding Weng would be of little consequence.

It was only after he was elected to Parliament that his continued interest in Ms Weng became more significant. The file notes suggested the two had sought each other's company whenever Paxton visited China – in 1997, 2000 and 2002. It was not clear if, or when, he had been compromised by Weng, but the file noted that his increased interest in a number of Pacific islands – Nauru and Tuvalu, especially – coincided with China's growing financial links with these tiny nations.

China was using its financial clout to try and broaden its political power base across the Pacific Rim as a counterweight to the might of the United States. Superpower against superpower. The Cold War might have ended, but the world was continuing to feel the wrath of hostile states playing a high stakes game of brinkmanship.

Had Paxton become a willing envoy for the Chinese? Gordon wondered. Men betrayed their country either for money or for sex. Looking at the intelligence gathered on Paxton, it appeared he may have succumbed to both.

'You've been a bad, bad boy,' Gordon quietly muttered, as a disturbing pattern was laid out in front of him.

The file then noted that Paxton appeared to have backed off and kept Ms Weng at a distance as his political career took off, with appointments to the Shadow Ministry and then as Minister for Defence. 'An eight-year hiatus has been observed by officers. Despite twice visiting Beijing over this period – in 2005 and then in 2008, as a guest of the Chinese Government for the Beijing Olympics – BP did not meet with Weng.'

However, there was no doubting the relationship had been rekindled during Paxton's most recent visit to China at the beginning of the year. The photographs did not lie. There they were at the Green Tea House, with its beautiful minimalism and wonderful high-backed chairs, both looking relaxed and enjoying the formal occasion, along with the Chinese Junior Minister for Defence, several of his attachés and the Australian Foreign Minister.

The Australian Ambassador was present too, along with several of her staff. No doubt one of them was assigned the task of keeping mental notes that would later be fed into the file, a dossier that could be deployed like a deadly missile if its masters so desired.

Bruce Paxton had walked straight back into a honey trap. And it all seemed so convenient – a Defence Minister with a known weakness for women seated so close to a former consort … Who'd arranged this liaison? Was it a set-up, a deliberate ploy to compromise the Minister?

Ben Gordon's mind was racing; he needed answers. Most of all, he needed to find out just who was aware of this dirty little secret.

August 15, 2011

There were days, long thankless days, when George Papadakis felt like Winston Wolfe, the Harvey Keitel character from *Pulp Fiction*, always cleaning up after someone else's mess.

The unbridled joy of helping run the nation gave way to the rank thought that being chief of staff to the Prime Minister was a lowly descent into the gutter minds of those MPs bent on a suicide mission.

Xavier Quinn, the gaffe-prone Education Minister, was one of the worst. But foot-in-mouth wasn't his only problem – his biggest liability was an inability to keep his penis in his trousers.

Why was it always the Catholics? Papadakis again gave quiet thanks for the Great Schism. The best thing his Greek Orthodox Church ever did was ditch those weirdo Latins in 1054. A thousand years on, it still looked like a good policy.

What bemused him with Australian Catholics was that a disproportionate number of them had sexual hang-ups. He traced some of the problem to the Western Church's idiot innovation of clerical celibacy. But that couldn't explain the particular Australian problem because he knew from experience the French and Spanish Catholics had a much more relaxed attitude to sex. So he blamed the Irish. Irish Catholicism was infected with the heresy of Jansenism, which saw humanity as depraved.

'*Odium corpus*,' he muttered to himself. 'Hatred of the body.'

He had found Australian Catholic men who had been endlessly fed messages during childhood that bodily things were bad reacted in one of two ways: they felt guilty all the time; or they simply rebelled and rooted like the world was about to end.

Xavier Quinn was the worst kind: he paraded his faith in public and in private banged like a dunny door in a cyclone.

Papadakis's theological musings were interrupted by a knock on his door.

'You wanted to see me, George?' It was Quinn.

'Yes. Sit down.' Papadakis wasn't about to waste time on niceties. 'Minister, do you recall a meeting we had in this very office the day before you were sworn in?'

'Yes.' Quinn shifted in his seat.

'Then you will recall one key message I had you repeat before I agreed that you would be included in the Ministry?'

'Yes.'

'What was it?'

'Don't screw the crew.'

Papadakis leaned forward. 'Well done, Minister. Yes, rule number one: don't screw the crew. Why? Because it causes more grief, more often, than you can possibly imagine. I don't care that you are serially unfaithful to your wife as long as you're careful, but Minister, screwing your chief of staff is a bad idea. It's a bad idea at any time, but it's a worse idea when she's married to the Assistant National Secretary.'

'Bullshit, all bullshit. I won't sit here and be talked to like this by you. It's simply not true. I know there are rumours about Connie and me but there always are when men and women work closely together. It's … it's … a kind of sexism.'

'Please, Minister, you of all people can't mount a feminist argument. I'm not surprised you just tried to mount it because, frankly, you would mount a knothole in a tree. That's the problem. So save the denials for your wife. Your chief of staff is leaving your office today. I'm doing a straight swap with the Industry Minister's COS.'

'What – Clare Jones? No way. She's a muff-diver and she hates me.'

'I know, she was even less keen than you … Until I told her that part of her job was to persecute you, with my blessing. That's all, thanks.'

Papadakis began making some notes as Quinn stood and shrank towards the door.

'Oh, and Minister.'

'What?'

'About the blow job from the prostitute in the back seat of that cab in Darwin …'

Quinn went white. 'Who knows about that!' he squeaked.

'Well, it turns out the cab driver is a party member. And, happily, rather than posting the security camera footage on

YouTube he sent it to me. It might come in handy one day. Now get the hell out of my office.'

Papadakis felt his spirit sink. That had been the easy meeting. He had always found it simple to punish people he had no regard for. A much harder task was asking good people to do difficult things. And David Joyce, the Secretary of the Department of Foreign Affairs and Trade, was salt of the earth and a fine public servant.

Joyce had been transferred from leading ASIO to try and keep Cate Bailey under some kind of control. He'd done an outstanding job, single-handedly keeping Australia's precious foreign relations in some kind of order while his mad Minister galloped from one country to the next in an endless quest to promote herself and her absurdly expensive ambition to win a seat on the United Nation's Security Council.

'George?'

Papadakis stood to meet his old friend. 'David, good to see you, mate. Would you like a coffee?'

'No, mate, thanks.'

'Have a seat. Look … I won't beat around the bush about your Minister.'

'Yes, very sad. The department's, er, well … they didn't wish that on her. But I guess I'm here to hear about a replacement.'

'Yes, er … well, not exactly.'

'Come on, George, you're not going to give it to the Trade Minister who's acting in the job. The guy couldn't find Tasmania on a map.'

'No, that didn't cross my mind. Of course not.'

'Thank Christ. Who then?'

'It's, well … the PM thought … and you know things are … difficult … for us politically, what with the hung Parliament and the loss of a vote in the chamber.'

'Yes.' Papadakis could tell Joyce's finely tuned spook instincts had begun to tingle. The man knew something bad was about to happen.

'Well, Cate Bailey can communicate, she's remarkably popular and there is a big push from the disability lobby to let her keep her job.'

'You are fucking joking, George!' Joyce leapt to his feet. 'You can't be serious! You can't do this to me! I had to babysit that hideous bitch for a year as she ran amok around the globe. Do you know how many disasters I averted? I'm surprised Mossad hasn't taken her out after she sold out Israel to woo Security Council votes from the Arab states. We threw a fucking party in my office the night she was taken to hospital and invited half the Canberra diplomatic corps. The French bought Bollinger. We didn't leave till dawn.'

'David, it's only until we can think our way through this. You'll be running the show. How much damage can she do from a hospital bed?'

'Heaps!' Joyce's face was going red. 'She's learned to text. She sends me about a hundred messages a day. And because she's borderline Asperger's she's memorised the mobile numbers of half the world's foreign ministers. She's bombarding them with her hare-brained ideas. She has to be stopped. I don't have the strength for this shit anymore. I'm fifty-six, I can take my super and run.'

'David, David … please. I will fix it, just give me a couple of weeks. I don't know how but I will fix it.'

'You'd better fucking fix it or this country's rooted and I'm moving to New Zealand.'

'Just for a few more weeks.'

'One month. Tops. After that find another idiot to do your bidding.'

'Thank you.'

Joyce slouched towards the door, opened it and stopped. 'What happened?'

'What do you mean?'

'What happened to Labor, George? You used to be a serious party. Now you're some kind of sad, faded circus act.'

August 15, 2011

YOU GOOSE!

Sydney's *Daily Telegraph* liked to start the morning screaming, preferably at someone it hated.

Alongside the massive headline was a picture of Greens leader Randal Wade looking suitably foolish and startled, snapped opening the front door of his Point Piper mansion in his animal-patterned pyjamas.

The three paragraphs below the enormous headline went straight for the jugular.

> Greens leader Randal Wade is under intense pressure to quit after being caught out illegally buying *foie gras*, a ritzy French paste made from the livers of force-fed geese.
>
> An outraged Lindy Byrne from Animals Australia said Wade, an avowed vegan, was a 'rank hypocrite'.

'Everyone knows *foie gras* is one of the cruellest foods in the world,' she said. 'And clearly he felt guilty about it because he has been trying to hide it. He has to go.'

The tabloid had detailed information linking Wade to the illegal importation and consumption of *foie gras*, including credit card bills, email trails and logs of phone calls. Someone clearly had access to private details that were very hard to get. The *Tele* pointed out that Wade had initially denied the story but, presented with the wealth of detail, had directed the paper to his lawyer. The lawyer had tried and failed to get an injunction preventing the story from being published.

The revelation was a double blow for Wade because in February the Australian Quarantine and Inspection Service had slapped an indefinite ban on the importation of poached and semi-cooked *foie gras* due to an outbreak of Newcastle Disease in France.

So not only was Wade morally culpable in the eyes of his peers, he had deliberately broken the law. And as an AQIS source pointed out, Wade's selfishness was a direct threat to the environment.

'We didn't ban this stuff because it was the food of choice for wankers,' the senior source said. 'Newcastle Disease is highly contagious. It could devastate Australia's avian industry and kill native birds by the hundreds of thousands. This guy is a selfish, dangerous clown. And a criminal.'

In several inside pages the *Tele* took Wade apart. There was a novice's guide to the horrors of *foie gras*. It detailed how ducks and geese are caged and force-fed several times a day – a mechanical feeder stuffed down their throats as a mixture of corn and oil is pumped into their stomachs. This blows up their livers to ten times their normal size, which is where the words *foie gras* come from, meaning, literally, fat liver.

After establishing the cruelty of the food, the *Tele* reprinted Wade's *Q&A* declaration that he was to become a vegan in the name of animal rights.

Finally, it detailed the cost of Wade's food perversion. Five hundred grams of poached whole goose *foie gras* retailed for $300. And it was usually eaten with champagne or a sweet wine like Sauternes or Monbazillac. An investigation of Wade's bin had unearthed an empty bottle of 1998 vintage Krug Champagne, which retails for $379. Also discovered was the butt of a Cohiba Espléndidos cigar, retailing for $83. The *Tele*'s total for one predinner splurge was $762, a figure it said could feed a Mt Druitt family of four for more than a fortnight.

It was devastating.

Sam Buharia forensically examined the paper to ensure there was not a single fingerprint on it that could lead back to him.

No. Job done. A perfect crime. And the cunt wouldn't see the week out.

August 15, 2011

It was one of Canberra's finest days, the crystal-cut clarity of the sky guaranteed to lift your spirits from the depths of winter. Unfortunately for Ben Gordon, he was locked in the confines of Defence's most secure facility and felt only the artificial climate of recycled air and harsh neon lighting. Adding to Gordon's grey mood, his ambitious boss had placed a series of files on his desk with firm instructions. 'I need answers by COB.'

Usually such an edict would be enough to stimulate his analytical brain into trying to solve whatever problem had been placed before him. But today he couldn't keep his mind on the job. Instead he was captivated by the unfolding mystery surrounding the pasts of Bruce Paxton and Catriona Bailey, pasts that, he was sure, were about to explode into the present.

And today there had been a significant development. Even Gordon's colleagues were intrigued by a smallish article buried in the world pages of the *New York Times*, quoting senior Pentagon sources who, according to the *Times*, were miffed by reports that Australia was about to pull back on the flagship Joint Strike Fighter program. One quote, in particular, stood out. 'A number of recent decisions by Minister Paxton raise the question of his commitment to ANZUS.'

In diplomatic terms, it was a definite shot across the bow. It was rare for US sources to be directly critical of a close ally like Australia. Something big was going on. He didn't know what it was, but Gordon was now sure that he and Dunkley were close to the epicentre.

It reminded him of the blunt message the Americans had sent in the lead-up to the dismissal of Gough Whitlam in November 1975. The head of the CIA had told his Australian counterpart that the US wanted Whitlam gone. Gordon was no raving leftie, but he could still recall his outrage and anger when, as a novice in the intelligence arena, he had first been alerted to the CIA's involvement in the Dismissal.

Why wasn't this on the history syllabus? Surely the Australian people were not so supine as to completely ignore this shameful episode?

For a while, Gordon had become obsessed with the issue, particularly after reading of the show trial of Christopher Boyce, the American who was sentenced to forty years imprisonment after being convicted of spying in 1977.

Boyce had learned that Pine Gap – the communications facility located in the Northern Territory that America had promoted as a joint facility with Australia – was in reality a CIA project. Incredibly, Boyce – whose misadventures were later turned into a film, *The Falcon and the Snowman* – claimed to have CIA cables outlining plans to dispose of the Whitlam Government for fear that it would close Pine Gap. The CIA was profoundly concerned by Whitlam's socialism and his wooing of China.

Eventually arrested for leaking information to Russia, Boyce was thrown into jail and never given the chance to explain why the US would betray one of its closest allies.

Gordon had studied the case carefully and considered it the most egregious act of interference by a foreign government in Australia's sovereign affairs. He could almost recite word for word Whitlam's lament to Parliament after the Dismissal: 'It is precisely because America is our principal ally that Australia must be satisfied that American agents are not acting in a manner contrary to our interests as a nation. Are we to let an ally get away with something that a rival would not be allowed to get away with? Alliances are not strengthened by covert operations or by condoning or covering up such covert operations.'

They were masterful and prescient words and they came flooding back as Gordon contemplated what he'd uncovered in the past few weeks – and what he suspected still remained hidden in the vault of secrecy.

Despite every keystroke at DSD being logged, Gordon was so enraged at the thought that the Americans were meddling in domestic politics – again – that his usual caution had cracked. He'd spent the last few hours trawling through the DSD's super computers looking for clues, but had sought to cover his tracks by embedding his searches within existing DSD projects.

When the end of the working day loomed, Gordon snapped back into official mode. He sent his boss a quick email promising he'd deliver the answers she wanted first thing in the morning.

For now he had more pressing matters to deal with.

Late that evening, logging on to his personal email account at home, Gordon hit the keyboard with a ferocity that surprised him, tapping out a few sentences to his friend.

> Charles, starting to look like shades of '75 here. What do our friends in DC think they are up to? Do they REALLY believe they can get away with it? Again! This is not the action of a friendly nation.
> Kimberley

He hit send, watching the email disappear into the ether, before closing down the computer for the night. It was late and he was planning an early start tomorrow.

A few kilometres away, in a small brightly lit room, two men carefully monitored their PC screens. Just after 11 p.m., they logged a short email.

> Charles, starting to look like shades of '75 ...

August 15, 2011

Elizabeth Scott gazed at the ocean and breathed in a long draught of the chill salt air. The moon hung full and low, skimming light over the waves as they rolled towards Manly.

The crazies will be out tonight, she mused, sending me mad messages. Immediately, she tried to erase the image from her mind. She needed to think clearly and not about one of the thousand pieces of ephemera that crowded political life. No one, except those who had done the job, could ever imagine it. The workload was crushing, relentless and largely thankless. Constituents, local branch members, businesses, donors, colleagues, the media – everyone wanted a piece of you. No, everyone demanded it. And believed your time was theirs by right.

If they didn't get what they wanted the threats were never far away: 'Won't vote for you', 'Will challenge your pre-selection', 'Will tell the media' – or the new narcissism: 'Will write about it on Twitter'.

Scott was used to high-pressure jobs but found politics suffocating. You could never lash out in public, no matter how rudely you were treated, or how idiotic the complaint. The mask was always on, and it chafed. She feared that one day she would forget how to remove it.

She could still be herself on this porch, looking out to sea, when the rest of the family was asleep. She had loved this house from the moment she saw the ocean. There were more expensive houses in her electorate of Warringah, with panoramic water views towards the city. But Scott was drawn to the top of Bower Street, nestled between the sea and North Head National Park.

The ocean was her escape. In moments of despair she could feel her spirits rise as she was drawn into the uncluttered vastness of it.

She took another sip of red wine and lit another cigarette: something else she kept from the world in this absurd, censorious age. She had smoked since her senior years at Abbotsleigh – it was her one vice and she wasn't about to give it up, so she hid it. As she hid so many things.

'Why am I doing this to myself?' It was not the first time she'd asked the question but, right now, the answer was more remote than ever. She had given up her freedom to be locked in the spotlight of the most thankless job in public life: Opposition leader.

From day one, everyone had questioned her motives.

'Only wants to be PM,' was the default assessment. She'd been branded selfish, power-mad, dictatorial, heartless, politically inept and uncaring by people who knew nothing about her. She barely bothered to read opinion pieces any more, so rote had the abuse become. And the cartoons. From the moment she stepped into politics she had been drawn wearing a tiara, with a silver spoon in her mouth, or dressed in a ballgown. That she had largely made her own wealth never seemed to matter. She came into public life as a spoiled rich girl cliché and she feared she'd never shake the image.

Yes, she was ambitious and that was never going to be sated in business. She was a nationalist and believed fiercely that Australia wasn't a lucky country. It had made its own luck and that luck would run out without good leadership. She had ideas and knew she could make a difference, if she ever got the chance.

But now that chance, like the night tide, was ebbing. Scott had made so many compromises that even she began to wonder if what people said about her was true: that there was nothing she wouldn't do to get to the Lodge.

And when she got there what would be left? A shell, echoing a cacophony of conflicting voices she had mimicked to talk her way to power.

She recalled one of the lines from her favourite play, *A Man for All Seasons*, where, in a debate between William Roper and Thomas More, Roper says he would cut down every law in England to get at the Devil.

'Oh?' said More. 'And when the last law was down, and the Devil turned 'round on you, where would you hide, Roper, the laws all being flat?'

In her six years in politics she had only met one person who really understood the terrifying dilemma of trying to balance conviction with the pursuit of power. He recognised something of himself in her, understood her conflicts, and knew she was a good person. Different from him, but good. It mattered so much to her that someone knew.

And the connection had been so strong it frightened her. But she couldn't talk to him anymore. Politics was killing all the things that she loved. She wondered if it would kill her. That, one day, she would sit on the porch, looking out to sea, and not be able to remember who she was.

2007

They'd been engulfed in silent uncertainty as the taxi drove them back to the Embassy Motel all those years ago.

It was a short fifteen minutes from the Elbow Room and they were both lost in the thoughts and emotions of the last hour.

Elizabeth Scott glanced at Martin Toohey as the passing Adelaide Avenue streetlights tracked across his face. He was a decent man; flawed, as she was, but decent. She hoped he saw that in her.

They climbed the stairs to their second-floor rooms, which the hotel's staff, as usual, had ensured were next to each other.

Scott didn't want it to end – for the brief, flirtatious moments of understanding to evaporate into another lonely night in an empty hotel room.

She dropped her keys. Toohey swept them up and turned to her. He stepped in and was closer than he needed to be. Much closer.

He put the keys in her hand and closed it, wrapping his fingers around hers. He stared into her eyes and Scott again felt that expectant tingle that had evaded her for years.

'Well ... er ... it's ... it's been just great. You are great. I can't tell you how important tonight was, how ... how it felt to ... well, just talk.' Toohey seemed to be finding it hard to focus; he seemed almost nervous.

'It was.' She didn't budge, didn't make a move towards the door. Half of her screamed, 'Ask me! Just ask me!'

'Well ...' He shuffled on the spot. 'Early morning and everything. I should get some sleep. So should you ... Not that you need it, you look just ... just great.'

'You too. Goodnight.' She kissed him on the neck, turned without looking back, opened the door to her room and walked in. Alone.

She rested against the door and heard the click of his door closing. Surely, she thought, this is the moment when I feel good about myself, when I congratulate myself for being faithful.

'So why do I feel so empty?' she said out loud. She surveyed the dreary decor and sighed. 'If this is what victory over sin feels like, God, then it's little wonder you lose so many battles.'

She threw her coat on the bed. There was a knock and she could have sworn her heart actually stopped beating.

She opened the door on his goofy smile.

'On indulgence, Madam Speaker, I'm sure there was something else I wanted to say ... I just can't remember what.'

She threw her arms around him and they kissed. A glow started in her face and spread the length of her body.

He gently pushed her into the room, closing the door. Tenderly, he brushed aside her hair and kissed the exposed skin. At the hint of his hot breath on her neck, all her nerve endings tightened.

He undid the tie on her wraparound dress, lifted it off her shoulders and let it drop to the floor. The stubble on his cheek rubbed across her bare shoulders as his hands lightly brushed over her bra.

She grabbed his tie and pulled him towards the bed. There it was her turn. She unbuttoned his shirt and dipped her head to softly bite his nipples. Then she pulled his pants down and they both kicked off their shoes.

They weren't teenagers, there was no hurry. Toohey kissed her breasts through her bra as he softly ran his fingers over her panties. He kissed her neck, shoulders and back, lingeringly, almost lovingly. He unclipped her bra and pushed down her panties.

He tugged off his own briefs and, rolling her over, massaged her back. He slid his lips the length of her body, lightly brushing her buttocks, thighs and the backs of her knees.

She turned over, pushed him onto his back and straddled him. 'This is the way I like it,' she whispered.

'Me too.' He arched up to kiss her nipples and reached around to feel the beautiful curve of her back.

She drove down and those thousand nerve endings exploded. Her body tingled with goosebumps and she threw her head back and gasped.

'Jesus,' he exclaimed.

'Let's leave him out of this.'

The night was a blur of passion. Both knew it would be their first and last time together. And neither wanted to leave anything unexplored.

August 17, 2011

Like many reporters his age, Harry Dunkley feared the great era of newspapers was coming to a close. Crusading editors who were prepared to send their charges into the field had been replaced by bean counters, hired to prune budgets and slash expenses.

There were only a handful of heroes left, and more sinners than saints. Christ, there were some days when Dunkley questioned whether there was any principle or honour left in his once noble profession, now controlled by the vapid minds of those who chased celebrity and preferred fluff and polemic over hard news.

But today, a bright winter's day in the national capital, Dunkley awoke with a sense that maybe, just maybe, he was about to make history. He sprang out of bed, ignoring the painful call of the cold on his body, leaping fearlessly into a shower before the water had a chance to warm. Some obscure Top 40 hit from the '80s was ringing in his head, refusing to fade to grey.

The trumpet blare of *A.M.* signalled it was 8 a.m. Bruce Paxton, a renowned workaholic who was rumoured to have spent the odd night on his office lounge, would have been at Parliament House for the past few hours, maybe longer, devouring briefs, talking strategy and fending off the latest barbs from his Department. The Defence Minister was in the full throes of his reform agenda, carving large chunks from the military's bulging arsenal of overpriced kit. Dunkley privately shared Paxton's zeal for taking on the Defence establishment, but this was not about sentiment.

As the kettle whistle blew, Dunkley consulted his 'Private' government directory, found the Minister's contacts page and punched the number into his BlackBerry.

Surprisingly, the phone was answered after a few rings with a gruff 'Paxton'.

'Minister, it's Harry Dunkley.'

There was a long pause. Clearly Dunkley was not the person Paxton was hoping for. 'Yes, mate.'

Despite his vast experience, Dunkley was still nervous. He wiped a sweaty hand on a tea towel. 'I need to speak with you, today, and … er … preferably alone.'

'Well, mate, I'm busy today. Parliament's in full swing, in case you didn't realise. Give Adam a call.'

Adam Tracey, Paxton's press secretary, specialised in stonewall tactics and was legendary for answering even the most simple questions with, 'Mate, by way of background, and strictly off the record, I have no comment.'

No, Dunkley thought, Adam Tracey didn't need to be part of this assignment. It was time to up the ante.

'Bruce, I need to see you. Today. I know you're flat chat but these matters can't wait.'

Paxton clearly sensed Dunkley's urgency and granted him twenty minutes of valuable Ministerial time.

It was nearly a quarter to four and there was still no sign of the Minister. Dunkley mentally paced the small waiting room. He'd pumped himself up, written and then rewritten his briefing notes and memorised the questions that needed to be fired at Paxton. 'C'mon, Minister,' he muttered, casting another glance at his watch.

An approaching swirl told him something was up, a flurry of bodies gliding by in the outside corridor and, finally, Bruce Paxton, Minister for Defence, swept in with two of his fawning advisers. He tensed up when he saw Dunkley, as if he suspected the next half-hour or so would prove as painful as extracting a tooth without anaesthetic.

'Mr Dunkley, give me a few minutes, would you?' Paxton's demeanour was pure business. It would need to be.

Dunkley shuffled in his seat, scanning inside his leather work bag, making sure his A4 notes and small digital recorder were there, for the umpteenth time.

A few moments later, he was ushered into the Minister's inner office.

'Righto, Mr Dunkley, what is it that couldn't wait?' Paxton got straight down to business. He'd taken a beating during Question Time and Dunkley noticed a slight twitch in his right shoulder, the body language of a man under severe pressure.

Dunkley motioned to Adam Tracey, sitting to Paxton's right. 'Minister, I appreciate your time, but I really want this to be just the two of us.'

'Well, you can get fucked, Mr Dunkley. Adam stays, got it?'

Dunkley briefly considered standing his ground, but the risk wasn't worth taking.

'Okay, Minister, Adam stays, as you wish.' He pulled a sheaf of papers from his bag, five A4 pages held together by a paperclip – a summary of a two-month investigation that had begun on the shores of Lake Burley Griffin in the murky freeze of that fateful June morning.

'Minister—'

'Just a moment, Harry.' Tracey leaned across. 'You don't mind if we record this?' He placed his own digital recorder between the two men, hitting 'record' with an exaggerated press of his finger.

'Sure, no probs. Minister, for the past two months I've been researching your time with the CFMEU and the United Mineworkers—'

'Oh, terrific, mate, I'm flat chat trying to reshape Defence and you're about to give me a fucking history lesson.'

'More than a history lesson, Minister. In 1982, you made a trip to China. You were WA Secretary of the Mineworkers at the time, correct?'

'If you say so, mate.'

'You made contact with Zhou Dejiang and Zheng Wang, two of China's up and comers. Mr Zhou is now in charge at the Ministry for State Security and Mr Zheng … well, the son of the Red Capitalist has done very nicely out of his various business ventures.'

Paxton's face was impassive.

'One of those ventures was Guangzhou Mining. Zheng set that up in 1982, supported by his father and the Chinese Government which deemed him a "safe" entrepreneur. He was a busy boy, our Mr Zheng, establishing Guangzhou as one of the vanguard Chinese export companies. He took tentative steps at first, forging links with the West … there were various projects in Brazil, the US … and Western Australia.

'And that, Mr Paxton, is where you come in.'

'Really? How exactly?'

Dunkley took a deep breath. This was the key moment and he wanted to get it just right.

'The United Mineworkers Federation – Workplace Reform Association.' Dunkley spoke slowly, deliberately. He wanted to emphasise its importance, and make sure that Paxton got it. From the slight grimace on his face, Dunkley gathered that he had.

'Guangzhou had big plans for its investments in WA – it was looking at iron ore, nickel and possibly gold. It had the backing of the Communist Party and an endless line of credit.

'You were briefed on those plans during another trip to China, late in 1983. At an informal dinner that Mr Zheng hosted for you and, let me see, three others. You sought him out some time after this, didn't you? You wanted to talk turkey and, by all accounts, he was eager to listen. Let's face it, Mr Zheng was keen to foster ties with those in the West who could help his business expand and you … well, as a senior union figure, you were exactly what he was looking for.'

Paxton interrupted. 'This is all very impressive, Mr Dunkley, but where's it leading? I'm running behind time thanks to the Coalition's brains trust – now, that's a contradiction in terms …' He smiled, for the first time in a while.

'Yep, I know Minister, but I need to spell this out, methodically. You made arrangements with Zheng, offered him a priceless deal – industrial peace, provided he gave you what you wanted: money. And he did.' Dunkley checked a figure on a page of his notes. 'To be precise, $385,900 paid into a Commonwealth Bank account held at the Northbridge branch in Perth. This was the account affiliated with the Workplace Reform Association, except its purpose wasn't to help the members of the UMF, was it? You wanted this money for much less noble purposes, like ensuring your re-election as State Secretary …'

Dunkley's confidence was growing. He had documents to back every word. 'Then there was the house, the nice pad near Freo, all paid for by Guangzhou. And then – the big one. As if it wasn't bad enough using Chinese money to buy union elections and personal property, you channelled nearly $80,000 into your '96 campaign to win Brand. Those nice Community Voice newsletters, the endless mail-outs to voters, those sponsorships of the local netball and footy teams – all paid for by China Inc. And you never declared one red cent, did you?'

The two men stared at each other, each loath to blink first.

Dunkley felt a surge of excitement. He knew he had his man.

The Minister started to clap, really slowly, the heavy hand of sarcasm.

'Well, Mr Dunkley, that is quite a story. Congratulations, it must have taken some time to piece it all together. I reckon you could enter that in the Walkleys, perhaps in the Best Fiction category. Tell you what, son, you might think yourself pretty fucking smart but you can't prove one word!'

Dunkley reached into his leather work bag, pulled out his digital recorder and placed it in front of the Minister's snarling face. He turned up the volume before pressing play.

'Good morning, my name is Douglas William Turner, Vietnam Veteran, 2RAR, and a former Assistant State Secretary with the CFMEU. This is my declaration before the law. For eight long years, I was a loyal bagman for Bruce Leonard Paxton. And I kept records of every transaction. Oh, and Bruce, if you're listening to this, you are a dead man …'

Dunkley watched as Paxton sank back in his chair, his usual bluster gone. He shook his head with the disbelieving look of a man headed for the executioner's chair.

The Toohey Government – already on the edge – was about to head straight over the falls.

August 18, 2011

George Papadakis didn't like surprises. And he really didn't like Bruce Paxton. For him, Paxton was another piece of garbage left over from the Bailey Government that he didn't dare pick over in case something nasty crawled out.

And something very nasty had just crawled out.

The PM's chief of staff had taken the call after midnight, just as he was drifting off after another day of tragicomedy on the Hill.

'George ... it's Bruce ... Bruce Paxton ...'

The Defence Minister was slurring his words, enough to confirm he'd been drinking most of the night. 'Something's come up, I need to meet with the PM, tomorrow ... today, I mean ...'

'When you say "something", do you mean the Yanks have decided to give us the stealth bombers for free? Or do you mean something bad?'

'Ah, the second one, mate ... something bad ... and not pretty.'

'How "not pretty" Bruce?'

'That fucker Dunkley from the *Oz* is out to get me,' Paxton whimpered.

Papadakis's blood ran cold. He knew and despised most of the press gallery but he had a grudging admiration for Harry Dunkley. If he had something on Paxton, chances were it was real and dangerous.

Over a torturous hour-long call, through a haze of booze and self-pity, Papadakis managed to wheedle all of the details out of Paxton. And they were horrifying.

The meeting was scheduled for eight.

'Prime Minister, the Defence Minister is here to see you.'

Martin Toohey didn't bother rising to greet Paxton, whose complexion suggested he'd endured a long and rugged night of drinking. The PM was sitting with his back to the courtyard, George Papadakis to his immediate left.

Paxton sat without being asked, his back to the door. He wore the crumpled look of a man facing his own mortality.

And Toohey and Papadakis weren't about to make it any easier. For ten drawn-out seconds, they said nothing, until the Prime Minister broke the silence, uttering just the one word.

'Well?'

For several hours, Paxton had been rehearsing the lines that he hoped would save his Ministerial career and steer him through this crisis. At 4 a.m., the arguments had sounded convincing and he had even allowed himself to imagine that he, Papadakis and Toohey would emerge to fight this battle together.

But as he began to speak the dream evaporated, and all he could muster for the two most powerful men in the country was a barely audible, 'I'm fucked.'

'The Prime Minister and I have already established that. What we need to ensure, Bruce, is that we are not all as fucked as you.'

Papadakis's voice was as cold as the morning frost. But he could not completely abandon Paxton; after all the Toohey Government was hanging by a thread – the Foreign Minister remained in a coma, and now a Ministerial resignation loomed. Papadakis knew the resignation would have the media baying for blood, the blood of this hapless Toohey Government.

The Prime Minister finally spoke. 'Bruce, this is what you're going to do. You will write a letter of resignation and say nothing to anyone until this story breaks. You will then retire to the backbench, but not from Parliament. You will be looked after. If any legal expenses are incurred, the party will pay. It irks me to say this but we cannot afford the loss of even fools like you before the next general election.'

With that, Paxton rose and walked from the room, receiving not even a cursory goodbye. The Minister knew that he had no choice. He would draft the resignation letter as instructed, without telling a soul. But even as he drifted from sight, past the security guard's cubicle, he was plotting. Plotting redemption and revenge. And not necessarily in that order.

August 18, 2011

'SHAME MURDOCH, SHAME.' A small group of sloganeering protestors greeted Harry Dunkley as he arrived at News Limited's head office in the inner Sydney suburb of Surry Hills. The phone-hacking scandal had filtered Down Under, providing a platform for these professional agitators to ply their trade.

It was a shade after 10 a.m. The drive from the national capital had taken nearly four hours, the last thirty kilometres a slow crawl along the M5. It had given Dunkley a chance to go through his strategy for explaining the import of the Paxton story to his editor and the company's fastidious inhouse lawyer. He had gone over its factual accuracy and, most importantly, the legal protection conferred by Doug Turner's statement, which backed up every piece of evidence Dunkley had gathered. In his mind, it was watertight.

But he knew there would still be a battle to get the go-ahead to publish.

He'd just ordered a coffee from the ground-floor cafe when his BlackBerry rang. It was Ben Gordon. Harry felt guilty – he'd noticed several missed calls from Gordon last night and this morning and still hadn't replied.

'Hey Ben ... sorry. I meant to call you back, but the last twenty-four hours have been busy as all get out.'

'Harry, where are you?'

'I'm in Sydney, mate, going to see the boss to discuss you know what.'

'We need to talk.' There was a hard edge to Gordon's voice, an urgency that snapped Dunkley out of his self-obsession.

'What's up?'

'We need to talk, not over the phone.'

'I'll be in Sydney all of today, maybe tomorrow as well. I'm sorry, Ben, I should have been in touch earlier but things have moved very quickly.'

'Harry, we need to talk, asap. There's a whole other side to this ...'

Dunkley saw Deb Snowdon, his editor, enter the cafe and head his way. 'Ben, mate, I've got to—'

'There's something else—'

'Harry!' For once Snowdon looked happy as she sat down beside him.

'Gotta go,' Dunkley said into the phone, his tunnel vision for the big scoop relegating his friend's plea for the moment.

He could just hear Ben on the other end, still talking. '—something about Bailey, Harry. Something unbelievable.'

August 18, 2011

Brendan Ryan was alone, as usual. The Labor power-broker liked to work late into the night, in the dark, with only the light from his computer screen illuminating his apartment on State Circle, the road that rings the Parliament.

He had shared the odd relationship in his thirty-eight years, but women usually found his introspection, intensity and complete lack of interest in anything but politics a turn-off. Coupled with an inability to tolerate people he considered dim – and that was most people – it didn't make him an engaging date.

From the time he was a teenager he had gone to bed well after midnight and risen late, but recently he'd found it hard to sleep at all. He was constantly anxious and his already poor health was worsening.

Everywhere the news was bad. It seemed as if the pillars on which he had built his life were all crumbling at once. The global financial crisis had accelerated the power shift from the West to the East and Ryan feared for the future.

The West had been on a suicide mission for a couple of hundred years, with its most influential thinkers endlessly chipping away at its foundations, weakening its political structures. They'd killed off the Christian God, taken an axe to the hierarchy of ideas, demonised the past and opposed development. They were the vandals in Rome. And Rome was burning.

Never a fan of the European Union, Ryan feared its splintering monetary system would bring the entire enterprise undone. He could have taken a sadistic pleasure in seeing Europe, the source of many of the worst ideas in Western thought, go belly up. Except it would probably drag the United States down too. And for Ryan that was an unalloyed catastrophe.

Ryan understood the flaws in the United States better than most, but believed, on balance, that the post World War II settlement guaranteed by US military might had delivered more good than evil. America had established and maintained the power structures that ensured prosperity.

So the shift in power from West to East disturbed Ryan. He hoped conflict could be averted, but deep in his soul he feared it couldn't. War was coming. In some ways it was already raging as, daily, China launched internet attacks. But it was only the beginning. War was coming and the West was weak.

At some stage in any life a man has to choose his friends. Ryan's were the US and Israel. Everyone else could go hang.

And Ryan had also chosen his great love: the Australian Labor Party. For Ryan, Labor was the supreme innovator in Australian political life, driving the projects that had delivered a just society: a living wage, public education, the pension, superannuation and universal medical care.

Now Labor was adrift. The same shallow ideas from the Left that had killed the West had infected and corroded his party. It had lost touch with its largely conservative blue-collar base as white-collar, inner-city lefties reinterpreted the party of Chifley and Curtin into some kind of endless gay Mardi Gras.

'If Chifley were alive today, the Left would have banned his fucking pipe,' Ryan muttered to no one.

His party was broken and, for the first time in his life, Ryan didn't know how to fix it.

August 18, 2011

The night was deathly still as a light mist crept round a row of poplars laid bare by Canberra's long winter. It was just after 9 p.m. and Telopea Park was empty and dark.

Ben Gordon liked it this way. He would often walk this lonely strip of green, finding its bracing cold and silence a perfect antidote to a frenetic day. The park was just a few minutes from his apartment, and after reaching its pathways he set his course towards the lake.

He could just pick out the distant chimes of the National Carillon, its bells ringing out a mournful tune from long ago. Schubert's *Serenade*, he decided.

The music of the Carillon usually worked as a balm, but not tonight. Instead its mix of metal and melody only added to a growing sense of alarm and trouble.

Gordon had stepped out into the cold to try and make sense of what he knew – how a hundred jagged pieces now pointed to an extraordinary conclusion.

The ring of his mobile, from inside his coat pocket, interrupted his thoughts. He ferreted the phone out but the number was unfamiliar and he didn't need the distraction anyway. What he needed was clear air and headspace.

Another thought had been nagging him, a fear that he had left his fingerprints as he pursued the key to this terrible secret.

He mentally marked out a series of possible missteps, privately chastising himself for being so stupid, so bloody amateur. First, he had used a work computer to download information – information locked in DSD's electronic vaults. He knew every keystroke would be logged, but had thought the risk worth taking. Then he had fired off a series of emails to Charles Dancer outlining his concerns about this deepening conspiracy.

He recalled how his home computer had slowed one night. And how he had heard two distinct clicks on the line during one of the dreaded phone calls to his mother. He'd been sloppy. Was he paying the price; was he being tracked through cyberspace? Were his phone calls being tapped? Had he, the hunter, become the hunted?

He shivered and pulled his cashmere coat tighter, hoping to ward off the cold and a growing sense of panic. He desperately wanted to share the intel with Dunkley, and looked forward to meeting with his friend.

He turned and quickened his pace, keen to put the park's darkness behind him.

A frightened possum scurried across his path and up a tree, its rasping cry piercing the quiet. His heart missed a beat as he came to a sudden halt.

There was something else. An echo. A scuffle of shoes on the footpath nearby.

He was not alone.

August 19, 2011

The din of the truck nearly tore a hole through Dunkley's sorry head. The paper-thin walls of the Sebel on Albion Street amplified the sounds of the early morning inner-city traffic. Dunkley blinked twice, staring at a small damp spot on the ceiling before remembering why he was there. He stumbled out of bed, noticing the time – 7.17 a.m. – as he carefully opened the door, fumbling around for the newspaper he'd ordered.

He placed it on the bed as he reached for his BlackBerry, noticing six missed calls – three from the same number. Probably 2UE, he reckoned, Jason Morrison wanting a chat about his scoop. He pushed the curtains back a few feet and unfurled the broadsheet to its full front-page splendour.

DEFENCE MINISTER IN UNION SLUSH FUND SCANDAL

The Toohey Government has been rocked by a fresh crisis after explosive revelations that Defence Minister Bruce

Paxton used a union slush fund, financed by China, in his first election campaign.

A special investigation by the *Australian* can reveal Mr Paxton spent at least $80,000 of union money to help him win his seat of Brand at the 1996 election. The funds were paid by a Chinese investment vehicle, Guangzhou Mining. But Mr Paxton appears to have broken electoral laws by failing to properly disclose the source of the money.

Mr Paxton refused to comment on the allegations. But the *Australian* has learned the Minister – who has been responsible for a major shake-up in Defence – has been ordered to deliver a full explanation to Prime Minister Martin Toohey by this morning.

The latest scandal will plunge the government deeper into crisis as it deals with yet another self-inflicted wound. And it comes as the Greens and crossbench independent MPs raise new concerns over the capacity of the Labor administration to deliver on its election promises …

Christ, thought Dunkley, marvelling at his handiwork. He really had plunged the knife in. He finished reading the splash before turning to the page four and five spread, which featured a graphic detailing Paxton's sordid dealings with the Chinese beside pictures of Doug Turner and Zheng Wang, tagged as 'Key players in Paxton scandal' by a not very creative sub-editor.

Just then his phone rang. It was Evelyn Shand from the Canberra online desk, part of the early morning crew whose role was to deliver 'value-add' to the paper's daily coverage of national affairs.

'Woohoo, great fucking story, Harry, it's going off. Twitter is in meltdown and three Opposition MPs have already called for Paxton to stand down … Hold on, this has just come through … from the Prime Minister's press office – I bet they're ecstatic with you – the Minister is going to hold a presser in the Blue Room, 9 a.m. What d'ya reckon? Will he walk the plank?'

Dunkley was pretty sure he would but couldn't be certain, given the precarious nature of the Toohey Government. One thing was clear, though: Dunkley wouldn't be at the press conference to twist the blade a little deeper and to bask in the adulation and jealousy of his press gallery colleagues. He'd been at News Limited HQ until late, getting the lawyers to sign off on the final story. And then he'd spent the early hours celebrating. Now he needed to leg it back to the national capital for the critical day two follow-up – and to meet with Ben Gordon to discover what he'd found out that was so urgent.

It took nearly seventy-five minutes to reach the outskirts of Sydney and the express lanes of the M5 for the trek back to Canberra. The BlackBerry had rung on a nonstop loop of congrats and radio requests. Christ, even Thommo had rung to see if Dunkley would appear on *Morning Glory* as part of a special Paxton package. He had politely declined.

It was nearly 9 a.m. and he wanted to listen in as Bruce Paxton fronted the media in Parliament's Blue Room, the cramped office thirty metres from the Prime Minister's suite where important matters of state were first relayed to the public via the media.

Dunkley had only one regret this morning – that he wouldn't be there, in person, to eyeball Paxton as he tried to put whatever spin he could on what was now a full-blown catastrophe for the Toohey Government.

August 19, 2011

'Minister, Minister ...' It was Sally Brown, that yappy photographer from Fairfax, imploring him to look dead straight into her lens, her voice a screeching whine above the others. A hundred flashes from a thirsty pack of mongrels.

Bruce Paxton knew they were 'just doing their job', but this morning, with his world collapsing around him, he felt like doing a Hawkie and telling them to fuck off. Caution got the better of him. After all, that outburst would be gold for the TV cameras and he wasn't about to give up all of his dignity yet.

This morning he had gathered his staff and personally delivered the painful message of his resignation. There had been stifled tears from the long-term faithful, and then the slow walk to the gallows with just his press secretary by his side. It was the most painful experience that a Minister of the Crown could face: the public shame, the sense of being fed to the lions. And that gnawing feeling that someone, somewhere along the line, had betrayed him. That really hurt.

He strode with all the purpose he could muster into the Blue Room and took up his position behind the lectern. A wall of faces met him from a bare few metres away. The room was crammed, despite it being an ungodly hour for journalists. He'd given a press conference in this same room just a few short weeks ago but that time only a handful of reporters, all of them Defence correspondents, had bothered to turn up. Now a smell of blood was in the air.

'Well, I'm glad to see my popularity is on the rise,' he said, mustering something like a smile. A few reporters laughed, though his attempt to lighten the mood had clearly not gone down well with two of the PM's overbearing media handlers who both shot him a death-stare from the back of the room. Fuck 'em all, he thought.

Adam Tracey handed Paxton a sheet of handwritten notes, speaking points to work from as he announced why he was about to take one for the team.

'Right folks, ready to roll? Good. This morning, I have tendered my resignation to the Prime Minister as the Minister for Defence.'

An audible gasp went up around the room, although it should not have come as a surprise. A few reporters tried to break in with questions, but Paxton silenced them with a defiant black-gloved gesture.

'I have done this not as an admission of guilt, but to protect the government, this good government, from these defamatory allegations, allegations that I plan to vigorously contest. The simple facts are these. Before I entered Parliament I was employed as a senior union official, charged with improving the lives of many working men and women who relied on a strong and resourceful union to protect them from the claws of greedy bosses. I did my job as best I could, and with passion, winning many a battle against employers who thought they were immune from the laws and statutes of this country; who thought industrial relations was a bad joke. We taught them otherwise, and of that I am immensely proud.

'Now, in relation to the specific allegations made by the *Australian*, let me say this. Yes, I was involved in helping to facilitate Chinese investment into Australia, including Guangzhou Mining, which, I might add, has employed thousands of Australians and paid hundreds of millions in taxes since we ... er, since it started operations here.

'But – and I must emphasise this strongly – any suggestion that I profited personally is sheer bloody nonsense.'

Paxton halted, taking a sip of water and scanning the room to gauge the mood. It remained hostile. He continued.

'I considered it the wise thing to do to resign from the Ministry and take my place on the backbench while I fight these allegations. The Prime Minister reluctantly agreed. Finally, I would like to say that in the years I have held this portfolio, I have sought to strengthen the security of this country while also implementing some very necessary reforms to the structure of the Defence forces. These I am immensely proud of, and I hope my successor, whoever it should be, can continue this good work in the best interests of the nation and taxpayers. Thank you very much.'

And with that sign-off, ex-Minister Paxton swept out of the room, leaving a dozen reporters flailing as they tried to get just one of their questions answered.

Paxton might have gone from the Ministry, but there was still plenty to play out, plenty to pursue as the press gallery, like a rapacious school of piranhas, moved in to pick this carcass to the bone.

August 19, 2011

From the early hours of the morning the Coalition's shock troops had been carpet-bombing the airways, decrying the latest Toohey Government scandal and demanding an early election.

The hard-Right's warrior queen, Emily Brooks, had been on to the ABC's News Radio from the moment Marius Benson arrived at work. An interview was put to air just after 6 a.m.

'This government is a sick joke and a disgrace – it has to go. The Prime Minister must sack his Minister then drive to Government House and sack himself,' she fulminated. 'The people of Australia deserve better than this motley rabble, this poor excuse for a government. The Coalition is ready to take over, and the people are demanding it. The time for change is now.'

It took a few moments for Benson to be able to break into the diatribe.

'But surely the resignation of a Minister will be enough. What will you do if the government carries on?'

'Shadow Cabinet has voted on this, Marius,' Brooks thundered. 'We will deny a pair to the Foreign Minister and block every piece of legislation. In the national interest we will shut this government down until it does the decent thing.'

'With respect,' Benson said, 'your leader, Elizabeth Scott, has repeatedly refused to back that tactic. Has she had a change of heart?'

'I'm quite certain she sees the sense of it now,' Brooks said.

Scott was scheduled to make an appearance on *Wakey Wakey* just after seven. She was equally strident in calling for an end to what she called 'the incompetent and illegitimate Toohey Government'.

'If the Prime Minister does not call an election will you deny a pair to the Foreign Minister?' asked the all-too-pretty male presenter.

Scott paused. Her staff had told her that Brooks had already been out trying to paint her into a corner. They were split on how she should respond. But Scott wasn't.

'No,' she said. 'There has to be some grace in public life. I will not deny a pair to a woman on life support. It would be monstrous ... I cannot lead a party that does not observe the basic rules of human decency.'

The Opposition leader had drawn a line in the sand. She would not concede to the demands of Brooks and her hard-Right cronies. Scott had finally found the point beyond which she would not compromise. There were some things in politics that were beyond partisanship, that required the human spirit to soar above the bloodthirsty demands of the party machine.

She had set the scene for a showdown with Brooks at the joint party room meeting on Tuesday. She had made her choice and now the party would have to make its decision: back her or sack her.

August 19, 2011

For nearly two hours, the radio had played a steady symphony of Bruce Paxton the Musical. The ABC had predictably gone wall to wall after the shock of the Paxton resignation, calling in its political hotshots to interview anyone they could get their hands on. The high-rating commercial stations, 2GB and 2UE, had devoted large chunks of their morning line-up to the scandal, too. That great court of public opinion – talkback radio – was in overdrive, with the punters evenly divided on whether Paxton should have walked the plank.

Dunkley had raised the temperature on the scandal during several radio interviews by phone while on the road, telling Neil Mitchell on Melbourne's 3AW that there was 'potentially more to come'. He'd regretted the comment immediately.

'What sort of stuff do you still have?' Mitchell had asked, a reasonable question from the broadcaster, but in truth Dunkley didn't know. He could only imagine and hope Ben Gordon had some dynamite in his kitbag. It had sounded like it on the phone yesterday. But Dunkley didn't know because he'd barely spoken to Ben in weeks. Journalism was a selfish business, but he'd make it up to his friend, his collaborator on this grand tale.

The shimmering haze of Lake George, flanked by a trail of giant wind turbines on its eastern edge, told Dunkley he was a half-hour from Canberra. The trip down the highway had flown, the adrenalin rush from the Paxton resignation acting like a turbo-charge for the small four-cylinder car he was driving. Several times, he had felt like winding down the windows and shouting into the wind 'I AM FUCKING ALIVE', but the temperature had roared out its warning, and he timidly withdrew.

Now, as a sign said Canberra was just forty kilometres away, he reached for his BlackBerry and hit speed dial for Ben Gordon. It rang loud and clear six or seven times, before a strange voice barked out a gruff 'Hello'.

'Ah, who is this?'

'Senior Constable Waters, Chris Waters. And who might you be?'

Dunkley's mind was racing. He checked to make sure he'd rung Ben's number. Yes, he had. Okay, keep it together.

'I'm a friend of Ben Gordon's … is everything all right?'

'You wanna tell me your name?'

'Harry … er, Harry Dunkley. Is everything all right?'

'Mr Dunkley, the *Australian*, right? I think it wise we meet, in person. You're in Canberra?'

'Not yet. I'm about twenty, twenty-five minutes away, depending on traffic.'

272

'I'm in Woden, the main police station. You know where we are?'

Dunkley kept his voice calm, despite his rising alarm.

'Yep, opposite the shopping centre, the newish building. I'll see you hopefully in half an hour.'

Dunkley hung up and wondered what on earth Ben had got himself into.

August 19, 2011

Even while Bruce Paxton was singing his death hymn, journalists were receiving a short email from the Prime Minister's media office.

Media alert. Courtyard. 10 a.m.

The PM's courtyard in the full grip of a Canberra winter was a desolate, grey place; an empty square of concrete where even the sun refused to go. So there was method in George Papadakis's madness, scheduling a presser there. He would keep the press waiting until they couldn't feel their feet and hands, then send the PM out. Twenty minutes in they would want the ordeal to end as much as the nation's leader did.

Martin Toohey and his inner circle of trusted advisers – Papadakis; senior political guru, John Foreman; legal expert, Sarah Franklin; plus his useless media adviser, Dylan Blair – had spent close to two hours war-gaming for the press conference, pausing only to watch the train wreck that was Bruce Paxton's resignation.

'So, George, what'll be the first question?' Toohey asked.

'When are you going to resign?'

'You think?'

'PM, I fucking know.'

'Do we have a good answer for that?'

'Depends on how you define good.'

'What about we run through all the bills that have successfully passed through Parliament?' offered Blair.

'Dylan,' Papadakis said, 'do us all a favour and go down to Aussies and tell Dom we're going to need lots of coffee.'

'I'll have a long black,' said Toohey.

The PM turned to the rest of his troops. 'Seriously, what's the answer? Has he broken any laws?'

'Don't think so, PM. The AEC has a three-year statute of limitations on election donations – section 315 – and this happened nearly fifteen years ago,' said Franklin, who was delighted to have an answer that offered a veil of legal cover.

'But there is no statute of limitations on being stupid and, let's face it, corrupt.' Toohey stared out the window. 'Still, the loss of a Minister does not – and should not – mean the loss of a government. In our system we hold power as long as we hold the confidence of the House. And we have the numbers.'

'There's still a question mark over that, PM,' Papadakis said. 'The Coalition's lunar Right is threatening to deny Bailey a pair. If that happens then we're in a much tougher place. You know Scott as well as any of us. Will she hold on that?'

'Who knows, and it's not today's main problem, although it'll come up in the litany of second-order issues we face.' He had a guilty flashback to their last meeting and regretted, again, his vicious parting words to her.

'Still, today we are the government. We have lost a Minister, we have to admit fault on that. But we will not cut and run from government just because it's hard. Government is supposed to be hard.

'And let none of you forget, the Labor Party is the party — the only party — that takes the tough decisions for the national good. We can't let the Tories take the low road to glory, as they always do. We don't shirk the difficult reforms, the ones that Hawke and Keating, and even Gough, made as they tried to craft a better Australia. So ... what's my opening line going to be?'

'Ladies and gentlemen, thanks for coming.' Toohey scanned the miserable array of badly dressed journos and wondered why he always said that. As if they wouldn't come to feast on the carcass of his government.

'As you know, the Defence Minister has offered his resignation and I have reluctantly accepted it. It is a profound disappointment. However, Mr Paxton agrees with me that his behaviour, no matter how long ago it occurred, is not compatible with the standards I demand from my Ministers. I recognise this is a blow for my government. But let me make myself perfectly clear. I intend that this government will go full term.

'Any questions?'

The Prime Minister was buried in a cacophony as a dozen gallery journalists all yelled at once, hoping to get in the first question, sensing this was a press conference where blood would be spilled.

Toohey picked out the man he knew would get straight to the point, the appalling Jonathan Robbie, the headkicking number two from Channel Nine.

'Why won't you do the decent thing and resign?'

'The Minister has done the decent thing and resigned. There is no reason for the government to follow on the basis of a misjudgement Bruce Paxton made long ago, before he was a member of Parliament. While I enjoy the confidence of the Parliament I am the Prime Minister and I intend to get on with doing my job. The decent thing for this country is to give it a decent future and I have always believed that only Labor can deliver that.'

The Prime Minister pointed to another inquisitor.

'Did Minister Paxton offer to resign from Parliament?'

'Definitely not.'

'Should he?' yelled another.

'The Minister ... er, former Minister ... faces no charges. He has been convicted in the court of public opinion. He has paid a high price for that. He will continue to support this government from the backbench and work to clear his name. And don't forget he doesn't admit any of these allegations. Michelle?'

The press gallery doyenne asked whether the PM was confident of his stricken Foreign Minister being given a pair by the Coalition.

'Well, that is a question you should be putting to the Opposition leader. My understanding is that she has committed to that on television this morning. Unfortunately, my experience in dealing with Ms Scott gives me no confidence that I can rely on her word.'

And so it went for thirty agonising minutes. Finally Dylan Blair, holding a now stone-cold long black, yelled, 'Last question.'

And then Toohey did something none of his staff had war-gamed.

'Finally, can I take this opportunity to say that from today our relationship with the Greens and the crossbench will be recast. I am ending the formal agreement with the Greens. We will propose Labor bills – it is up to the Greens whether they support them, try to amend them or vote them down. The Greens' new leader can decide if she wants to back a progressive Labor Government or if she wants to hand over the reins of power to the Coalition. That is a decision only she can make.'

With that, the Prime Minister turned on his heel and walked inside as a dozen voices yelled in his wake. Turning into his office, he shut the door and was greeted by a grinning Papadakis.

'Well, Martin, that was unexpected. Welcome back – I've missed you.'

'George, my friend, I have had the last cucumber of compromise shoved up my arse. That deal with the Greens was a disaster, as you predicted. We stand or fall now on our own.'

August 19, 2011

Woden Police Station, all steel and gleaming glass, took minimalist chic to a whole new level. It was just twelve months old and stood on the fringe of the southern suburb, home to one of Canberra's busiest shopping malls and several battalions of public servants. Harry Dunkley wasn't much in the mood for admiring architecture, though, as he pulled up shortly after 11 a.m.

The last half-hour had been a blur, a numbing trek into Canberra along a highway marked by scattered crosses erected for accident victims by families unwilling to give up the ghosts of the past. Dunkley had tried to keep it together as his mind raced like an out-of-control speedway rider, round and round and round.

He'd rung the Sydney news desk, trying to explain to an infuriated online editor why he couldn't file updates on Bruce Paxton's resignation for the *Australian*'s web pages.

'Christ, it ain't rocket science,' the editor had shouted after telling Dunkley he 'lacked commitment' to the broadsheet's burgeoning online business.

Dunkley's rejoinder – 'I have something more urgent to attend to' – apparently meant little.

Chris Waters, a senior constable with fifteen years experience in the Australian Federal Police, had left instructions at the front desk for Dunkley to be ushered through to his office as soon as he arrived. Within a few minutes, he was in an upstairs room being offered a cup of tea.

Harry's heart started to beat faster. Something was clearly wrong. He sensed that Ben wasn't just in trouble; it was worse. Far worse.

Waters seemed to confirm it when he sat down opposite him, looking as if he'd rather be anywhere else.

'Mr Dunkley, I'm sorry to inform you that Mr Gordon was found, close to 1 a.m., at the southern end of Telopea Park, Kingston, near Wentworth Avenue. He was deceased. And while we don't have the autopsy results, it's pretty clear to us he was bashed and strangled.'

Dunkley was stunned. Ben Gordon, dead? It wasn't possible. 'How … who found him? Why …'

'Mr Dunkley, I'm not at liberty to provide too much detail at this stage, given the sensitivity of the … ah … matter. I don't need to tell you that what appears to be another gay-bashing crime will need to be handled with the utmost sensitivity.'

Waters flicked open a manila folder, reading from some notes. 'I am told that you are the executor of Mr Gordon's estate … I presume you know this?'

It took Harry a while to respond. It all seemed so unreal. 'Ben doesn't have much family, or at least family he was close to, and I agreed a decade or so back … I never thought it would happen, though …'

'Well, I can get someone to show you through his apartment after we've signed some papers. The family has been notified of the death, and I believe his mother and sister are on the road to Canberra as we speak. You may prefer to speak with them first?'

'Not really. To be honest, I've only ever met them briefly.'

Dunkley struggled to think clearly. He prided himself on being able to stay calm in a crisis. But, until now, that had always been a crisis for someone else.

'Listen, Senior Constable, this is a great shock, but I have to get to work at Parliament House. Can I arrange to meet someone later at Kingston, say 7 p.m.?'

'That can be arranged, sure.'

Dunkley left his details with Waters and departed in a daze. Ben dead? A gay bashing? Found around 1 a.m.? It didn't make sense. Ben had often told Dunkley that he was too old to be running around chasing the sort of casual anonymous sex sought by those who visited Telopea Park at night.

Something didn't fit. He needed answers and a visit to the Kingston apartment was a priority.

But it would have to wait until later that day. The biggest political yarn in years was going off on the Hill and he needed to get back and reclaim ownership of it. His job was just about all he had left now.

Just after 7 p.m., a police car pulled up outside the Argyle Apartments. Streetlights flickered weakly and two constables got out of the vehicle, donning their hats. Harry Dunkley had arrived a few minutes earlier, still numbed by the news of Ben's death, but also determined to get access to Ben's apartment to search for clues.

What had Ben meant the other day when he'd said the Paxton stuff was 'bigger than you know, maybe much bigger'? And what had he said about Bailey? Had Ben told others? Or had their project been infiltrated? Had their phones been tapped, their computers accessed by prying eyes?

The two constables had the keys to the apartment and followed Dunkley as he led them across a ground-floor courtyard to the entrance.

He was trying to work out a way to access, discreetly, Ben's safe, which he knew was in the spare bedroom. It had to contain a clue to what Ben had discovered.

'Mind if I take a look in the spare room?'

The constables were nearing the end of a busy shift and as far as they were concerned, Dunkley, as executor of Gordon's estate, could have access to whatever he wanted – as long as they were done and dusted within half an hour.

Dunkley had looked up the code Ben had entrusted to him all those years ago and took little time to punch in the safe's combination, the door opening with a sudden click.

Inside was a stack of documents, some jewellery, a leather pouch tied with a red ribbon and an old fob watch.

Dunkley leafed quickly through the pile of papers until he found a folder marked 'BP'. He checked to make sure he was still alone, then flicked through its contents.

There were the notes and clippings that Gordon had shown him or spoken to him about during their trek for the truth. But one item was missing, something that was more valuable than all the other contents combined.

Someone had taken the original black-and-white photo which had kicked off this mad chase that had now claimed the life of his friend.

Dunkley vowed, then and there, that he would track the bastards down.

August 23, 2011

Elizabeth Scott gazed up at the historical guard of honour, at the men, the good men, who had led the conservative forces through the last half-century. Menzies, Howard, Fraser – each a hero in his own way, all paid-up members of the Liberal pantheon.

She would join them one day, her black-and-white portrait emblazoned with the words 'First female Liberal leader'. But on this Tuesday morning, with her restless colleagues circling, Scott had more immediate things on her mind.

Most weeks, the meeting of the joint parties – the Liberals and Nationals – was a mundane affair, punctuated by jovial banter and the odd policy stoush. But today, a pressing question needed to be asked and answered. Would the Coalition back the government's request to give the stricken Foreign Minister Catriona Bailey a parliamentary pair? It was a vote that would help decide whether the Toohey Government survived or not.

Scott was preparing to demand that her party back her judgement and say yes. It was a question of decency, she believed, but the Shadow Cabinet had baulked when she'd sought its support. So she was going to take the issue directly to her colleagues. It was a rare thing to do – to ask the party room to vote on a question of parliamentary tactics – but these were not normal times.

The main hurdle was Emily Brooks, the hard-Right warrior who had been courting the support of the Nationals and the conservative flank of the Liberal Party, and whose tough-as-nails approach in the Senate and the media had been credited with bringing the Toohey Government to its knees. In contrast, Scott knew there was growing unease with her own leadership style, and her failure to put sufficient distance between her small-l liberal view of the world and that of the discredited Labor brand.

So, she mused, it would come down to this: high principle versus brutal pragmatism. She would demand a vote to back her stance, with the implied threat of standing down if the party overruled her. It was a calculated, high-stakes gamble. But she didn't believe the Coalition would risk a leadership change when the Toohey Government was on life support.

She was wrong.

The press gallery began getting a sense of the unfolding drama when the joint party meeting ran into its second hour. Then some MPs and Senators started texting their media favourites with messages like 'Things not going well for Scott' and 'It's fucking unbelievable in here. Very heated.'

The television networks scurried to stake out the hallway outside the Coalition party room. They were joined by a gaggle of scribblers. The 24-hour broadcasters began to speculate that the leader had been rolled.

Finally, the doors opened and Alex Jacobs, the Liberal Whip, emerged alone, to be immediately consumed by the media crush.

'Ladies and gentlemen, please,' Jacobs pleaded. 'I have a short statement and I won't be taking any questions. There will be press conferences shortly.

'Today, after a debate on parliamentary pairs, Senator Emily Brooks moved a motion of no confidence in the leadership of Ms Elizabeth Scott. The ballot was tied. Ms Scott then stood down. Senator Brooks was elected leader.'

The gallery pack was dumbfounded. Scott had rolled the dice and lost. Like John Gorton in 1971, she had then done the honourable thing and resigned. The Scott experiment was over.

As the Whip finished speaking, a triumphant Emily Brooks emerged from the party room, an entourage of beaming followers in tow. Half the journalists in the group split off to record the first words of the new leader while the others stayed poised to witness the bitterness of the vanquished.

Cameramen positioned themselves in front of Brooks while journalists bombarded her with questions.

'How do you feel?'

'I am honoured and humbled.'

'Do you feel sorry for Elizabeth Scott?'

'Ms Scott is a great Australian and will be a great member of my team.'

'How can a Senator be leader of the Opposition?'

'Read the Constitution. Nothing stops a Senator from being Opposition leader or Prime Minister. But I will have more to say on that shortly.'

'What does this mean for the Prime Minister?'

'His worst nightmare.'

She swept past the cameras, making for her office on the Senate side of Parliament House.

Moments later Scott emerged with a couple of her staunchest supporters on either side. Her face was set, she looked tired, but in a triumph of will, she held her composure.

From his suite, Martin Toohey watched as Scott made her dignified way back to her office. It was only about seventy metres from the party room but she was slowed by the crush of media.

'The Via Dolorosa of loss,' he said as he watched her journey, feeling every pain-filled step.

Scott said nothing except, 'We'll have a press conference after you've heard from the leader.'

'Well, Ms Scott,' Toohey whispered. 'You're a better man than I am.'

Emily Brooks arrived back in her Senate suite, shut the door to her office and punched the air. She had ousted her hated rival and could now focus on taking the battle up to Martin Toohey and his dreadful administration. There would be no quarter given.

The Coalition would have one aim – to destroy Labor, quickly.

First, she would have to deal with her status as a Senator. The Westminster convention is that the Prime Minister be a member of the chamber where government is formed – the House of Representatives. But that is not demanded by the Constitution. At her first press conference, half an hour later, in the same room where she had executed Scott, Brooks outlined her plan. She would stay in the Senate until the general election was called, then she would resign and contest a lower house seat.

'But that's ridiculous!' shouted one journalist.

'Why? Because you say it is?' Brooks barked. 'I don't agree. It's perfectly manageable. And you should remember two things. I expect an early election. And when it's called I will not ask any of my colleagues to stand aside and hand me a safe seat. I will contest the Treasurer's seat of Lilley. To win government we need to win Labor seats and I intend to play my part in that.'

It was a bravura performance. Brooks exuded confidence – some would say cockiness – but no one questioned that she was a stone-cold political killer and that Toohey now faced a much tougher challenge.

By contrast, Scott's press conference was muted. When a party leader falls, even the press gallery feels a sense of pity.

Scott appeared stunned, but was determined to hold it together. She had seen other leaders shed tears and thought it would only invite ridicule if she cried.

In the end it was a kind of out-of-body experience. The crushing pressure she had felt since taking the top job was gone.

In its place was the bitter hollowness of loss, coupled with a primal sense of relief.

'What will you do now? Will you recontest?'

The question seemed almost to come out of a fog.

'I'm going to take my time and have a think about it.'

'Will you serve Emily Brooks on her front bench?'

'No, I won't.'

When it was over, Scott made her way back to the Opposition leader's office to find that her staff was already packing. Her personal assistant tearfully smiled at her.

'The calls have started to flood in,' she said. 'Most of them congratulating you for showing some character and doing the right thing. They say it's rare in politics now and they've changed their opinion of you.'

'Pity they didn't tell Newspoll that,' Scott said, wearily opening her personal office door. Sitting in the middle of her desk was a magnificent vase of flowers.

'Those came a few minutes ago,' the assistant said. 'Here's the card.'

Scott opened the envelope and removed a card bearing the handwritten words of a verse from *Paradise Regained*.

> *For therein stands the office of a king,*
> *His honour, virtue, merit and chief praise,*
> *That for the public all this weight he bears.*
> *Yet he who reigns within himself, and rules*
> *Passions, desires, and fears is more a king...*

She felt a lump grow in her throat as she read the beautifully familiar verse to the end. Her eyes glazed with tears. It was Martin Toohey's handwriting.

The assistant looked at the card.

'Who's it from?' she asked.

'Nobody you'd recognise.'

August 24, 2011

Harry Dunkley scanned the rows of the mourning, uniform in their grief, and thought, what a pitiful crowd. Fewer than two dozen were seated in the spacious chapel.

In the front row, Gordon's soberly clad mother and sister sat solemnly, eyes rimmed with red, occasionally speaking softly to each other. Behind them, Ben's small community of cross-dressing buddies huddled together in gloomy counterpoint, their too-short black skirts, killer heels and platter-sized hats seeming almost grotesque in broad daylight, as if they'd staggered out of the bar scene in *Star Wars*.

In the second-last row, a man in a dark suit was sitting alone. His face was vaguely familiar. Dunkley made a mental note to seek him out when the service was over.

Ben's brother, Michael, had started to speak, welcoming the sparse crowd for what would be a short memorial. 'And the eulogy today will be delivered by Ben's oldest and dearest friend, Harry Dunkley …'

Dunkley rose, feeling as if he was floating off the ground. He needed to get a grip. He had spent hours trying to write something meaningful, but still felt a guilty pang of inadequacy.

'I have spent my entire adult life crafting words …' He paused and cleared his throat. 'Trying to find exactly the right phrase for exactly the right moment. But there are some places where words run out. I find myself in such a place now. I do not have the skill to find the right words to do justice to the life of my friend Ben Gordon. But I will try.

'Ben and I were friends for nearly thirty years, and from the moment we met, in the Manning Bar at Sydney Uni, we instinctively liked each other. Ben was the sort of friend who stuck with you through thick and thin, who could be counted on to help out if you got into a tussle on the rugby field, or if your life was turning to mud.

'He wrestled his whole life to come to terms with who he was, who he should be. He felt cheated by nature, and I never really realised until now what a heavy load that must have been for him. It would have crushed a lesser man, or woman.

'I do not know what Ben was meant to be. I just hope he was at peace with himself when he died. But I do know this. Ben was my friend and his love was as reliable and constant as starlight. No matter how profound or painful his struggles, he never wavered as a friend. If anything, I failed to be the kind of friend he needed. He had asked me for years to call him Kimberley and, to my shame, I find it hard. Even now.'

Dunkley paused. 'His death is hard to understand. The police report says it was another gay bashing in Canberra. That he died simply because he was the wrong kind of person in the wrong place at the wrong time.

'But I don't believe it …' Dunkley glanced at his notes, composing himself before looking out into the crowd. He noticed that the man in the suit was crying. He continued, turning his gaze to the plain white coffin, draped with a garland of brightly coloured flowers.

'Ben Gordon was taken from us too early, a beautiful, brilliant man who strayed into the path of some evil, twisted mind. But his spirit, his irrepressible spirit, will live on. And I will not rest until I find out the truth …' He fought back his own tears before uttering a word he had resisted for years: ' … who killed our friend … Kimberley, and why.'

Dunkley bowed his head for a moment. Then he looked back from the coffin to the crowd and noticed the man in the dark suit had gone.

August 25, 2011

GETCHA!

It was a cheeky nod to one of the most famous newspaper headlines of all time, the 'GOTCHA' announcing the sinking of the *General Belgrano* by the Brits during the 1982 Falklands War.

Now another Murdoch tabloid had grabbed it, on the other side of the world. It wasn't a warship that had copped it, but Jamie Santow, that sanctimonious high priest of online outrage. Oh, and he'd taken it where it really hurt, by the very medium on which he'd built a virtual empire.

One misdirected tweet from Santow to one of his co-conspirators at *GetSet!* had been sent to each of his 100,000 followers.

> The cripple crusade has gone off. Maybe we need to get some spastics on board 2. What U think mate?

In the short history of Twitter, it was perhaps the biggest cock-up of all; well, at least since US congressman Anthony Weiner had sent a picture of his penis to his army of followers.

Maybe there is a God after all, George Papadakis thought, as he scanned the tabloid that was otherwise full of dire news for the Toohey Government.

Santow had desperately tried to lay the blame elsewhere, even suggesting his Twitter account had been hacked à la the *News of the World*. But the twitterati were having none of it, and the calls for his resignation were getting louder by the tweet. In a final act of online irony, one infuriated *GetSet!* member had kicked off a petition on the group's website to have Santow replaced – on the grounds he had brought the organisation into serious disrepute. There were already 1400 backers for this, and the numbers were building steadily.

The online beast of discontent that Santow had helped create was about to devour him.

August 25, 2011

Emotionally shattered, physically drained. Harry Dunkley had been working on pure adrenalin for almost a week, trying to keep focused on the biggest political story of his life, while feeling overwhelmed by the loss of his friend and the shadow of guilt it had cast.

Dunkley closed down his PC, grabbed his keys and quietly slipped out of the parliamentary building. Checking his watch, he calculated it would take him no more than five minutes, ten max, to reach the rendezvous.

His car was parked in its usual place on level four, deep in the bowels of the Senate. The remnants of a discarded cigarette stained the stairwell, its odour still lingering in the concrete walls. The time had clicked over to 8 p.m., the temperature barely registering above zero.

The Toyota coughed a few times and began the slow climb out of the Senate car park onto the one-way road that ringed the

Parliament. Security on their mountain bikes were rugged up against the cold, still patrolling the precinct, despite the hour and the freeze.

The drive tonight was so quick that the car's aged heater barely had time to crank out any warmth. Red Hill was one of the highest points in Canberra, and a favoured meeting place for fitness freaks who would slog up its paths on foot or by bicycle. It was also a trysting place for lovers, particularly those seeking illicit liaisons away from the city's watching eyes.

Dunkley had last been to its pinnacle a year ago, dining at Beyond Red with a Shadow Minister whose ambitions clearly outweighed his talent. Tonight food would have to wait. A quarter past eight came and went, and the few vehicles that eased up the hill disgorged only hungry diners heading for the restaurant. A tune played on the CD, Jeff Buckley's 'Hallelujah' with its soft ode to lovers past. Canberra's night lights danced and an approaching vehicle flashed its high-beam twice. It was the signal.

Finally, after two months of intrigue and subterfuge, Dunkley was to meet Mr DFAT, the man who had initiated the downfall of Bruce Paxton.

A slight man emerged from a late-model Citroën, his face partly obscured by a fur-lined hood. He walked the few metres to Dunkley's passenger door, nervously checking to make sure no one was close by, and then got in. It was close to 8.30 p.m. The man lowered his hood and looked straight into Dunkley's eyes. Dunkley was speechless for a few seconds.

'Well, well, the man at the funeral, second-last row, dark suit.'

'Not bad, Mr Dunkley, not bad at all.'

'And you're Mr DFAT, the one who first rang me more than two months ago. It is you, right?'

'One and the same. Might I say, you delivered a very nice eulogy the other day.'

Dunkley offered a handshake to his source. 'Harry Dunkley.'

It was accepted without hesitation. 'Charles Dancer.'

'Charles Dancer? I've been around this place for a very long time and I've never heard of you.'

'I'm flattered, I pride myself on being invisible.'

How strange then, Dunkley thought, that this nervous-looking man, evidently steeped in Canberra's bureaucratic ways, was now outing himself as the mother of all Deep Throats.

'I have one trivial question to start with,' Dunkley said. 'What was with the diplomatic plates and the Embassy of Taiwan envelope?'

'Oh, come on, Mr Dunkley. A man must have some fun; it was a theatrical flourish, nothing more.'

'So why me? What was this all about? And why are you here now? And, not to put too fine a point on it, who the fuck killed my friend?'

'Correction, Mr Dunkley ... *our* friend. Kimberley and I were close, though we had a different kind of relationship to the one you shared. Perhaps a tad more fractious, too. So that answers the question of why I am here. And why I am potentially risking a two-year stint in jail for breaching the Official Secrets Act.'

'You did that when you handed over a picture that came from an ASIS file.'

'I had permission to do that, from serious people – that's my job.'

'Why?'

'Because Bruce Paxton was a real and present danger to the realm. He threatened the alliance with the United States and he was clearly a security risk. And, Mr Dunkley, he was in bed with Chinese intelligence, literally.'

In the half-light of the car interior, Dunkley's confusion was apparent.

'Let me make it simple for you. While you chased one face in a thirty-year-old photo, our friend Kimberley was pursuing the other. And that man, Zhou Dejiang, introduced Paxton to one of his best – and most alluring – spies. From the Chinese perspective, it worked a treat,' Dancer said.

'Paxton had been compromised for thirty years. We would have let it pass … but then he rekindled that relationship earlier this year. That dalliance in the Orient was the tipping point – how could we allow a Defence Minister like that to continue?'

'What do you mean *we*? Who is we?' Dunkley was getting annoyed. 'The Prime Minister? He gets to decide who serves, doesn't he? Who are you talking about?'

'I'm talking about the people who will be here as a half-dozen Prime Ministers come and go. The patriots who serve this country in silence and who defend its interests, and those of our allies.'

'What, faceless bureaucrats and diplomats? Is that who you're talking about? And who else? The Yanks?'

'Well, the Americans certainly had an interest in the lustful habits of Paxton. But theirs was a more fundamental concern, as was ours.'

'Which was?'

'The Alliance, Mr Dunkley. Paxton was a risk to this country's security, pure and simple. He had already triggered major concerns in Washington with his plans to wind back the Joint Strike Fighter program. Added to that, he was sleeping with a skilled Mata Hari. That's some double act, I would say.'

'And did your employers and their mates kill Ben?'

'No ... well, I don't think so.' For the first time Dancer seemed genuinely distressed. 'I'm as confused as you are about that. It doesn't make any sense. It's not ... it's not our style.'

'What about the Americans? They don't seem to have an issue with capping inconvenient people.'

'They are capable of it, certainly. But it's not usual. They'd do it in Pakistan maybe, or Colombia. But here, never, and we would not take it as the act of a friendly nation.'

'Well, who then? And what did Ben have that was so damaging that someone wanted him dead?'

'I want to know as badly as you do.'

'Well, what if he had information that linked the United States and senior Australian bureaucrats to a plot to topple a democratically elected Minister?' Dunkley asked. 'I would say that's pretty damaging, wouldn't you? People would want to keep him silent, wouldn't they?'

'Yes, they would, but believe me, there are other ways to discredit a story. And Kimberley had some certain disadvantages when it came to being a credible source. We could have destroyed her credibility. Worst case scenario, we'd plant kiddie pictures on her computers and have the police raid her house. Game over. That's also my job.'

'That's some job, your job.'

'This nation has many enemies, Mr Dunkley. I help guard it. You might not like my methods but you sleep soundly in your bed because people like me stand watch.'

Dunkley felt rage boiling inside him.

'Even if it kills me, I will find out who killed Ben. Give me a number I can contact you on. This isn't the end of our conversation. It's the beginning.'

August 26, 2011

It was the end of August, and the day dawned fine and mild in the national capital. The first sprigs of wattle signalled the approach of spring. Canberra had yielded to an uncommon beauty, the kind of day that explained the allure of the bush capital.

From its lofty perch, the Australian flag that normally flew proud above the Parliament hung limp, seemingly ashamed of unfurling its full banner to the skies. Perhaps it was a silent message to those men and women below who bickered and fought over the laws governing this nation. Because, for the past fortnight, the flag had stood sentinel over one of the most explosive – and tawdry – periods in the history of Australia's century-old Federation.

Defence Minister Bruce Paxton had resigned in disgrace, his past finally catching up with him. Elizabeth Scott had rolled the dice and lost, another in the long line of Opposition leaders to have been killed off by an impatient party room. The Toohey Government was reeling as an energised Coalition engaged in bare-knuckle politics, led by Emily Brooks, one of the most effective street fighters the Parliament had seen. 'A rabid rottweiler on steroids,' a Liberal colleague had dubbed her.

The parliamentary pantomime had descended into pure farce as the resurgent Coalition tied the House of Representatives in procedural knots, refusing to grant a pair for stricken Foreign Minister Catriona Bailey.

'It's a joke. This is now a place where getting stuck in the dunny could see the government fall,' one long-serving Labor MP was heard to moan.

Only skilled manoeuvring by the Leader of the House had seen the government survive to week's end. But the games in the chamber had dashed any chance of getting business done. It was political gridlock and some of the nation's most experienced commentators were predicting the government would fall by Christmas.

Martin Toohey's decision to rip up the accord with the Greens had contributed to the instability. Firm friends had turned into mortal enemies and the Greens' new leader – emboldened by a recent Newspoll showing the Greens' primary vote surging to 15 per cent – had launched a campaign targeting Labor's inner-city base ahead of the next election. That, in turn, had seen a revolt by sections of the Labor Left, who were agitating for some kind of symbolic action to win back the luvvies.

'So what do we do now?' an exhausted Toohey asked George Papadakis, as the two sat in the prime ministerial suite, attempting to wash away some of the grime from the last fortnight.

'Pray, my friend. It won't work but nothing else we try does either.'

August 26, 2011

It was 3 a.m. and John James Hospital was switched to silent. The night staff went about their work, all quiet efficiency. In dim rooms medical machinery softly hummed as patients dozed between rounds of routine monitoring.

In Room 43, Catriona Bailey was ignoring the hour, keeping watch as a battery of screens relayed unfolding world events. On CNN, Israel's Prime Minister was addressing a press conference. Bailey dashed off a Tweet cautioning him against a pre-emptive strike on Iran's nuclear sites.

The Foreign Minister was by herself, but never alone, plugged into the outside world through a phalanx of wires and modules, plotting and scheming while the national capital slept.

She turned next to finessing the finishing touches on her latest 8000-word piece for *The Monthly*. In typically overblown prose the essay, 'Renewing Labor', mapped out a path for her shattered party. She traced its fall to the malign influence of factional bosses and union warlords and said there was now no choice but to hand it 'back to the people, where it belongs'.

What Labor needed most, now more than ever, she argued, was courageous leadership. By the man – or woman – made for the age. As usual, in closing she threw in a religious allusion. 'A prophet is not someone who can see the future,' she wrote. 'It is someone who sees the present, with perfect clarity.'

She grinned, internally. *She* was the perfect political prophet for the global 24/7 internet age. Unsleeping, all-seeing and hard-wired into the virtual universe. This little effort would set the cat among the pigeons nicely.

Bailey now saw her life in Messianic terms. She had been crucified by the party, and been laid in the tomb. She had appeared to be dead – but was not.

The fuel that coursed through her veins and sustained her was revenge.

And she would rise. Again.

August 26, 2011

The quiet ambience of the Tulip Lounge, a smart boutique bar in Manuka, was the perfect tonic for a spent Harry Dunkley.

He collapsed into one of the feather-soft couches and thumbed through a generous cocktail menu, searching for something a little more serious than a Fluffy Duck. He finally reached a list of imported ales, most of which he had never heard of.

But this wasn't just a social outing. He was waiting for a contact. *The* contact. In two decades covering the gory spectacle of national politics, there were few people he trusted more.

He and the contact had an unwritten agreement – Dunkley would call only in times of crisis. The last time the two had talked was a little over a year ago when Dunkley rang to confirm a tip that Labor was preparing to dump Bailey as Prime Minister.

The journalist glanced at his watch, confirming that his contact was late. He was always late. But Dunkley wasn't going anywhere. He was searching for answers and suspected this was his best means of getting them. No one was better connected in Canberra, whether it be about the factional plays in Labor, the latest manoeuvrings within Defence or the musings of the US administration.

Almost an hour after the agreed appointment, the untidy figure of Brendan Ryan shambled up the stairs.

'Sorry, I was held up,' Ryan said, sweeping up the drinks menu with one hand as his other plunged into a bowl of salted nuts.

'No problems, mate. You've had a bit on lately.'

'Yeah, you might say that. You can't accuse us of making politics boring.'

'Yep, you guys are good for journalism.'

They shared a small laugh and chased down the waiter.

The odd thing about Ryan, Dunkley mused, was that he was usually a vault. But once persuaded to talk, he seemed to enjoy it – and was a trove of information.

'Do you reckon you can hold on, with the numbers in the House the way they are?'

'Well, right now Simmo is talking to that grubby Queensland Liberal, trying to persuade him to break ranks. He might do it too, 'cause he won't get preselected again.'

'But surely you can't win another election? You're gone – it's just a matter of time, isn't it?'

'Never make bold predictions, Harry, you know that. If we can endure, we can turn this around. Sure, mate, it's like trying to land a spaceship on a snowflake, but that's the plan. And this new Liberal leader, she's a nasty piece of work … mate, in time people will grow to hate her.'

Ryan paused. 'Sorry about your friend, Harry.'

'Thanks, mate, that's really why I'm here.'

'I know.'

'How much do you know?'

'More than you, but not everything, not by a long chalk.'

'So tell me about the Yanks. It's been suggested they were behind the leak that destroyed Paxton. Are my sources solid?'

Ryan took a slow sip of beer. 'The Americans were concerned, mate. And they had every right to be. Our own people were deeply concerned. Washington might have sped the process up, but Paxton, well, he was gone from the moment he hooked up with that Tibetan girl – again. Harry, we simply can't afford a Defence Minister, with unfettered access to such sensitive information, so deeply compromised.'

Another scoopful of nuts disappeared into Ryan's gaping mouth, before he continued.

'I don't know if he ever told the Chinese anything useful, but it doesn't really matter. That fucking fool was threatening our nation's ability to defend itself. He wanted to cut back Defence spending, not increase it. And this at a time when we need to be expanding our military. We have to prepare, Harry, for future conflict – a war with China which, in my judgement, is inevitable. Our people had been dragging their feet on Paxton for nearly two months. Give the Americans credit, mate, they know how to finish the job.'

Dunkley digested the explosive information, realising he'd taken the wrong fork in the road. 'So I missed the big story. I followed the money and found a crook.'

'Well, that's still a story. It's just not the most interesting one. And it had the desired effect. So thanks. Your country salutes you.' Ryan mockingly raised his glass before finishing his beer, looking for a waiter to order another.

'But weren't you concerned that getting rid of Paxton might bring the government down?'

'No, mate. We don't need Paxton as Defence Minister, we just need his vote in the parliament. Of course it was bloody embarrassing, but it was essential to secure the defence of the realm. Some things, my friend, are beyond politics.'

'Does the Prime Minister know about this?'

'No.'

Dunkley signalled a waitress and ordered two more beers, before turning back to Ryan.

'Who killed Ben?'

'I don't know for sure, but I – we – suspect the Chinese.'

'Jesus, Brendan, that's just bullshit. What possible reason could they have?'

'I can't prove this but we suspect the Chinese were on to your friend and his little, er, theory. About Bailey.'

Ryan carefully scanned the surrounding lounges, before lowering his voice and continuing. 'Do you remember the phone call from Ben last week? He said to you that there was something else he had to tell you. "Something unbelievable about Bailey."'

Dunkley was stunned. 'Mate, how do you know that?'

'We were listening, Harry, and clearly we weren't the only ones. We didn't move against Ben because we wanted him to help you. From the start we knew he would. That's why you got the photo. And Harry … I know you're wondering, but we've got it back, safe and sound where it belongs.'

'What was Ben going to tell me about Bailey?'

'Well, he did say "something unbelievable". And he was dead right. Didn't you ever think that the reason we gave for shafting that bitch Bailey was a bit thin? What? That she was a crazy control freak who was hard to work with? We've had maniacs in office before and lived with them. Name a PM who isn't hard to work with. Ask Gary Gray about Captain Whacky. Sure, Bailey was riding low in the polls. But if that was the reason for killing a Prime Minister, well then Toohey would have gone months ago.

'Don't forget our main problem in that abortion of an election campaign was that we couldn't explain to the Australian people why we dumped our leader. We were just lucky that Scott was such a lousy politician or the Coalition would have hosed us.'

Ryan moved in close.

'We got rid of Catriona Bailey because she's a … *spy*.'

Dunkley wore a what-the-fuck expression that could have been seen clear across the lounge.

'Harry, you look startled, but let me go on. She was recruited by the Chinese when she was a language student in Hong Kong in the early 1980s. Honkers was a rich breeding ground then for the Commies. And they really hit the jackpot.

'All the time that Bailey was working her way up through Labor ranks, building her contacts in Washington, she was also feeding intel back to Beijing. She pretended to take a hard line against China on human rights, but she was always acting in their interest. It was a convincing performance too. We – us and the Americans – only found out when it was too late.'

Dunkley struggled to absorb this impossible information. It was as if Ryan was speaking another language.

Outside, the orderly nature of the Canberra evening continued, a steady procession of public servants returning to their neat homes after another day performing the tasks necessary to keep the Commonwealth of Australia ticking over. No more, no less.

'I don't have any evidence that the Chinese killed Ben,' Ryan continued. 'But I do know that no one on our side did. I think the Chinese intercepted Ben's call to you, panicked, and decided to act.'

Ryan fell into silence and Dunkley didn't know how to fill it. Finally, he spoke.

'Well, that's the most extraordinary tale I ever heard, Brendan. But I could never write it … unless I turned my hand to fiction.'

'Why not mate?'

'Because … nobody would ever believe me.'

Steve Lewis arrived in Canberra in late 1992, and has been tormenting the nation's political elite ever since. He worked for the *Australian Financial Review* for fifteen years before joining the *Australian* as chief political reporter, and since 2007 has been breaking news and causing mischief as national political correspondent for News Limited's big-selling metropolitan dailies – the *Daily Telegraph*, *Herald Sun*, *Courier-Mail* and *Advertiser*.

Chris Uhlmann is one of Australia's best known and most respected political broadcasters. He began his career in journalism at the *Canberra Times* as the world's oldest copy-kid, after failed stints as a student priest, storeman and packer and security guard. He was editor of the *Canberra Weekly* before joining the ABC in 1998. As political editor of the ABC's flagship current affairs program, *7.30*, he has earned a reputation for his fearless pursuit of the nation's politicians.